PRAISE FOR SARA GOODMAN CONFINO

"Aspiring journalist Judy Greenberg is not in pursuit of an MRS degree. Smart, savvy, and unapologetically ambitious, Judy is a young woman ahead of her time with big dreams and even bigger obstacles in Sara Goodman Confino's captivating new novel *Off the Record*. It's 1962, and women aren't considered 'real reporters.' Instead, they are sidelined to the typing pool. But that won't stop Judy from chasing the story behind the story. As she inches closer to a dangerous scoop, sparks fly with newsroom charmer Jack Fields, and the stakes climb fast. When Judy uncovers a headline-making story, she's forced to choose between safety and ambition, love and leads, silence and the truth. Buckle up: *Off the Record* is hot off the press, packed with romance, intrigue, and suspense—and is Confino's best yet."

—Lisa Barr, *New York Times* bestselling author of *The Goddess of Warsaw*

"Reading a book by Sara Goodman Confino feels like settling in for a girls' night full of laughter and juicy storytelling—and *Off the Record* might be my new favorite. Judith is the kind of heroine I adore: determined, sharp, and unwilling to accept the limits others place on her. When she stumbles across a story no one else has uncovered—one with the power to upend everything—she dives in headfirst, and I was right there with her. Smart, spirited, and utterly captivating."

—Jenni L. Walsh, *USA Today* bestselling author of *Death Was Not on the Guest List*

"By now fans of Sara Goodman Confino know to expect feminist stories chock-full of humor, Jewish joy, and family dynamics that are as familiar as our own living rooms, only more entertaining. With *Off the Record*, Confino takes it up a notch with mystery and danger that had me on tenterhooks. Lovable protagonist Judy Greenberg has enough chutzpah to fight an army of overpowering Jewish mothers, and flirtatious and sweet Jack is her perfect match whether she likes it or not. As for me, I didn't like it; I loved it!"

—Meredith Schorr, *USA Today* bestselling author of *Roommating*

"There is nothing not to love about *Off the Record*, Sara Goodman Confino's latest gem. It has everything readers have come to expect from this expert storyteller: humor, heart, wit, romance, and a plucky heroine who isn't afraid to chase her dreams. Add Washington politics and Cold War intrigue, and you have a madcap adventure that just might be Confino's best yet!"

—Samantha Greene Woodruff, bestselling author of *The Trade Off* and *The Lobotomist's Wife*

"A sharp, spirited, entertaining tribute to investigative journalism—and the women who refused to stay on the sidelines. Confino captures the thrill of chasing a story in this girl-power page-turner."

—Alexandra Robbins, *New York Times* bestselling author of *The Teachers*

"It's 1962, and all the 'good girls' are clamoring for their MRS degree—all except for one, that is: aspiring journalist Judy Greenberg. Smart and determined, Judy knows that she has what it takes to make it as an investigative journalist, and one handsome reporter in particular certainly agrees. So when Judy intercepts a suspicious phone message meant for her boss, she and Jack Fields embark on a mission where the stakes couldn't be higher—and soon discover that it's what happens off the record that changes everything on it. Fans of Sara Goodman Confino will delight in this scintillating story where secrets, danger, and matters of the heart collide."

—Heidi Shertok, author of *Unorthodox Love* and *Match Me If You Can*

"When ambitious journalist Judy Greenberg landed the interview that could launch her career (against her old-school parents' wishes), she wanted more than to be part of the 'typing pool'—her dreams were much larger. While demanding respect and going rogue, she didn't expect to run into a trail of secrets that refused to stay 'off the record.' Razor sharp, fast-paced, and with brilliant plotting, *Off the Record* is Confino's best yet! Full of heart and grit, this compelling, high-stakes historical thriller about loyalty, and the price of telling the truth, will tug at every emotion."

—Jaime Lynn Hendricks, bestselling author of *Their Double Lives*

Off the Record

OTHER BOOKS BY SARA GOODMAN CONFINO

Behind Every Good Man

Don't Forget to Write

She's Up to No Good

For the Love of Friends

Good Grief

Off the Record

A NOVEL

SARA GOODMAN CONFINO

This is a work of fiction. Names, characters, organizations, places, events, and incidents are either products of the author's imagination or are used fictitiously.

Published by Lake Union Publishing, Seattle

www.apub.com

EU product safety contact:
Amazon Media EU S. à r.l.
38, avenue John F. Kennedy, L-1855 Luxembourg
amazonpublishing-gpsr@amazon.com

ISBN-13: 9781662537554 (paperback)
ISBN-13: 9781662537561 (digital)

Cover illustration © Philip Pascuzzo
Cover image: © CSA-Images / Getty

Printed in the United States of America

For Kevin Keegan
You were right: The harder I worked, the luckier I got.

1

"You're going to be late!" my mother yelled up the stairs as I finished buttoning up the jacket of my suit.

Technically, it was my sister's suit from last year, but she was currently seven months pregnant, and therefore I had a few months before she demanded it back.

Then again, she didn't know I had taken it either. But desperate times called for desperate measures, and I had landed an interview for my dream job. Kind of. It was a start anyway.

"Judy!" my mother called again more insistently. I slipped on my shoes, adding a solid three inches to take me to a respectable five foot three, grabbed my handbag, and went running down the stairs.

"I'm coming!" As if there were any scenario short of the president himself hiring me that would make me late for this interview.

Of course, my mother thought I was interviewing at my uncle's law firm. Yawn.

"You're going to have to take the bus," she said crossly. "Your father left already."

I pretended this was a hardship and not my plan all along. "I'm so sorry, Mom. I just wanted to look perfect."

She picked an imaginary piece of lint off my sleeve and straightened the pillbox hat that I had also nicked from my sister's closet. That, she *would* miss.

"Very professional," she said. "Your uncle Gil will have to hire you."

I was less certain of that than she was, especially considering that I wasn't going to that interview unless I somehow botched this one. And I was *not* going to mess up my chance to work at *The Washington Digest*.

Even if my first foray into journalism *had* broken up Uncle Gil's marriage. That was the other reason he didn't have to hire me. But that was his own fault, quite honestly. If he hadn't been having an affair with his mistress at the same hotel where I had skipped school to try to get a picture of Truman Capote with my Brownie box camera, he wouldn't have wound up in the background of the photograph that *The Montgomery Gazette* ran, and he would still be married to Aunt Dorothy.

Technically, she wasn't my aunt anymore.

Just like how technically it wasn't *my* fault his marriage ended. But I wasn't his favorite niece, and I knew it. So working at his law firm didn't exactly have the same appeal as working at a professional newspaper.

Of course, my mother didn't care about any of those technicalities. She wanted me working at the law firm to earn the MRS degree that I had failed to procure in four years at the University of Maryland. My sister, along with most of my female classmates, had dropped out after earning hers, but I was determined to leave college with a degree in journalism. And no finance major with a receding hairline was going to sway me.

So I smiled at my mother, kissed her cheek, and assured her that her little girl would be returning gainfully employed.

"Psh," she said, waving a hand in the air. "Come home engaged. Then we'll celebrate."

I blinked. "Might be a tall order for an interview with my uncle, but I'll do my best."

She patted my arm, and I left the house, shaking off the weight of her expectations as I walked to the bus stop, my heels clacking on the sidewalk of our Rosemary Hills neighborhood in Silver Spring, Maryland. A ride into DC with my father *would* have been quicker. But then I would have to duck into my uncle's building, hope no one who knew me saw, wait for my father to leave, then dash three blocks to *The Digest*'s office. Fewer chances to mess this up on the bus—even if the old woman who sat down next to me did smell like onions, and—I glanced at her fur-covered sweater—yes, that odor was cat food. I scooted as far over as I could, hoping the light spritz of Chanel No 5, which I had forgone a textbook to buy, would hold up against the stench. I was sure even my mother would agree that it was a better investment than economics of the non-home kind.

I stepped off the bus on K Street and walked the remaining two blocks to *The Digest*'s office. One block down and three over from the building *The Washington Post* had moved into twelve years earlier in 1950.

The Digest wasn't as grand as the empire Mr. Wainwright and his father-in-law had created, but it was a step in the right direction. And they were hiring, which *The Post* wasn't. Well, *The Post was* hiring, but they explicitly told me they had no openings in the women's section, which was the only place a woman could expect to write.

I grinned up at the building, which stood the full 130 feet that DC law allowed, so as not to block out the Washington Monument, the letters of the sign seeming to wink at me in return. This was the start of my new life. I just knew it. I would save up for a few months and make enough money to pay for a room in a boardinghouse for women—in cash, of course. My father would never sign off on a lease—neither of my parents could fathom a girl wanting a life where the end goal wasn't a husband and children.

I wasn't *opposed* to the idea of a husband. Eventually. But whoever he was, he would have to understand that I wanted a career too.

And a husband like that wasn't so easy to find.

Besides, if I was husband hunting, I would have worn a dress, not my sister's suit, which was a decent knockoff of a number the first lady wore last year. My brother-in-law having family in the garment industry up in New York had its benefits, which I was happy to pinch when my sister wasn't looking. No, this was about showing off that I could be a serious journalist.

So I stepped purposefully through the revolving door, told the older man in a security uniform that I had an interview, walked past a group of young men smoking in the lobby, and approached the desk.

"How can I help you?" a middle-aged woman asked, taking a puff of her own cigarette. I fought the urge to wave my hand in front of my face to clear the smoke.

"Judy Greenberg," I said, attempting to lower the timbre of my voice and holding out my gloved hand. When she made no move to shake it, I lowered my arm. "I'm here for the interview."

She looked me up and down, then turned back to her typewriter. "Third floor. Ask for Mrs. Kelly."

Not the warmest welcome, but I would take it. If *The Diamondback*, the University of Maryland's student newspaper, had been any indication, women still weren't *popular* in newsrooms. But I was determined to change that. Alone if I had to. I marched to the elevator bank and pressed the up button, tapping my foot with nervous energy until the elevator arrived.

Once inside, I waited until the doors opened at three, depositing me into a large typing pool of women. Which I supposed made sense for interviews—they would need a secretary there to keep it all straight. I stopped at the first desk I saw. "I'm looking for a Mrs. Kelly?"

The woman at the desk glanced up sharply. She was maybe two or three years older than me. She took me in, then shook her head. "Best call her Miss," she said. "If Dolores downstairs told you to call her Mrs., it means she doesn't like you."

"Doesn't like me? She doesn't know me."

"Doesn't matter," this woman said, sliding a fresh sheet of paper into her typewriter and rolling it into place. "It's that door at the other end of the room. And *Miss* if you want to get anywhere. The old battle-axe isn't married. You'll see why."

"Thank you," I said, meaning it. Having a friend in the typing pool would definitely be useful on deadlines. "I'm Judy."

"Patricia," she said, shaking my proffered hand. "Good luck."

I refrained from saying I didn't need luck. My journalism degree and clippings from college surely spoke for themselves. Instead, I thanked Patricia, walked to the door she had indicated, and rapped three times with my knuckles.

A raspy voice said to come in, and I pushed the door open. "Miss Kelly?"

"If you can't read, I can't help you," a severe-looking older woman in horn-rimmed glasses said, pointing to her name on the door. She finally raised her eyes to look at me. "Who are you and what do you want?"

And that would be why she's not married, I thought, mentally thanking Patricia. "I'm Judy Greenberg, and I'm here to interview for the—"

"Shh," she hissed. "Close the door. She doesn't know she's getting the axe yet."

Trying to keep my eyes from widening, I closed the door as instructed. Miss Kelly indicated for me to take the seat across from her desk. The job advertisement did not specify that it was for the newspaper's women's section, but it also didn't prohibit women from applying, so I was a bit surprised when she held out her hand and demanded my résumé, but I assumed she was screening applicants for whoever would be doing the actual interview.

Or maybe *The Digest* was more progressive than I had even hoped.

She scanned the document I handed her, then lowered her glasses and fixed me with a hard look over them. "No, you won't do at all."

"Excuse me?"

"There's no fraternizing here," she said bluntly. "Which is exactly why we have an opening. I don't know why you'd want to marry a journalist anyway. They're never home and don't make enough money. Go apply at a law firm or something like that."

I blinked rapidly at her, taken aback by her assessment of my intentions at *The Digest.* Time to set the record straight. "Actually, my mother thinks I'm applying at a law firm today for that very reason," I confided, leaning forward. "But I'm *here* because I'm *not* looking to—fraternize. I want to be a reporter." I reached into my bag and brought out a manila envelope. "I think if you'll look through my college clippings, you'll see—"

"A reporter?" she repeated, barking out a short laugh. "You're at the wrong newspaper."

"But—the job listing—"

"Didn't even take into account that a woman might think of applying," she finished. "How's your typing?"

"Excellent," I said, confused. "Ninety words a minute."

"And your accuracy?"

"Over 99 percent."

"But you didn't attend secretarial school?"

"Miss Kelly, I have a bachelor's degree in journalism, with a minor in government and politics. I graduated with a perfect 4.0 GPA and was the first female section editor at my college newspaper, as well as—"

She held up a hand. "Like I said, *The Digest* isn't looking for a female reporter. I can offer you a job in the typing pool, but with the express caveat that it will *not* lead to a reporting job." She hesitated, and I leaned in closer. "Here. I don't want to get your hopes up, but we did have one girl leave us to go work for the women's section at *The Washington Post*."

The Post. This was a stepping stone to *The Post*. No, working in the typing pool wasn't anything close to the job I wanted, but it was a foot in the door.

"Yes or no?" Miss Kelly asked. "I don't have all day, and if you don't take it, I need to list the job immediately."

"I'll take it," I said quickly.

Miss Kelly's face turned somehow even more stern. "I will warn you again: There is to be no fraternizing with the male staff. The girl you'll be replacing is about to learn just how serious I am about that."

"Miss Kelly," I said, placing a hand over my heart. "Thank you so—"

"That'll be all," she said, balling my résumé up and dropping it into the nearly full wastepaper basket at the side of her desk. "You begin Monday at eight. And I do *not* tolerate tardiness."

I nodded, fighting the urge to rescue the document I had worked so hard on from its fate. "Yes, Miss Kelly. Thank you, Miss Kelly."

"Tell Louise Clark to come in here," she said.

I had no idea who Louise Clark was, but I was sure my new friend, Patricia, would help me learn the ropes quickly.

It wasn't exactly the outcome I had hoped for, but I was still one step closer to my goal than I would be at my uncle's law firm, that was for sure. Besides, my mother didn't need to know about the no-fraternization policy. And a pathway to *The Washington Post*! Though I was certain even *The Digest* would see the skills I had. It would be impossible not to.

When I got home, the house was empty. My mother had either gone shopping or to see a friend and my father was still at work, so I decided to change out of my sister's suit and then walk over to her house—ostensibly to see how I could help prepare for the baby's arrival. Really to steal some more clothes for my new employment. *Everything's coming up roses,* I thought merrily.

2

Laden with garment bags that I told Betty I would store at my house to help her make room for the new baby, I practiced my story for my parents.

I didn't, however, expect to see Uncle Gil sitting in the living room, chain-smoking furiously with my father.

"—a major problem," he was saying. "When I go out of my way to make an effort, and she doesn't even—"

I tried to sneak past them and make it up to my room undetected, but a gust of wind—*likely from Uncle Gil's fat head,* I thought—made the door shut too loudly, and he and my father turned to look at me.

I smiled innocently. "Hi, Daddy. Uncle Gil."

Neither returned my smile.

"You better not have been shopping again," my father said sternly, inclining his head toward the bags in my arms.

"Of course not," I said, insulted. "These are Betty's clothes that I said I'd keep for her because she needs her closet space right now."

"And I don't suppose you'll be wearing them for her too?" Not much got past my father.

"Well, keeping them in rotation *is* cheaper than mothballs."

He shook his head. "Would you care to explain why you didn't go to your interview that your uncle went to great lengths to set up for you?"

I draped the garment bags carefully over the club chair in the corner of the living room—if the clothes were wrinkled, I would have to iron them before I could wear anything to my first day of work, and heaven knew I didn't pick up ironing skills in college.

When I looked back up, with great poise I may add, my mother had entered from the kitchen with glasses of brown liquor for the two men and an expression on her face that told me she was in no mood for my games.

"I'm terribly sorry, Uncle Gil," I said, though I wasn't in the slightest. "I had every intention of being there today." *Lie.* "But you see, Daddy left before I was ready, and I took the bus downtown, and there was this woman who smelled like cat food—"

"The point, Judith," my father said.

"I suppose I'm burying the lead, but honestly that detail is important, because I was so distracted by the cat food lady that I missed the stop and rode too far—"

My mother's eyebrows were approaching her hairline. "You'd think you'd want to get away from her quicker," she muttered.

"Oh, I did! But I was so nervous that I would smell bad for my interview that I just wasn't thinking clearly. You know me—a total flibbertigibbet." She pursed her lips but didn't argue the point. I was anything but a scatterbrain, but they never quite saw that I had a plan. Sometimes it worked in my favor—I could get away with them saying, *Oh, that's just Judy. Don't take her seriously.* Which I hated, but that attitude had gotten me out of more than a few pickles over the years. Uncle Gil's divorce included. "Anyway, I was walking the five blocks back to Uncle Gil's office when I passed *The Washington Digest* building. And on my honor, I thought nothing of it, *until* I heard two men—oh, Mom, you should have seen them. So handsome. Not a wedding ring in sight." I lowered my voice, saying, "One of them even looked Jewish!" Back to normal tone. "They were talking about a job opening at *The Digest*. And well, I *do* have a degree in journalism, and I had a little while before I had to be at Uncle Gil's office, and I thought, *Why not just* see *what the job is?* And wouldn't you know it? They absolutely loved me and hired me on the spot!"

"As a reporter?" my father asked skeptically.

"Well, no, not exactly. Not *yet* anyway. I'll be starting in the typing pool, but I thought one clerical job is probably just as good as the next for finding a husband and all—"

My mother moaned faintly and slid down onto the sofa next to my father. "She could have married a lawyer or a doctor and she chooses a journalist?"

"To be fair, they have lawyers at the paper, Mom." I didn't know if that was remotely true. "And I'm not exactly engaged to *anyone*. But why not enjoy my work while I look around?" Uncle Gil's face darkened. "No offense, Uncle Gil. But I *did* get a degree."

"Only because you didn't find a husband," my mother said.

"Young lady, I put in a good word for you," my uncle said, "and you made me look foolish."

I sighed. "Uncle Gil, you did that yourself by setting up an interview for me in the first place."

Okay, I didn't say that. I *thought* it. I didn't say it.

"I am so sorry, Uncle Gil, and I appreciate you *so* much. I truly do. But imagine if instead of becoming the high-powered attorney that you are today, your parents forced you to go to medical school and become a doctor. You wouldn't wish that kind of unfulfillment on your niece, would you?"

By the look on his face, yes, he clearly would. Time to switch tactics.

"I'd be terrible at keeping things confidential. What if you lost a client over my inability to be discreet?" Another lie. I was far more discreet than any of them would ever guess. But better to play into my flighty family reputation for now.

"No," he said gruffly—and hopefully realizing he had dodged a bullet by me standing him up. "That's true. You're far from reliable." He downed his drink and stood. "It's just a shame that your sister never needed a job. *Betty* would have done me proud."

My mother looked like she wanted to argue, because having three children by age twenty-five was the exact achievement she wanted for both of us. And at twenty-two, unless I got married tomorrow and popped out three kids in rapid succession, that wasn't happening.

"Betty is pretty perfect," I agreed. "But don't you worry, Uncle Gil, as an employee of *The Digest*, I promise to scour every picture to be sure you're not in one doing anything untoward. This time." His face turned purple, and he started sputtering as I skipped out of the room, snatching the garment bags and dashing up the stairs. Enraging Uncle Gil wasn't the best way to get my parents off my back, but sometimes it was just too fun to resist.

3

Outfitted in my sister's finest pink-and-brown twill suit, I stood outside *The Washington Digest* looking up at the building. It wasn't an impressive structure, and the sign hadn't actually winked at me Friday—the neon in the *e* was clearly on its last legs. The sidewalk rumbled slightly under my feet, indicating that . . . something . . . was happening deep in the bowels of the edifice. Or it could have been my own excitement that I was practically vibrating with.

Yes, I was starting in the typing pool. But I believed in myself and was determined that I was going to be writing articles before the calendar flipped to 1963. It was June—six months was more than enough time to prove myself and make them see the value in a female reporter. Times were changing so quickly that they would be fools not to keep up. Between Dorothy Butler Gilliam making waves at *The Washington Post,* Helen Thomas becoming a fixture as a White House press correspondent, and Barbara Walters joining the *Today* show, we were clearly becoming important in the world of journalism. And I was sure I had what it took for my name to be up there with theirs someday. I just had to figure out how to get the editors at *The Digest* to give me a chance.

It became increasingly clear as my first morning on the job progressed, however, that no one *else* knew I was destined for journalistic greatness.

Starting with the fact that I hadn't yet been issued a security pass. The security guard lumbered over when I walked in. "You in the typing pool now?" he asked. He was probably over sixty, and wasn't tall, but was broad shouldered in a way that gave him a bulldoggish silhouette. His nametag read "Frank."

"I am," I said, holding out a hand. "Judy Greenberg." He didn't shake my hand.

"Make sure they give you a badge," he said gruffly, heading back to the chair he had been sitting in when I entered.

Not the most auspicious start, but I went to the elevators, pressed the button, and waited for the doors to open. Patricia greeted me as I stepped out into the typing pool.

"Miss Kelly told me to get you set up," she said, taking me toward a desk a few over from hers. "This is where you'll be working." She pointed to the sterile wooden surface that had a typewriter, a ream of paper, and a box of number 2 pencils sitting on it. I glanced at the other desks around me to make sure that bringing in some personal touches would be allowed. Most had framed pictures. A few had flowers or plants—though I assumed those were fake as the only windows were on the far wall and the fluorescent lights that flickered intermittently as the building rumbled weren't exactly conducive to life, plant or otherwise.

"What *is* that?" I asked on the third or fourth combination of vibrations and flickering.

"What is what?" Patricia asked, looking around.

"When the building wobbles?"

"Oh." She shook her head. "You'll get used to that. It's the presses warming up for the evening run. Wait till they start printing around five—the whole place feels like a Magic Fingers motel bed."

"A what?"

Patricia laughed. "How old are you anyway?"

"Twenty-two—I graduated last month from the University of Maryland."

"And you haven't spent time in a motel? Oh, honey, you have a lot to learn."

I glanced at her, suddenly shy, to make sure she wasn't mocking my lack of experience, but her expression was friendly. "Strict parents," I said with a shrug. "And Miss Kelly said no fraternizing—"

Patricia took my arm and pulled me into a closet by my desk, shutting the door firmly behind us and tugging on the cord to a single lightbulb that hung in the center of what I could now see was a supply room, lined in floor-to-ceiling shelves with paper, scissors, rubber cement, typewriter ribbons, correction fluid, and oh-so-many pencils.

"Listen," she said. "*No fraternizing* means don't get caught. And definitely don't get knocked up."

My eyes widened. "So the girl I replaced . . . ?"

Patricia nodded. "A diaphragm is your friend. And whatever you do, don't mess around with the married ones. Louise wasn't the first to learn that lesson." She leveled a finger at me. "If you're smart though, she'll be the last."

"I'm just here to get experience and move up to being a journalist. I don't have time for boys anyway."

She chuckled. "Well they're going to make time for you—these reporters love the fresh-off-the-farm new girls. Just do try to be clever about it. Miss Kelly has eyes in the back of her head."

"I am *not* fresh off a farm. I live in Silver Spring!"

"Which, compared to the city, might as well be Kansas." She peered at my face as the building rumbled again. "I'm not being mean—just warning you, that's all."

"I appreciate it," I said. And I did. But I also meant what I said: I wasn't here to meet men—and based on Patricia's description of the newsroom's proclivities, even my mother was going to agree with Miss Kelly.

"Great," Patricia said, reaching for the cord and plunging us into brief darkness before she opened the door again. "So when you run out of paper or need anything else," she said loudly as we exited the closet, "this is where you get it. Just make sure you sign the sheet by the door. They account for every pencil here." Without even looking at her, she then added, "Good morning, Miss Kelly. I'm getting Miss Greenberg situated like you asked."

I turned around, straightening my posture—I wasn't sure how Patricia knew Miss Kelly would be standing there. The woman had materialized out of thin air. But I decided to take that as a lesson: Miss Kelly was everywhere, and I should be prepared.

Miss Kelly nodded crisply. "She says she can type ninety words a minute. And she has a journalism background so she should know editing symbols. Get her started on Don Withers's column for tomorrow." She didn't acknowledge my presence beyond that and turned on her heel, marched right over to another girl's desk, yanked the sheet of paper out of her typewriter while she was still typing, balled it up, and threw it away. "Editorial just cut this one. Go grab another."

"Tyrant," Patricia muttered. "Come on. I'll show you the assignment board."

She walked me over to a large bulletin board organized in columns by urgency. Articles, covered in penciled editorial markup, were tacked to it, with a set of wire boxes, organized by when the articles were due, for finished articles to be placed in. I had never seen anything like this—at my college newspaper, we were responsible for typing and retyping our own articles.

Patricia handed me Don Withers's latest column, which was a misogynistic mess about the foolishness of sending daughters to college, with instructions to type a clean copy according to the markup provided by the editors upstairs. "Then it goes to print?" I asked.

"Depends—they usually go through a few rounds. But it's worth proofing your work before you turn it in. If they're on deadline, you don't want to be responsible for a typo."

I skimmed the page in front of me—a list had an Oxford comma between the last and second-to-last items, which wasn't used in journalism unless absolutely necessary for clarity. "What do I do if there's a mistake they haven't caught?"

Patricia shook her head. "Leave it. Type everything exactly how it's marked. You don't want to be the reason they print a mistake. We're expendable down here—to them anyway—and if they can prove you made a change, you're gone."

I chewed the inside of my bottom lip, contemplating this. I *was* right about the comma. While it was likely that *The Digest* had its own stylebook, that was universal. *I've got to start somewhere,* I thought, sitting down at my desk. Even if that somewhere was just removing an errant comma.

I had the article typed and ready to go back to Editorial in under ten minutes. I placed it in the finished bin, and a kid who couldn't have been more than sixteen or seventeen grabbed it promptly and then left the room.

I went to Patricia's desk. "What next?" I asked.

She looked up at me, confused. "Finish the column."

"I did."

She glanced at her wristwatch. "Okay, second important lesson of the day—don't work that fast. At least not if you want any friends here."

"But—"

"Yeah, I know, you think they'll see how great you are and give you a writing assignment. It doesn't work like that, doll. You're just making everyone else look bad."

I was torn. I wasn't here to make friends, just like I wasn't here to find a man. And the harder I worked, the more they *had* to see that I was overqualified for the typing pool. But I had been in a sorority, and I knew how easily a group of women could ignore the best of intentions if they felt slighted. "Sorry," I said, shrugging meekly. "I'm just excited to be here."

Patricia pulled a cigarette from a Pall Mall box on her desk and then offered me the pack. I shook my head as she placed her cigarette between her lips and lit it. She took a drag, turned her head to blow out a plume of smoke, and removed the cigarette, which came away with a ring of red lipstick that matched the nails on the fingers it was held between. "See if you're still saying that by the end of the day. For now, go look at what's next on the board. You never want Miss Kelly to see you without work at your desk. Just cut the pace some, huh? No one is counting your words per minute here."

By lunchtime, it felt like I had typed half the newspaper's articles, even at my reduced speed. What I had learned so far was that a lot of socializing, nail filing, and smoking happened when Miss Kelly left the third floor to go speak to Editorial. The conversations dried up, the files disappeared under desks, and the cigarettes were stubbed out when she returned. Everyone worked hard when she was in the room. But I wanted her to see that I worked hard even when she was gone—without alienating myself from the other women, who were eyeing me with curiosity at best.

"You're new here," a male voice interrupted both my thoughts and my typing as I keyed his words in the middle of a sports piece about how a record-breaking fifty-four single-day home runs had been hit league-wide in baseball the day before. It was clearly a slow news day.

I blew out an annoyed breath, plucked the tainted article from the typewriter, and rolled a new sheet into it, preparing to start over. "No," I said grumpily. "Been here for months. You just never noticed."

"I definitely would have noticed you," the voice said, and I finally looked up to see who it belonged to. He didn't tower over the desk, standing at probably five foot eight or nine, though he would dwarf my five feet even if I stood up extra straight. No one would confuse him for Rock Hudson, but he was undeniably handsome, with a straight nose, defined jawline, and warm hazel eyes that crinkled at the corners as he smiled.

"But you didn't," I said, returning to the typed sheet with editing notes in the margins that I needed to transcribe. There were a whole lot of baseball players listed whom I had never heard of, and I needed to get their names right.

The man at my desk wasn't fazed. "Then where did you sit before Louise left?"

Oh no. He thought I was flirting. I peered around anxiously to make sure Miss Kelly was nowhere to be seen. Based on the plumes of smoke and peals of laughter in the room, I was likely safe for now, but this man needed to be on his way before she came back.

"In class. At the University of Maryland," I said. "Now if you'll excuse me—"

He grinned broadly, showing even, white teeth. "Class of fifty-eight," he said, a thumb pointed at his chest. "If you were a year older, we'd have overlapped."

"But I'm not, so we didn't. And I do need to finish this before Miss Kelly returns."

"Nah," he said. "Louise usually typed my stories—she never had a mistake. Unless you count"—he moved a hand in a rounded gesture over his stomach—"you know."

"I'm afraid I don't," I said primly. "Now if you'll excuse me, Mister—?"

"Jack Fields," he said, holding out a hand. My fingers remained hovered over the home row of typewriter keys. When I didn't show instant recognition, he continued. "Junior White House correspondent." I raised an eyebrow at the *junior* part, but he ignored it. "And you are?"

"Judy Greenberg," I said, giving up. "Now, really, Mr. Fields, I do need to finish this article." I resumed typing, hoping he would take the . . . Well, it wasn't exactly a hint. But he remained at my desk.

"What'd you major in?" he asked. "You type awfully well for someone who didn't go to secretarial school."

"Journalism," I said with a sigh.

"Huh. You any good?"

I looked back up at him and not for the first time marveled at how much easier it must be to be born a man. Get hired for any job you want just because you can pee standing up. Have the audacity to interrupt a woman at work with no consequences for you, and no worry of what consequences it would have for her. Even his little pregnancy gesture for Louise Clark—that was *her* mistake, not whoever knocked the poor girl up. *He* didn't get asked if he was any good—*he* just got to cover the White House of all places! By virtue of a chromosome, he got to stand where I wanted to be, next to Helen Thomas, while she thanked the president.

"Are *you* any good?" I asked tartly.

He inclined his head with a grin. "I like to think so."

"Of course you do. Now, if you'll excuse me, Mr. Fields, I really do need to finish this."

"Throw it back on the board," he said.

"Excuse me?"

"The president is addressing the Yale graduation today, and I snagged a copy of his speech. If we can get this in tonight's edition, we'll have scooped everyone. I need it typed up immediately." *The Digest* still printed a morning edition and a smaller evening edition with updates from the day.

"How did you get his speech?"

Mr. Fields winked at me. "A good reporter never reveals his sources. Now come on. Let's see what you can do."

Curious, I took the sheets of paper he handed me. "There's no markup on these."

He leaned down close enough that I could smell his Canoe cologne and a hint of Wint-O-Green Lifesavers. "That, Miss Greenberg, is the secret of why Louise was so popular upstairs. Well . . . apparently one of the reasons. But as a journalism major, you should make short work of correcting mistakes—if there are any, that is."

"Hah," I said drily, but I put a fresh sheet in the typewriter again.

"Attagirl," he said, taking the sports story from me to return to the board. "I had a feeling you would be up for a challenge."

"Fields, leave her alone," Patricia's voice said from above my head. "It's her first day. She doesn't need you sniffing around."

"Who's sniffing?" he asked. "I've got our front-page story that needs typing."

"And you take that to the pretty new girl instead of someone who you know can type? Sounds fishy to me." She turned to me. "Come on, Judy. Let's go to lunch. I'll introduce you to the girls."

"I really need this upstairs as soon as possible," Fields said. "No one knows we have it yet."

"Then why don't you run on up there and tell them that they'll have it after lunch."

"How many words is it?" I asked Mr. Fields.

"Eight-fifty."

"Ten minutes?" I asked Patricia.

She rolled her eyes. "Fine. But if you're a minute past that, I'm leaving without you." She went back to her desk, where she lit another cigarette.

"Ten minutes? With edits?"

"Well, not if you stand here talking to me."

Fields grinned again. "Don't worry. If you miss that deadline, I'll take you to lunch."

I looked back at the pages he had given me. "Thank you for the offer, Mr. Fields, but that won't be necessary. I have plans with Patricia, and I'll be ready for them."

He stood there watching me as I made my way through the first page, changing awkward phrasing and inconsistent punctuation as I went. Then I made a shooing gesture with my right hand, and he finally stopped hovering, chuckling as he threaded his way through the typing pool.

4

“Come on, doll,” Patricia said. I glanced at the clock. She was nearly a minute early, but it was fine. The typewriter dinged to indicate I had reached the end of the page, but I had also finished the article. Except for the lead, it hadn’t needed much work. As a graduate of the same journalism program I went through, Fields wrote tightly. And a good chunk of it was lifted directly from the speech that the president would have—I looked at the clock again—just finished delivering in New Haven. I had particularly liked his line about myths being the enemy of truth rather than lies. It was, after all, a myth that women wouldn’t be as strong journalists as men, as I hoped to soon prove.

“Let me just put this in the bin to go upstairs,” I said, pulling the page from the typewriter and adding it to the stack.

“No need,” Fields said, appearing out of nowhere. “I’ll bring it up myself.” He leaned down as Patricia pulled on her gloves. “Nine minutes and eighteen seconds,” he said quietly. “Assuming it’s not actually a recipe for brisket, I’m impressed.”

“Mr. Fields, I have a degree in journalism, not the culinary arts.”

“I suppose that answers the question of why you’re working here and not married.”

I stood up quickly—too quickly, as I banged my knees against the desk in the process—and opened my mouth to tell him what he could do with his opinions, but he was engrossed in the pages he had taken from my desk.

He let out a low whistle. "You *are* good," he said. "I'll give you that."

"Judy," Patricia said. "We'll lose our table if you keep talking to Fields."

I made sure to give Fields a disgruntled look, though I wasn't entirely sure he meant the marriage comment as an insult, and, if we were being honest, I hadn't actually been insulted, though I knew I should be. Then I grabbed my handbag and pulled my own gloves—fine, Betty's gloves—from it to put on as well, though I was hatless. Betty had noticed the loss of her pink pillbox, and my mother was returning it today. It was a shame her head didn't swell when she was pregnant, but a hat was something I could buy myself once I was getting paychecks.

Which reminded me, money was going to be extremely tight until that first payday. "Where are we going?" I asked Patricia, trying to keep the concern out of my voice. Clothes were one thing, but if I nicked so much as a dime from my mother, she would notice. In fact, I was surprised my mother hadn't sent me off with an egg salad sandwich, like she did for my father.

"Duke's," Patricia said.

My family didn't keep strictly kosher, but we also didn't eat out all that often. A big splurge tended to be a trip to Hofberg's deli or *maybe* O'Donnell's if it was a really special occasion. Though I didn't know whether that had more to do with money or the fact I wasn't known for my mealtime etiquette as a child. At twenty-two, I had *just* moved to the adult table for holidays, and even then only because my mother didn't want my niece and nephew picking up bad habits. Entirely uncalled for, I might add, as I hadn't thrown food or stuck green beans on my teeth to make walrus tusks in at least ten years.

"Duke's?" I repeated, not having any idea what that was.

She turned to face me. "You really *are* fresh off the farm, huh? Duke Zeibert's."

"Oh," I said, surprised. I had certainly heard of the Jewish restaurateur whose clientele included DC's elite as well as the commoners.

Everyone who was anyone ate at Duke Zeibert's. And apparently, I was now someone who would as well. "Duke *Zeibert's*. Of course."

Patricia looked me over, then elbowed me playfully. "We tend to splurge when there's a new girl. Besides, lunch there is the best husband-hunting ground in the city."

We walked the three blocks to the restaurant at the corner of L and Connecticut, where a group of six vaguely familiar-looking women in jewel-hued dresses gathered near the front of the line to get in.

"Just in the nick of time!" one called out merrily to Patricia. "You know they won't seat us if we're not all here."

"Just have Gladys flirt with Duke again," Patricia said. "He always comps her something."

"Please," a girl in a robin's-egg blue shift dress said, shaking her head. "It was *one* time and I'd forgotten my wallet."

"Mmhmm," another girl said. "And the free order of onion rolls last time?"

Gladys wrinkled her nose. "There aren't enough Lifesavers in the city to get that smell off your breath. Couldn't he have sent over some dessert instead?"

"He was just marking his territory," Patricia said. "As long as you smelled like onions, everyone else stayed away."

"My mother would run me out of town if I married a—"

Patricia cleared her throat. "Ladies, I want you all to meet Judy *Greenberg*," she said with emphasis on my last name. "Miss Kelly hired her to fill Louise's spot."

Gladys's eyes widened. "I didn't mean anything by that—my mother just wants me to marry a good Protestant boy, that's all."

I fought the urge to press my lips together as I realized how she had intended to finish that sentence about her mother running her out of town. Being a woman wasn't going to be my only hurdle at *The Digest*, apparently.

"It's okay," I said, though I wasn't at all sure it was. Best to play it friendly. "My mother would run *me* out of town if I brought home a Protestant boy, good or not."

Gladys smiled broadly and linked her arm through mine. "I like you already," she said firmly. "I'm Gladys. This is Connie, Helen, Theresa, Maggie, and Carol."

I blinked at the rapid-fire introductions, attempting to commit them to memory. "I'm going to do my very best to remember all that," I said, prompting chuckles.

"Do you know Duke?" Gladys asked. "Since you're both Jewish."

It was better than being asked if I had horns, but the assumption that we all knew each other was tiring. I shook my head. "It's a small community, but not *that* small."

The door opened, and we were ushered into a large dining room outfitted with square tables, white linen tablecloths, and light-brown chairs all on a blue-and-brown carpet. The host brought us to a pair of tables pushed together and set for eight toward the front center of the restaurant, where menus and water glasses appeared in front of us. But I couldn't have cared less about the menu because on the way to our table, we had passed Jack Kent Cooke, the businessman who had just recently purchased a huge stake in the Washington Redskins, House Majority Leader John McCormack, and heiress Anna Wainwright, the latter of whom set my heart rate racing. Her husband owned and operated the largest and most respected newspaper in DC.

And I was about to eat lunch just ten feet from her.

I tried, rather unsuccessfully, not to stare as she and the impeccably dressed woman across from her chatted and laughed.

A balding man in his fifties came over to the table, carrying a plate of rolls. "Onion rolls on the house for my favorite ladies of *The Washington Digest*," he said, pinching Gladys playfully on the cheek. The girls all exchanged knowing smirks.

"Thank you, Mr. Zeibert," Gladys said, though she looked like she could have done without the pinch.

"I told you, it's Duke," he chided. Then he looked around the table and noticed me. "I don't believe I've had the pleasure," he said in a New York accent.

"This is Judy Greenberg," Patricia volunteered. "She just started work today."

"Greenberg," he repeated, closing one eye as he looked at me. "Your father Gil Greenberg?"

"My uncle, actually," I said.

"Ah, you must be Leonard's daughter, then." I nodded, and the girls around the table tittered. So much for the Jewish community not being *that* small. "I'd say a round of drinks on me, but I know Ann Kelly doesn't want you drinking before going back to work, so let's make it dessert, then. You tell your father and uncle I say hello."

"I will, Mr. Zeib—Duke," I said, marveling both that Miss Kelly had a first name and that he was on that sort of basis with her.

"That's a good girl," he said, putting a hand on my shoulder before moving on to another table where—yes, that was Helen Thomas. I didn't even need to eat. I just wanted to sit there and eavesdrop on all the conversations happening around me.

"I think our table just moved a few feet closer to the front next time we come," Connie said conspiratorially.

"What do you mean?" I asked.

"Seating isn't exactly a meritocracy at Duke's. You're seated in order of importance. We were farther back, despite how cute we are, until Gladys flirted."

We were currently at the back edge of the front third of the restaurant.

"For heaven's sake! I didn't *flirt*," she said. "I honestly forgot my wallet and didn't want to put any of you out."

"Speaking of putting out," Maggie said, "I assume Patricia warned you about Louise's fate?"

"Patricia did, Miss Kelly did, that Jack Fields did—"

"Of course Fields came around already," Carol said with an eye roll.

"He's an odd one," Helen said. "But I think he's harmless."

"Well, *I* heard it wasn't William Herman's baby, and that he got mad when he found out she was also messing around with—"

"Ladies," Patricia said, clapping her hands together once. "The walls have ears here, as you well know. I suggest we order."

I glanced around, and while no one seemed to be paying particular attention to us, there *were* a lot of prominent journalists nearby. Everyone at our table picked up their menus, and I did the same, taking care *not* to order the matzo ball soup, though it was one of the more affordable items on the menu. I wanted to blend in as much as my last name would allow because this was definitely the world I wanted to occupy.

5

Back at the office, I resumed grabbing stories from the board and typing them until I noticed that the sound of typewriters had ceased. I got to the end of the line I was on and looked up to see the girls packing their things in unison. A quick glance at the clock on the wall—I would have to see if Betty had a watch she wouldn't miss—told me it was the end of the day.

Then the building began to shake in earnest. Nothing like the mild rumblings I had felt off and on all day. This couldn't be the presses. It was an earthquake. I grabbed on to my desk for dear life, wondering if I was supposed to hide under it or if that was just for nuclear threats.

I was peering underneath to see if I could fit without ruining my stockings when I heard Patricia laugh.

"It's just the presses," she said. "You'll get used to it."

"How does the building stay standing with this kind of shaking?" I asked, straightening.

"Good question. But it hasn't fallen yet, so I doubt it will today." She peeked over at my typewriter. "That one doesn't have to be done until tomorrow. You can finish it in the morning."

"Is that allowed?"

She smiled. "It's up to you, of course. But there's no overtime. And Miss Kelly isn't rewarding you for working late—though she will dock you if you don't arrive on time tomorrow."

"Good to know," I said, looking around to see if other girls had left articles half finished in their typewriters or if they stored them somewhere. The typewriter seemed to be the place of choice, which did make sense—you would have to start from scratch if you pulled it out or it would never line up perfectly.

"Do you have plans tonight?"

I studied her profile, wondering if she lived at home with her parents too. I doubted it because she had talked about spending time in motels. My parents would actually die if I did something like that. And they would be sure to take me with them.

"No. I have to get home for dinner or my parents will worry."

Patricia chuckled, but there was no malice in it. "You're going to want to fix that situation in a hurry. Come on, doll. I'll walk out with you." In the elevator, she put a hand on my arm. "Let me know if you need a recommendation for a doctor."

"A doctor?"

"Diaphragm," she whispered. "You do *not* want to wind up like poor Louise."

I honestly wasn't sure which would kill my mother quicker—finding a diaphragm in my drawer or me coming home in Louise's condition. Then again, I wasn't sure she knew what a diaphragm was. She would probably use it as a bathtub stopper when she bathed Betty's kids. I grinned at the idea of Betty discovering her children bathing with a birth control device.

"I'm okay for now," I said. "But I'll let you know if that changes."

Patricia shrugged. "Just try to steer clear of the editors. They're all married, and none of them are leaving their wives, no matter what they tell you in the heat of the moment." She cocked her head. "We all speak from experience on that one."

"All? But Miss Kelly—"

"Made that rule for a reason," Patricia finished. "Look, we were all green once. You should have seen me when I first got here."

"Where are you from?" She didn't have a discernible accent, and I had trouble picturing her as "green."

"Carroll County," she said, naming an extremely rural area of Maryland about an hour and a half north of the District.

"So when you said I was fresh off the farm—?"

Patricia let out a merry peal of laughter. "Born and raised. And took off the first chance I got." She spread her arms wide as we stepped out of the building into the early evening heat of June in DC. "And look at me now. As city as they come. I haven't milked a cow in six years, and I never plan to again."

I tried to picture this cosmopolitan young woman, with her sleekly bobbed hair, fashionable dress, perfect button nose, and talk of obtaining birth control without a husband, milking a cow. It was a jarring contrast to be sure.

But I told her I would see her in the morning and made my way toward the bus stop, tired but content. I was on my way.

~

"Fields isn't a Jewish name," my mother moaned over dinner. "Didn't you meet any other men?"

I sighed, my appetite vanishing rapidly. If I told her about my conversation with Patricia, she would stop asking—though she would also forbid me from leaving the house again, so that tactic would backfire too.

"It was my first day," I said. "I need to actually do my work, so I *have* a job at which to meet men." The smell of onions wafted over from a dish at the end of the table, jogging my memory. "Oh—I did meet a Jewish man today."

"You did?" My mother beamed. "Tell me all about him."

"Daddy, he knows you—we went to Duke Zeibert's for lunch. He says hello to you—and Uncle Gil."

My mother's face turned thunderous. "Duke Zeibert is older than me and married," she said. "You know perfectly well what I was asking, young lady."

My father held up a hand, his face far more indulgent, and my mother stopped. "Duke's is actually a respectable place to meet someone far more successful than a journalist," he said. "Not the most frugal of lunch options though."

"Who cares about frugal if she meets a wealthy man there?"

"I walked right past Jack Kent Cooke," I said, seizing on my mother's enthusiasm. If lunch gave them reason enough for me to keep working—and perhaps with some extra pocket money slipped into my purse for meals—I was willing to milk that for all it was worth.

"Psh, a goy," my mother sighed, lamenting that he wasn't Jewish.

"The richest goy in the city," my father said, and I watched a debate play out across my mother's face. I considered pointing out that he was also older than my mother. And married. But none of that would help my case.

"It's okay," I said. "I was going to pack myself a sandwich for tomorrow. You're right, Daddy. I should be more frugal."

"Not so fast," my mother said, as expected. "We can spare a little money for lunches."

I hid a smile behind my water glass. This was easier than I had thought. If I didn't have to spend my own money on lunch, that women's boardinghouse got closer by the day.

6

I hadn't been issued a badge yet, so I made a pit stop on my way to work and picked up a box of doughnuts, which I presented to Frank, the security guard in the lobby. I didn't have the money to spend, but it never hurt to get on people's good sides, and he had been underwhelmed by my lack of a badge.

"For me?" he asked, his face lighting up. I nodded as he selected a cream-filled one and took a bite. He closed his eyes and let out an *mmm* sound. His eyes were shining when he opened them. "These remind me of the *quesitas* my *abuela* made when I was a kid."

I didn't know what *quesitas* or *abuela* meant and did a bit of a double take at the unfamiliar language. "Where did you grow up?"

"Puerto Rico," he said fondly. "These are the only doughnuts with the same flaky texture."

"Then Frank is short for . . . ?"

"Francisco. But here . . ." He shrugged. "Better everyone thinks I'm from Italy—the southern part." I felt a surge of compassion for him. I, of all people, knew what it was like to be rejected from a job based on a demographic factor.

I patted his arm, told him his secret was safe with me, and found myself smiling as I rode the elevator up to the typing pool. There were few problems a box of Montgomery Donuts wouldn't fix. Maybe I should bring Miss Kelly some. And when I reached my desk, there was a copy of the previous evening's edition of *The Washington Digest* sitting on the keys of my typewriter with a piece of paper clipped to the front page.

I picked it up, squinting at the messy pencil script on the note. "Your first front-page story," it read. "Thanks for the edits! -JF"

My lips curled up into a wide grin, which I quickly adjusted to a neutral face as I saw Miss Kelly watching me with a raised eyebrow. Besides, I told myself, it wasn't like I *wrote* the story. I'd had front-page bylines in *The Diamondback* with some frequency, despite the grudge the editors held against me for the error of being born a woman. This was nothing.

Except it wasn't, and I knew it. I could feel it. I was going to break into the actual newsroom. And something told me I wouldn't have to go to *The Washington Post* to do it. And then? Who knew. Maybe even *The New York Times* wasn't entirely out of the question. I thought of Patricia spreading her arms and declaring herself a city girl—but hacking it in Washington was a world away from doing the same in the city that never slept.

"Miss Greenberg." Miss Kelly's crisp voice interrupted my daydream of a prewar brownstone and the most renowned newsroom in the world.

I shook it off. "Yes, Miss Kelly?"

"You're here to work," she reminded me. I looked around—more than half the desks were still empty. Even without owning a watch yet, I knew I was early.

"Yes, Miss Kelly," I said, trying to imbue in my tone that I felt properly chastised. But I also kept the note from Fields out of sight. I wasn't fraternizing—especially not in the sense *she* meant it now that I knew all about Louise's fate. But I got the impression she wouldn't approve of me using my degree to edit either. I pocketed the note, moved the evening edition to the side, and sat, resuming work on the article I had left unfinished the previous afternoon. She stood over me for a few seconds, then crossed the room to a girl I hadn't met yet who apparently wasn't typing fast enough for her liking. At least that wasn't an issue for me. I glanced down at my fingers flying over the keys on the workhorse of an Underwood at my desk. I preferred my teal portable

Royal from college, but the keys of the newspaper typewriters did have a satisfying click to them.

A couple of hours passed somewhat tediously before a hand slapped several pages down next to me. I looked up to see Fields offering a winning smile. “Feel like another front-page story, college girl?”

“What is it?”

“Cuba again. The president wants to tighten the trade embargo even further. Choke Castro some more.” He leaned closer. “Between you and me, it’s all vindictive after the Bay of Pigs.” The failed attempt by the CIA to remove the new dictator the previous year—and subsequent declaration of a Communist state—hadn’t gone over well with our commander in chief.

I couldn’t put my finger on it, but something about his demeanor just made me itch to take him down a peg. “Trade embargoes are boring. And you’re awfully confident it’ll wind up on the front for someone who overuses em dashes when a comma would do.”

He laughed. “A Communist government ninety miles off our shore is never boring. But this is why we’re such a good team. Guaranteed above the fold with you on my side.”

“I’m not on anyone’s side.”

He leaned down closer. “Not even your own?”

I looked at him sharply. “What’s that supposed to mean?”

His shoulders lifted in a shrug. “Nothing. I just assumed you wanted to use that degree of yours to write.”

“Eventually,” I said primly. I pulled the page I had been working on from my typewriter, even though it meant I would have to start again from scratch, and wound a fresh sheet through the roller. “A girl’s gotta start somewhere.”

I picked up the first page and got to work, then realized he was still standing over my desk. “Are you going to watch me type the whole thing?”

“Does it bother you?”

“Yes,” I said tartly. It was impossible to type with accuracy with someone watching you. Everyone who had ever sat at a typewriter knew that.

"Sorry," he said, suddenly looking embarrassed. "I'll—uh—I'll be back for it, then."

"I can just put it in the pile to go upstairs."

"No, I uh . . . I like to take it up myself."

I thought back to him reading through my handiwork as I left for lunch the previous day. "You mean you like to check and make sure I didn't mess anything up."

"No—I mean—I—"

"Fields, leave her alone," Patricia said. "Do you just like this desk or something? There are twenty girls here who can type your articles for you."

"There are twenty girls here who went to secretarial school," Fields said. "There's one who has a journalism degree. And I like my work perfect."

"Everyone in here is perfectly capable," Patricia said. "Now go on. You're going to get Judy in trouble if Miss Kelly catches you down here."

"I can handle Miss Kelly."

"Can you?" Patricia asked. The two of them stared at each other for a few seconds, and if Patricia had been a man, I had the feeling it would have come to blows. There was no love lost between the two of them, that was for sure.

"How long do you need?" Fields asked me, folding first. "I'll come back."

I looked at the pages in front of me. "Seven hundred words?"

He let out a low whistle. "You're good. Seven twenty-two. But it's supposed to come in at seven, give or take five."

"You want me to cut twenty-two words?"

"Seventeen would do. If you can. If not, the copyeditors will."

I rolled my eyes. "Give me fifteen minutes."

"You did yesterday's in under ten."

"Yesterday's was three-quarters the president's words. This one, I assume, is all yours."

"Touché," Fields responded. "I'll get a cup of coffee and come back."

Patricia was still standing at my desk when he walked away. "Why don't you like him?" I asked once he was safely in the stairwell.

She made a wry face. "I'm not 100 percent convinced he wasn't the one who got Louise in trouble."

"Fields?" I asked, incredulous. Yes, he was cute, but in the same way a Jack Russell terrier was. Enthusiastic, sweet, and yappy as hell. And while I was somewhat enjoying lobbing insults his way, I couldn't picture him abandoning a problem he had made.

Patricia shrugged. "I don't know. I just know he doesn't follow the rules like the rest of the reporters do."

"I thought you said they're *all* trying to 'fraternize' with us typing pool girls?"

She shook her head with a grin. "I didn't mean *that* rule. I meant he just comes down here and picks and chooses who types his articles—like the rest of us aren't good enough. And the way he said he'd handle Miss Kelly if he got you in trouble—you'd be out of a job, and he still wouldn't think it was his fault."

She had a point. Though I minded his version of rule-breaking less than she did—as long as it didn't get me fired. In my experience, journalists who followed rules often missed out on crucial story leads. I thought back to how I had snuck into classes I wasn't enrolled in to see if there was any truth to rumors that students were cheating. I could see Fields fibbing his way into something if it meant he'd break an interesting story. And I could respect wanting someone with a keen eye reading his work—especially when that someone was me.

But the reality was, that didn't matter. The clock was ticking, and I wanted to have this article done before Fields returned to claim it. I didn't think he would have much sway with the editors as a junior reporter, but it didn't hurt to have someone male in my corner who was going to praise my abilities.

7

After lunch, a buzzing passed through the typing pool. I looked around, assuming it was Miss Kelly.

I was right—she was walking with a man whom I hadn't seen before, but who carried himself with the air of someone in charge.

Granted, that was most men in a roomful of women.

But both the cut of his suit and the way he seemed to be ordering Miss Kelly around spoke of a position of power. Miss Kelly was far from cowed in her plaid dress, belted to show off a slim waistline, and sensible shoes. But it was a good reminder that while Miss Kelly ruled the roost in the typing pool, she wasn't the final word in who wrote for *The Digest*.

"Who is that?" I whispered to Carol, whose desk was closest to mine.

"John Worthington," Carol whispered back. "The third." She offered no other information.

"Is he an editor?"

Carol looked at me askew. "He's the publisher," she said quietly. "This whole organization is his."

I smoothed my skirt, though I was still sitting, and did my best to look industrious, while also watching him from the corner of my eye, hoping to be noticed and plucked from obscurity.

Which didn't happen, of course. The silver-haired man didn't even look at anyone besides Miss Kelly that I could see. We were invisible. Worker bees, keeping the hive going, but otherwise insignificant.

He said something Miss Kelly didn't like, and she fixed him with an absolutely withering stare. For a moment, the two glowered at each other, then he bowed his head slightly and retreated to the elevator. She scowled after him in annoyance—though I had yet to see her smile. For all I knew, that was the only face she made. Then she strode through the typing pool purposefully. She walked past me and Carol, stopped, and from the clicking of her low heels, I could tell she was coming back.

"Miss Greenberg. My office. Now."

My nerves jangled. What could I have possibly done wrong? I had typed articles nonstop since my arrival except for two lunch breaks, neither of which I was late returning from. I hadn't even taken a smoke break because I was the rare modern woman who didn't smoke. *Fields,* I thought. She must have seen him at my desk again. Patricia said she had eyes in the back of her head. But I hadn't encouraged him—quite the opposite. And what was I supposed to do if he came to my desk? Ignore him?

The real answer was likely tell him to follow protocol. But that could backfire too because all it took was him complaining to someone above Miss Kelly that I had refused to type his article, and my journalism career would end before it began.

I suddenly understood why Patricia didn't like him. I wasn't such a fan myself as I trudged into Miss Kelly's office, hoping this wasn't my last time in there.

"Shut the door," she instructed without looking up from her desk.

I did as she said and stood across from her desk. She hadn't yet told me to sit, and I wasn't sure I was supposed to.

She handed me three pages, paper clipped together. "Did you type these this morning?"

The byline read "Jack Fields," and I recognized the lead immediately—which made sense. I had reworded the whole thing.

I nodded. She looked up, and I realized she hadn't seen or heard my response. "Yes, ma'am."

"Sit," she said finally. I complied, crossing my legs demurely at the ankle and fighting desperately to avoid fidgeting.

"I've been reading Jack Fields's work since he started here," she said. "This wasn't how he gave it to you."

"No, ma'am." My voice was so quiet that it was barely a whisper.

"You know we have an editorial staff for a reason?"

"Yes, ma'am."

"Do you also know he's taking credit for your work?"

I raised my eyes to meet hers. "Excuse me?"

"He walked into the newsroom today waving this around and challenging the copyeditors to find a correction."

"Were there any?" I asked before I could help myself.

A ghost of a smile crossed Miss Kelly's face, gone so quickly that I wasn't sure I hadn't imagined it.

"No," she said. "Miss Greenberg, I appreciate that you want to write. Believe it or not, I was young once, and running a newspaper typing pool with an iron fist wasn't my childhood dream."

I tried to imagine what dreams this woman, whom I could see going up against Josef Stalin and coming away the victor, could have possibly had besides overseeing an empire. I could no more picture her wanting to do something else than I could picture her young.

"But," she continued, "I did warn you that *The Digest* is not progressive enough to hire you. Nor to give you credit for your work on Fields's articles."

"What—" My voice came out too high pitched. It was squeaky on a good day, but this was a level only dogs could hear. I stopped and lowered it. "What am I supposed to do when he brings me articles, then?"

"Whatever you'd like," she said, sitting back, and again I swore I saw a hint of amusement. "If you tell him to put them on the board like everyone else does, I will support you. If you want to continue editing his work, that is your prerogative. But if you're the girl I think you are, knowing he's getting all the credit for your work won't be appealing, will it?"

"No, ma'am," I agreed. Making Jack Fields look like a far better writer than he was while I rotted away in the typing pool until I was Miss Kelly's age was the *last* thing I wanted to do. What he deserved was a quick kick to the shin. And while I had a sneaking suspicion Miss Kelly would secretly agree with that course of action, I doubted she would back me to the higher-ups if violence were involved.

She picked up another piece of paper and a pencil, crossing out a line. Then she looked up, surprised to see me still sitting there. "Back to work," she said sternly. "We don't dillydally in this office."

"Yes, ma'am. Thank you, ma'am."

And my mother thought I had no manners. Granted, Jack Fields was about to feel the same way about me, but he didn't deserve manners.

Miss Kelly nodded, and I left, shutting the door behind me.

Sixty eyes watched me exit her office, all typewriters silent. I stopped short, unsure if I should address the room, finally settling for sitting back at my desk and resuming the article I had been working on, typing with an unrestrained fury until Patricia appeared at my desk, Gladys, Helen, and Maggie in tow. Everyone was still looking at me.

"What was that about?" Patricia asked quietly, sneaking a glance at Miss Kelly's door to make sure it was still shut.

"Fields," I said with a grimace.

"She didn't—?" Helen asked.

I shook my head, understanding the implication. Then I offered a half smile. "I guess she figured two days wasn't enough time for me to wind up in Louise's shoes."

Everyone close enough to hear me let out a laugh. The others leaned in, asking neighbors what I had said, and a wave of delayed chuckles followed.

"He was taking credit for my edits," I said. "That's all."

Patricia's face darkened. "I knew he was trouble. I told you that."

"He's a man," I said, thinking of my uncle, who still blamed me for breaking up his marriage.

Another round of laughs.

"What are you going to do?" Gladys asked.

I didn't know the answer to that yet. Did I want credit for my work? Yes. Of course. I was *really* good at this. I knew it. My professors knew it. Even the editors at *The Diamondback*, who were so threatened by my lack of male genitalia, knew it.

Jack Fields clearly knew it too.

Hell, even Miss Kelly knew it.

But it didn't matter if the editors knew it. This wasn't college, where I was grudgingly granted an equal education. It was the workforce. And if the bosses upstairs didn't want me writing, I wouldn't be.

And worse, if they knew I was editing, I was likely to be out of a job too. Miss Kelly may have recognized that I could edit as well as the men upstairs, but those men weren't going to take that news in the same stride that she did. And while I was confident in my work, one mistake and I was done.

Which meant I either just typed articles exactly as they were delivered to me, or I continued to work with Fields and let him take credit for it all.

I didn't like either option.

But I also likely wouldn't have to decide until the following morning, when he brought me his next article.

"I don't know yet," I said. "Miss Kelly said she'll support me whatever I choose."

This turned heads that had started to lose interest. "She did?" Carol asked from the desk next to mine. "You're not in trouble?"

I smiled wryly. "Not yet, at least. But give me until the end of the week."

Miss Kelly stuck her head out of her office. "I don't hear typing," she said, and everyone scattered back to their desks.

8

The next morning, I dressed in my favorite of Betty's dresses—a baby-blue belted sheath with the slightest of flared ruffles at the bottom. It fit like it was made for me—Betty was three inches taller than I was, and I begrudged her every one of those inches, except when I wore this dress, which didn't hit at her waist and made her look boxy.

Though I was sure she would prefer boxy to her current shape. Poor Betty. It didn't matter how many cigarettes she smoked or how much coffee she drank—all at her doctor's orders—when she was pregnant, she just couldn't help gaining weight. Her best friend, Gertie, had proudly gained only seven pounds with each of her babies. Betty had come home inconsolable after her last appointment when the doctor had told her she was up a whopping twelve pounds.

Watching my sister go through that didn't exactly make pregnancy seem appealing. Yes, I would likely have babies *someday*. But I wasn't in any rush to lose my own figure. Or freedom. Or chance to make it as a journalist. No, I didn't know that I would choose work over having a family as Helen Thomas had. I wasn't opposed to either option—as long as they were *my* options.

And after I had slept on it, Jack Fields was about to learn that I was a woman who absolutely made her own choices.

I wished I had the matching hat to go with the dress, but Betty had given me a strong talking-to about taking her things after discovering her pink pillbox missing. Which was rather ironic considering the lecture was given as she was packing up the clothes that now constituted my work wardrobe for "storage" purposes. But what Betty didn't know wouldn't hurt her. And while my mother *had* to know I didn't have permission to wear her clothes, she said nothing that morning as I went to leave for work, only straightened my collar, kissed my cheek, and told me to go meet an eligible man.

She would probably loan me her own jewelry, which had been strictly off limits since I borrowed some for a formal sorority event in college, if it would help me catch a husband. I had returned it all intact; she was just miffed I hadn't asked first. But if I had asked, the answer would have been no, and I preferred to beg for forgiveness than be denied permission.

Another newspaper sat on my typewriter when I arrived, a note paper clipped to it. I picked it up in a gloved hand—thankfully Betty was running too hot to wear gloves this summer, and I had pointed out that drawer space was about to become precious with *three* children in the house. "You're my lucky charm," the note read.

I felt my jaw tighten. My favorite journalism professor liked to say, "The harder you work, the luckier you get." So yes, I was his lucky charm because *I* worked hard. He, on the other hand, could go take a flying leap into the Potomac River.

In concrete shoes.

I balled the note up and dropped it in the wastepaper basket next to my desk. But I did slip the newspaper into my handbag. It may not have been my name on the article, but it *was* my work. That lead was all me. The third paragraph, where I had restructured the description of the Bay of Pigs into something more palatable to both the casual reader and the experienced newshound. The way I had cut the unimportant part of one quote to blend it with one used lower down to complete a thought effectively. If I squinted enough, that *J* for *Jack* in the byline could almost be for *Judy*. I might vindictively cross out Fields's name, but I wasn't going to throw it away.

More of the typing pool came by to introduce themselves when they took smoke breaks throughout the morning. I wasn't sure if it was the support of Miss Kelly, the fact that I got the room to laugh, or if they just wanted front-row seats when I eviscerated Jack Fields later, but I would take any camaraderie I could get.

Sure enough, just after eleven, Fields came striding back into the room, a smile on his face as he slapped his pages down on my desk.

I continued typing and ignored him. But the collective sound of keys slowed to a near stop around me. He cleared his throat, and I continued to type.

"Hey, Judy," he said, crouching down to be at my level.

"Miss Greenberg," I corrected coolly. I still hadn't looked up at him and definitely made a typo as I saw him tilt his head like a confused puppy in my peripheral vision. I didn't actually care that I would have to retype the article I was working on, but I didn't want him to notice that he had caused the error.

"Right," he said. From the corner of my eye, I saw him put a hand to the back of his neck. "Miss Greenberg." He leaned in closer. "I've got a doozy of an article for you today."

"Do you?" I asked, conveying as little interest as I could in my voice. "I suggest you put it on the board. If no one else takes it, I may later."

"I—what? No. You don't—" He lowered his voice to a whisper. "This one is extremely sensitive. I need a professional set of eyes on it."

I pulled the paper from my typewriter roll, putting it on the corner of my desk like I was going to turn it in, not throw it away and redo it, and finally turned in my seat to face him. "Mr. Fields, I believe they have editors upstairs who are paid to fill that role. Unless, of course, you want them to think that my work is yours?"

He colored slightly. "I—you heard about . . . that?"

"I did."

"It's—it's a testament to you, actually, if you think about it. They couldn't find a single edit that needed to be made."

"Except you said it was a testament to your own work." I leveled him with a withering glare, fully aware that the whole typing pool was straining to hear us. "And quite frankly, I've seen better leads than yours in a high school newspaper."

He stood up, towering over me at my desk. "I'll have you know—"

"Mr. Fields—in the future, if you'd like my help, ask for it. I work for Miss Kelly, not you. And there's a reason we have a system in the typing pool. I suggest you use it from now on."

He stared at me for a long moment, but I stood my ground. If I were a man, I would have taken his job already. But I wasn't. And this was the best I could do—which, thanks to Miss Kelly, was more than most women in the workplace could say.

"Right," he said eventually. "I—I'm sorry." But he still stood there, paper on my desk, as if he expected that to fix the situation.

I inclined my head toward his article. "As I said, that belongs on the board."

"But didn't you just finish—"

"Is anyone ready to go to lunch?" I asked the office, every head of which was turned in our direction.

For a few seconds, no one responded. "I'll go," a girl who had introduced herself as Linda said, standing up.

Patricia rose next. "Don't go without me," she said.

"I'm ready," Carol added.

I smiled at him as patronizingly as I could. "I suggest you put it on the board, Mr. Fields. I'll be a while."

And with that, I took my purse from the bottom drawer of my desk and swept past him, my new friends following.

9

"The nerve of that man!" I exclaimed for about the third time.

In the end, we formed a group of twelve girls for lunch, and we grabbed sandwiches from a deli to eat outside in Farragut Park. We lacked a picnic blanket, so we crowded onto the low wall surrounding the statue of the Civil War admiral, who, the plaque told us, coined the phrase "Damn the torpedoes—full speed ahead."

I looked up at the statue's face, thinking I detected a hint of a grin. As annoyed as I was at Fields, the camaraderie of the typing pool ladies made the sun seem to shine brighter.

"I told you I didn't like him," Patricia reminded me.

"Yeah, but you thought he knocked Louise up."

Most of the girls laughed. "He isn't Louise's type at all," Connie said. "She liked them older and married."

My mouth dropped open.

"Oh, honey," Gladys said. "Don't look so shocked."

"Be nice," Patricia said, elbowing Gladys. "It's her first week. The old men upstairs don't even know she exists yet."

"Are you serious that Louise got pregnant by a married man?" I asked. "What's she going to do?"

Carol shrugged. "Take care of it or hope he takes care of her."

Of all the girls I knew who had found themselves in trouble, only one didn't get married. Granted, a girl who lived on my floor in college got married quickly after and it was *not* to the boy whom she had been seeing prior to missing her cycle. Betty once whispered to me that that was why religion came down from the mother's side. A father wasn't a guarantee.

And the one who hadn't gotten married, well, her mother had taken her to a special doctor, and suddenly there wasn't a problem anymore. So I knew these things happened. But the blasé nature with which they were being discussed by women in the working world was a bit jarring.

Still, I felt for Louise, despite not knowing her. She had made a mistake, but the options left for her future were dismal at best, with zero consequences for the man who was just as much, if not more, at fault. He was the one who had taken—and broken—vows after all.

Not that I would be taking Patricia up on her diaphragm advice. Keeping my legs closed was enough, thank you very much.

"So if we're not allowed to fraternize, and the editors are married—"

"Most of the reporters are too," Deborah chimed in.

I involuntarily pictured Fields's ink-stained hands. I didn't remember seeing a ring. But then again, if he wasn't Louise's type because he was young and unmarried, there wouldn't be one, would there?

I grinned devilishly. "Then who, exactly, are you using that diaphragm with, Patricia?"

Everyone burst into whoops of laughter. I looked over to make sure I hadn't offended her, but she was laughing hardest of all.

"This month? Or last?"

Gladys elbowed her. "You're terrible."

"And what are *you*?" Patricia asked.

"Terrible," Gladys said, laughing merrily.

"It's not like the old days," Connie said. "We might as well have a little fun before we settle down and get married and start popping out babies."

I thought of Betty, pregnant with her third and just a couple years older than me, and agreed.

Though my idea of fun was different from theirs.

I looked up at the statue behind me again as we stood to leave. I had no idea what he had done besides say that line. But I doubted *he* would let another man take credit for his work.

Then again, who knew if he had actually said, "Damn the torpedoes"? Maybe he just took the credit himself and now had a statue while the poor slob who had *actually* said one of the most famous military quotes in history rotted, forgotten, in a rural cemetery.

I may not have had much power in this field or this world overall, but as I looked at my coworkers, all in bright, colorful dresses, most arm in arm walking back to the office, I realized we had more sway than any man in there gave us credit for. And maybe more than we ourselves thought too. If we walked out, the newspaper would shudder to a halt until they could replace and train an entirely new typing pool.

Not that any of us would do that. We all worked here because we needed the money, myself included, even if my main motivation was to move up the ladder to reporter.

And realistically, I wanted Fields's job. Well—okay, not *junior* White House correspondent. I wanted to be the real deal. I didn't want to be reporting solely on women's issues, which most of the few female reporters out there did. My mother may have devoured the For and About Women section of *The Washington Post*, but my father, Uncle Gil, and Betty's husband wouldn't touch that section with a ten-foot pole. I wanted to write stories that everyone read.

With my name on the byline. Front page. Above the fold.

"Judy!" Patricia said, and I realized from her urgency that it wasn't the first time she had called my name.

"Sorry," I said. "Head in the clouds."

She nodded toward the front door of *The Digest*, where Fields stood, a bouquet of wildflowers in hand.

"Think you have an admirer." The girls tittered.

I rolled my eyes. "An apology so he can keep taking credit for my work isn't the same as an admirer. Besides, imagine me bringing home someone with the last name Fields. My mother would lock me in the house and never let me out again."

Real laughs this time. Their mothers would be equally horrified if any of them brought home a Jewish man, as Gladys had pointed out on my first day—was that really only two days ago? So much had happened since then. I felt worldly and wise compared to that naive girl.

"You'll need a better bouquet than that, Fields," Patricia said as she passed him.

"Aw, lay off me, Patti," Fields said.

Patricia laughed and pinched his cheek. The two of them stood about eye to eye with Patricia in heels. I would have had to stand on an apple box to do the same.

I tried to walk past him, but Fields grabbed my arm. "Listen, Judy, I—"

"Miss Greenberg," I reminded him. "I'm not on a first-name basis with thieves. Now if you'll excuse me."

"I'm not a thief," he said, wounded. But he hadn't dropped my arm.

"Are you okay?" Carol asked me.

I debated saying no and letting the typing pool overpower Fields. But even with Miss Kelly's promised backing, making a full enemy in the newsroom didn't seem smart. So I nodded and told her I would see her inside in a minute.

"Give him the old right hook if he gets handsy," Gladys said to riotous laughter.

I shook my head and shooed them with my free hand. Then I turned back to Fields. "What do you want, Fields?"

"To apologize," he said. "I didn't mean any harm. You did really great work, and I was impressed. If you think about it, it was actually kind of a compliment."

"A compliment," I repeated. "To make everyone think *you* did such great work on your own?"

He smiled painfully. "Okay, well, when you put it that way . . ."

He sounded sincere. But I was so tired of having to fight for everything that he was handed just because I was a woman. "Good day, Mr. Fields." I wrenched my arm free and started toward the door.

"Judy—I mean Miss Greenberg, wait." I stopped but didn't turn around. "You're—you're good. You've got a really good eye." I turned halfway, which encouraged him to continue. "Why don't you go get a job at one of the papers with a women's section? I'm sure someone would hire you in a second."

In a flash, I was in front of him.

"So I can write about fashion and hairstyles and how to get a stain out of a pair of your husband's trousers?"

"Well, I don't have a husband, but—"

"Because I don't *want* to do that. I want to cover the news. The real news that *everyone* reads. Not just my mother and her friends. How many women are there in the White House Press Corps?"

"One," he admitted.

"Helen Thomas," I said. "That's it. And she got hired as a reporter during the war because so many male correspondents were overseas. Now everyone is home, and we're just expected to stay in our kitchens or write about what to do in one."

"There are plenty of women who have done important work in journalism though. What about—"

"I swear to God, if you say Nellie Bly right now . . ."

He shut his mouth.

"Exactly," I said. "You can name two."

"Anna Wainwright worked at *The Post* before—"

"Before she got married," I finished for him. "And her father *owned* the newspaper. Why isn't she running it now?"

He closed his mouth again.

"I wasn't born an heiress. I live with my parents in Silver Spring. There isn't a war going on to clear the newsrooms. And I don't have Joseph Pulitzer funding my crazy adventures. What I have is a good work ethic, strong writing abilities, great typing skills, drive, and grit.

And when a man like you tells everyone that you're the one doing what I can do, it makes it harder for me to get ahead. Do you understand yet?"

For a long moment, he said nothing. Then, very quietly: "I do. And I'm sorry."

"Yeah, well that and thirty-five cents will buy you a cup of coffee." I looked down at the flowers, still in his hand. "Did you pick those yourself?"

He nodded. "From Franklin Park."

"Which is federally maintained. So that was illegal." He blanched, and I felt a little sorry for him. But a quick glance up showed me that the typing pool was watching us through the lobby windows, and I didn't want to show weakness in front of them. "Have a nice afternoon, Mr. Fields. I have work to do."

And with that, I swept into the building, leaving him gawking after me.

"Lovers' spat?" Frank asked at the door.

I scowled. "Absolutely not."

Frank chuckled.

Later, at my desk, I found my mind wandering to his apology. It had felt genuine. And it wasn't like anyone upstairs—except Fields—was going to believe the work was mine anyway. But I shrugged. I had slammed that door closed, and I doubted he'd be back with an article for me anytime soon. I might as well focus on what was in front of me.

10

My family wasn't religious. I set foot in synagogue exactly four times a year if no one had a baby, a bar mitzvah, or a wedding. Twice for Rosh Hashanah, twice for Yom Kippur. And we kept what we joked was called "Maryland kosher," meaning we *basically* kept kosher in the house, but crabs were the exception. Because those were eaten off newspaper, not plates, and typically outdoors at a picnic table, they didn't upset the balance.

At least that's what we told ourselves.

But every Friday night, we all gathered at my parents' house for Shabbat dinner. Me, my sister, her husband, their growing brood, occasionally Uncle Gil, and always my grandmother Sylvia, who lived with us. She came to America when she was five from some town in Russia whose name seemed to contain the entire alphabet.

It didn't matter what plans I had—and that included when I was in college—my presence was expected. Demanded. Required. And no, attending Shabbat at Hillel on campus did not qualify as good enough.

So the first week of my employment was no different. Some of the girls from the office said they were going out for drinks and invited me to join them, but I had to explain that Friday nights were nonnegotiable. I doubted that would change even if I moved to New York—they would expect me on that train home every Friday afternoon.

"I get it," Carol said. "If I miss church on Sunday, my parents will disown me."

"Yeah, but you have a *lot* to confess to," Gladys said.

"I'm not Catholic!"

"Maybe you should be—you could use a clean slate."

We all laughed. But I still left promptly at five, watching as the girls walked in the opposite direction while I went to catch the bus home.

The job wasn't all I had hoped for—typing all day was tedious and I longed to interview people and collect information, sifting through and slotting it into the inverted pyramid to make sure readers got the most important information first. It drove me crazy when an article buried the lead or put unimportant details too close to the top. But it wasn't my place to fix these errors—and unlike with Fields, who wanted feedback, if another reporter traced an overhaul of their work to *me*, not Editorial, I'd wind up out on my behind pretty quickly. I did regret losing that single avenue to enjoying my work. Loath as I was to admit it, reworking Jack's articles had been a highlight of my week.

But I maintained hope that it would lead to more. I couldn't give that up. I had to believe things were going to change—even if not as quickly as I wanted them to—so that I could have a chance to achieve more than a secretarial job as a pit stop on the way to marriage. I wanted more than that so badly I could taste it. Yet it was still dangling out of reach, a couple of floors above my head.

I got home, called a quick hello, and ran upstairs to freshen up, change out of Betty's dress before I got caught, and scrub the typewriter ink off my fingers. If I was smart, I told myself, I would start wearing my own dresses on Fridays, so I wouldn't risk Betty spotting me in hers.

The house smelled of fresh challah, my mother's brisket, and the onions that seasoned various potato dishes. There was no better scent than a Jewish household on a Friday night, and I hurried back downstairs, hungry, tired, and ready to fall into bed after dinner, where I was greeted with my alternative to success.

I stopped short at the sight of a man sitting next to my seat at the table, which had been rearranged to squeeze in the extra spot. I glanced at my mother, bustling around the dining room, placing dishes of food, and my sister, who was helping her, though she snaked a hand behind herself to rub her lower back frequently. My mother caught my eye and inclined her head toward my chair, telling me to sit. I obliged but wasn't happy. As much as I didn't want to be serving the food after a week of working, it was infinitely preferable to my family staring at me during an attempted fixup.

"Hello," I said cautiously.

He looked over at me, and my heart sank. This was not some dashing stranger who would understand my desire to have a career before a family. He was at least ten years older than me, not much taller, heavyset, and balding. He wore glasses, behind which were a pair of mildly crossed brown eyes, over a nose that a girl would have had fixed by now. If I had children with this man, they would be doomed, even with the obligatory sweet sixteen nose job.

"Hello," he said around a mouthful of my grandmother's mock chopped liver.

And he talked with his mouth full. Nope. Absolutely not. I may have been twenty-two, unmarried, and employed—a trifecta of *shandas*—or shames—according to my family, but I did have standards.

"Judy, meet Gordon Levy. He's a cantor." My mother was brimming with pride.

"Shouldn't a cantor know to wait until we say the *motzi* to eat?" I clapped a hand over my mouth. I hadn't meant to say that out loud, and the consequences would be—

"Judith!" My mother was horrified. Uncle Gil's lips were pursed in dissatisfaction though not surprise. Betty blinked heavily and shook her head. Her husband, Reuben, slapped a hand to his forehead. Only my father and grandmother looked amused, though my father quickly replaced his almost smile with a stern look after a glance at my mother.

"Sorry," I said. "It's been a long week. I'm overtired. I shouldn't have—"

"You're not wrong," Cantor Levy said amiably. "But I find that deference to elders is more important than blessings, and your grandmother insisted I try her chopped liver."

"Mock," I said. "It's made of lentils."

"Don't give away family recipes unless you're planning to marry him," my grandmother said. She reached across the table and put a hand on mine. "I don't think we're worried about that tonight though."

"Sylvia!" My mother said.

But I was bolstered by the support.

"Your parents tell me you started a new job this week," Cantor Levy said. "At a newspaper?"

I nodded. "*The Washington Digest.*"

"Oh," he said noncommittally. "I subscribe to *The Washington Post.*"

So did we, but I didn't like the way he was shrugging off my new job. Never mind that *I* didn't even read *The Digest.*

"We subscribe to both," my father said.

"We do?" I asked.

He winked at me. "As of this morning. Delivery starts Monday."

My heart swelled in my chest. As mad as he should have been that I didn't bother with Uncle Gil's interview, he was proud of me.

My mother pulled a matchbook from the credenza, and the table quieted as she lit the candles and then covered her eyes to say the traditional Shabbat prayers. We all said, "Shabbat shalom," and then she asked if Cantor Levy would like to lead us in the motzi—the prayer said before eating.

Not that we literally ever said it except on Friday nights or as part of the Passover seder. But Cantor Levy opened his mouth, and his clear tenor rose, far too loud for our dining room, in a voice that was better suited to *shul* than a family dining table. I wondered, as he drew the syllables out longer than any human needed to, who was singing to his congregation tonight.

I also wondered how such an ugly man could have such a lovely voice, but I supposed it balanced out.

Dinner was easy enough—largely because I was too exhausted from the week to do much to put this man off. But when the meal was finished, and I stood up to help my mother clear the table, she stopped me.

"You should take Cantor Levy to the living room," she said. "Get to know him a little."

The only times I had been allowed to sit on the white sofas in our formal living room were when I was in trouble—big trouble—or when my parents were telling me someone had died. Betty's kids weren't allowed to play on the furniture in there. And I hadn't graduated to sitting unless I had crashed the car and needed a stern lecture. Or—I glanced at my grandmother—no, she was definitely still breathing.

"Mom, I'm awfully tired and—"

"Be polite to our guest," she hissed at me.

I looked to my dad for help, but he pretended not to notice. He would subscribe to a newspaper for me, but stand up to my mother? That was uncharted territory full of unknown perils.

I was on my own.

"Cantor Levy, would you like to join me in the living room?"

"I'd be delighted," he said, rising and offering me his arm. I pretended not to notice. It was all of a ten-foot journey after all. Though I did note that I was a smidge taller than him in my three-inch heels. For me, that was quite the feat.

"My parents must like you," I said wryly as he sat on the sofa. I opted for an armchair. The white sofas gave me the heebie-jeebies after so many years of lectures on them.

"Why's that?"

"I'm not allowed in this room."

He chuckled. "How old are you anyway? Nineteen?"

My mouth turned down. My mother had probably knocked a couple of years off my age to lure him here. I was bordering on spinster territory according to her after all.

"Twenty-two. I graduated from the University of Maryland last month."

"Really?"

"Is that so surprising?"

"To still be unmarried, well—yes."

Here it was. "Cantor Levy—"

"Gordon," he said amiably. "We're not in *shul* tonight."

"Yes, well, you should know that I have no interest in getting married anytime soon."

He looked confused.

"I want to make a name for myself in journalism."

"Why?" The question was said without disdain but with genuine incredulity.

"Because I love it," I said. "Why did you become a cantor?"

"Well"—he puffed out his chest, and the resemblance to a bespectacled toad became uncanny—"you've heard me sing."

"Yes, well . . . that's how I write. Like how you sing."

"That's hardly a realistic comparison."

I wondered what would happen if I yelled for my father and said this man had put his hand up my skirt. He'd show him the door—unless my mother insisted that was grounds for marriage. Not worth the risk. Though it had worked when I was seventeen and Uncle Gil had come to dinner with a girlfriend and her creepy son.

But a cantor was a different story altogether.

I was saved by my grandmother wandering into the room and plopping down on the other, unoccupied, sofa. "In my day, an unmarried man and woman needed a chaperone," she said. Then she belched, closed her eyes, and began to snore.

Loudly.

Too loudly.

In fact, every time Cantor Levy started to speak, the snores got louder, to the point where it was a futile endeavor and he eventually rose to leave. My grandmother opened one eye and grinned at me before resuming her fake snores.

"I suppose I should be going," he said, standing. "Shabbat services in the morning and all. You should come—Temple Beth Shalom."

Beth Shalom was an Orthodox congregation a couple of miles away. Men didn't sit with women, and services there could go five or six hours easy. I would absolutely not be doing that.

"Thank you so much for the offer, but I'm afraid I am otherwise engaged tomorrow morning."

His brows came together. "On Shabbat?"

"Yes. Orthodox life just isn't for me."

He opened his mouth to argue, and my grandmother let out a little sleep shriek that I was sure was actually a disguised laugh.

"I see. Yes, well, if you have plans on Shabbat, I suppose this isn't going to work anyway."

"No, Cantor Levy, it is not. Good night."

"Tell your parents I said thank you for the lovely meal."

I told him I would, but I remained in the living room while he left. The second the front door closed, my grandmother's eyes sprang open. I plopped down in the spot next to her on the forbidden sofa and leaned my head on her shoulder. "Thank you."

She put an arm around me. "You'll marry a man who behaves—and looks—like that over my dead body."

"Grandma!"

"What?"

"Don't say that in here! I'm only allowed on these sofas when I'm in trouble or my parents need to tell me someone died."

She reached up and pinched my cheek. "It'll take more than a white sofa to kill me. Though your mother might come after *you* for rejecting a cantor." She pulled a small wrapped chocolate from her pocket, rubbed it between her hands like she was trying to start a fire, and then opened it. With a hand on me to steady her, she stood up, went to the other sofa, and smeared the now-melted chocolate on the seat.

"What are you doing?" I asked, panicked. I was going to get blamed for this. I knew it.

"*Bubbelah*, do you think this is my first time dealing with your mother? We're going to tell her he stained her good sofa. And I doubt she'll smell to see that it's chocolate. He won't be back."

I laughed merrily. The rest of my family may have thought I was pure trouble, but if anyone questioned where I came from, they needed to look no further than my grandmother.

"Now," she said. "Tell me everything about this job. Do you know I had a job when I first came here? I worked as a soda girl, and I loved every minute of it." I did know that, but I let her reminisce before I told her all about my adventures from the week. Though I did leave out Patricia's birth control advice. We *were* still on the white sofas after all.

11

Monday morning, I was about to go catch the bus when my father told me to wait. I glanced at the door impatiently. Waiting could mean the difference between being early and being late, and a conversation that needed to happen before I left the house was never a good sign.

But he merely set his coffee down, took his sports coat from the back of his chair, kissed my mother goodbye, and said, "I'll drive you. It's only a little out of my way."

His office was up in Woodley Park, which was actually a long drive from *The Digest* in rush hour traffic, but I wouldn't turn down a ride. I hadn't seen cat-food woman again, but the rest of the people who rode my bus to work were not a dramatic improvement.

"So," he said as we took Sixteenth Street down into the city, "work is going well?"

Unlike with my mother, I could be a little more honest with him. "It's a little . . . repetitive," I said. "I'm just typing all day. For now."

"Do you think they'll let you write your own articles soon?"

"I don't know." The raw honesty in my voice surprised even me. "But I'm going to try my best."

"Good. Your mother—" He cleared his throat, and I looked at his profile in the car. I had my mother's nose, jawline, and chin, but my father and I shared our wide brown eyes, pale skin, and dark hair. Betty and I were like a negative image that way. She had my father's nose and face shape but my mother's reddish hair, freckles, and hazel eyes. Yet we somehow still looked enough alike that no one ever questioned if we were sisters. "Your mother wanted you at your uncle's office so he'd look out for you. You know how—men—can be—and . . ."

I didn't like where this was going one bit.

"I'm there to work," I said firmly. "I plan to be a reporter, and no one is going to derail that."

He swallowed visibly. "Some men aren't good at taking no for an answer."

We stopped at a light, and he didn't look over at me. "Dad, I may be small, but I am scrappy as hell, and you know it."

"Language," he said reflexively, but his posture loosened slightly.

"Listen—a reporter had me edit his work and tried to take credit for it. You'd better believe I put him in his place."

He finally smiled. "I do believe you did just that." Then he flipped on the radio, eliminating the need for a further awkward conversation.

When we finally pulled up to *The Digest*'s office on L Street, I went to get out of the car and thanked him. "You don't have to drive me in the mornings," I told him. "I know you would have cut through Rock Creek Park to get to the office if you hadn't."

His head tilted. "I would have. But then I wouldn't have gotten time with you. I won't be able to drive you if I have any early appointments, but I don't mind saving you the bus fare when I don't. Now go give those reporters hell."

"Language," I said with a smile.

My father winked. "I'd assume you hear worse than that in a newsroom."

I was grinning when I walked in.

But when I got to the third floor, Miss Kelly was standing at my desk. It was still ten minutes to eight, so I wasn't late. *Fields,* I thought. She had told me she would back me whatever I decided, but that either hadn't extended to my tirade last week or else someone above her had heard I was editing and wasn't happy.

"Miss Kelly," I said with a nod. Maybe this was nothing.

"You're up on seven today."

"Excuse me?"

"Mr. Pullman's secretary is ill, and he needs a girl from the typing pool to fill in."

George Pullman was a managing editor. And in theory, if he warmed to me, this could be my chance.

But I also had zero secretarial training and hadn't a clue of what I would be expected to do. The thrill of the typing pool had worn off within days, but at least I understood the work and it was journalism adjacent. This was far outside my area of expertise.

"Wouldn't one of the girls who completed secretarial school be—?"

"Do you see them here?" she asked curtly. "He needs someone now. You'll answer phone calls and take messages—unless it's Mr. Worthington or Mrs. Pullman, he is unavailable. Type any memos he dictates, show people who have meetings on the book into his office, and fetch his coffee. One cream, two sugars. Don't bother him. Don't talk to him unless he talks to you. Got it?"

I did not. But I nodded.

"Good. Go up now. Seventh floor, directly above my office." She turned to leave.

"Is it just for today?"

"I haven't the faintest of ideas," she said, walking into her office and shutting the door.

As the elevator crept slowly upward, I cursed the luck that my father had driven me, getting me to the office early.

But just as the door opened on seven, I also realized that she had been standing at my desk. Maybe—maybe this was her way of putting me in the path of Mr. Pullman because it could lead to a writing opportunity. A hint of a smile returned to my face. Miss Kelly wasn't so bad as long as you did as you were told.

And it certainly felt like it wasn't only my father rooting for my success now.

12

The desk in front of the office Miss Kelly had directed me to was empty, though it had a framed photograph of a young man, who could have been a boyfriend or a son depending on the age of Mr. Pullman's secretary. He was handsome, whoever he was.

That might have been the real reason Miss Kelly sent me though. Powerful men tended to like pretty secretaries, and my father's words rang in my ears about men not always being good at taking no for an answer.

I peeked in the top desk drawer and saw a sharp, silver letter opener. Worst case scenario, that could serve as a firmer no than my voice. Though if I had to resort to something like that . . . well . . . my time at *The Digest* was going to be short.

I shut the drawer and looked around for a clock. It was a little far away and I had to squint, but it was just about eight now.

The elevator opened and several women stepped out, chatting with each other before taking their places at desks outside other offices. None of them so much as looked at me. Apparently there was a hierarchy among the women at *The Digest*, and the typing pool was beneath the editors' secretaries. But I had a sneaking suspicion that some of them must have started in the typing pool as well.

The phone at my desk rang loudly, startling me. "Mr. Pullman's office," I said, realizing I had no idea how I was supposed to answer.

Washington Digest? George Pullman? Managing editor? Who even *had* this phone number?

"You're not Myrtle," the voice said accusatorily.

"She's—uh—she's sick today. I'm filling in." I hoped Myrtle was Mr. Pullman's secretary and that this wasn't a wrong number.

"Put me on with George."

"Mr. Pullman isn't in at the moment. Let me take a message, and he'll get back to you as soon as he can." I had no idea if he was in his office or not.

"Bull—"

"Your name?" I cut him off before he could prove my father right that I would hear worse language.

"Willis," he said angrily. "Bob Willis."

"Yes, Mr. Willis. Can you tell me what this is regarding?"

"He knows damn well what this is regarding and if he wants more access to the secretary of defense, he's going to call me back quickly if he knows what's good for him."

Access to the secretary of defense, I wrote on the telephone message pad I had found on the desk. *Call back requested ASAP.* "And your phone number?"

"He has it," the man said and hung up.

"Well, that was unpleasant," I said out loud.

The girl at the nearest desk looked over, uninterested. "I'd keep your opinions to yourself if I were you," she said before rolling a sheet of paper into her typewriter.

So much for the camaraderie I had found in the typing pool.

The elevator opened again, and I sat up straighter as five men, all about my father's age, walked out. The editors had arrived.

The tallest of them approached my desk. "You're not Myrtle," he said. I stood up, and he looked me over from head to toe, an admittedly short trip.

"No, she's ill today. Are you Mr. Pullman?"

"I should hope so," he said, moving past me to enter his office.

"A Mr. Willis called for you," I said to his back.

He stiffened. "I'll take a cup of coffee, before I deal with that. One cream—"

"Two sugars," I finished. "Right away, sir."

He looked back over his shoulder in approval before shutting his door. And I looked around for a coffeepot.

"Second door on your left," the secretary nearest to me said without looking up. "No ladies' room on this floor either. You have to go down to five for that. And best make sure someone watches your phone for you if you do."

"Can you watch it while I get Mr. Pullman a cup of coffee?"

She sighed, clearly not meaning herself, but nodded. Then ignored me again. I did *not* have faith in her dedication to answering Mr. Pullman's phone, so I hurried to the second door on the left. I kept the door open, my ears alert for ringing, and went to the machine on the counter of the tiny kitchenette. My parents still had a percolator. This was a newer drip coffee model, and I had no idea how it worked.

A tall, buxom blonde came in as I dug through a drawer hoping to find an instruction manual. "What are you doing?" she asked, a cigarette in one hand.

"Please tell me you know how this coffeepot works," I said, wiping at a bead of perspiration on my forehead with the back of my hand.

She smiled at least. "You're in for Myrtle today?" I nodded. "Easy. You fill this with water." She took the pot from me and brought it to the sink to demonstrate. "Then you take a filter"—she reached into a cabinet and brought out a flimsy paper cone—"and put it in this top part. Scoop the coffee in, pour the water, turn it on, and wait. Mugs are in this cabinet. Cream in the refrigerator. Sugar over here."

"Thank you," I said, suddenly ashamed that I didn't even know how to use a coffeemaker from this decade.

"They just got it a few months ago," she said. "We all had to learn." She took a drag of her cigarette. "I'm Florence."

"Judy."

"Cigarette?"

I shook my head. "I don't smoke. But thank you."

"Can't make coffee, don't smoke—you sure you're in the right place, hon?"

I laughed. "No." There was something friendly in her manner, and I found myself being honest. "I belong in the newsroom."

She looked at me appraisingly, then the corners of her mouth turned down. "Not here, unfortunately."

"That's what Miss Kelly said too."

"She would know," Florence said.

My eyes widened. "You mean Miss Kelly wanted to write?"

"I have no idea. She just seems to know how everything works here. I think the whole paper would shut down if she took a sick day."

What an oddity that a woman was that integral to the running of the organization, yet women weren't allowed to do more than type articles, fetch coffee, and answer phones.

Then again, how different was that from a household, really? At least here I didn't also have to cook, clean, and diaper babies.

The coffee gurgled and hissed as drops began to fall, and soon black liquid filled the glass carafe.

I reached for it, but Florence told me to wait. "Give it one more . . ." Another few drops fell. "There. Now you can pour it."

I filled the cup and then added cream and sugar. "Thank you," I told Florence. "I owe you one."

"No problem," Florence said, filling two cups and immediately taking a sip of black coffee from one of them. "We're allowed as much as we want too," she said when she saw me watching her.

I didn't really drink coffee either. Though I supposed another few weeks here and I would be drinking coffee and smoking as well.

I thanked her again and started back toward Mr. Pullman's office, when she touched my arm. "Keep the door open whenever you're in his office." Her voice was low, a warning in her tone.

"What if he tells me to close it?"

She shook her head. "Find an excuse. Though he prefers leggy blondes. Miss Kelly may have picked you on purpose."

Florence fit the definition of a leggy blonde. I could feel my nostrils flare in distaste and wondered if everywhere in the working world was this bad for women. I didn't want to be in the typing pool, but at least I was safe there, surrounded by other women.

I told her I would be careful, then went back to Mr. Pullman's office, where I knocked on the door. I could hear him talking to someone, and he didn't seem to notice the knock—my options were to let his coffee get cold or slip inside as inconspicuously as possible and deliver his drink. I opted for the latter.

He was facing away from the door, his chair swiveled toward the window, where the Washington Monument was visible over a few buildings. "I told you already—I don't care what the second lady does. We only care what *he* does." A pause. "*Everyone* knows that. I'm sure even *she* knows that." I placed the coffee on his desk and backed out of the room as quietly as I could.

My day passed in a blur of transcribing notes from his IBM Executary dictation device, fetching coffee, and answering calls. At five on the dot, he came out of his office, a hat on his head, and walked past me. Then he stopped and turned around. "I don't even know your name. Who are you?"

"Judy Greenberg, sir."

His mouth turned down slightly. "Greenberg, you say?"

I stood my ground. "Yes, sir."

"Well, as long as you're not handling money, I'm sure you'll do fine. Tell Miss Kelly you can come back tomorrow."

I bristled at the jab, but nodded. "Yes, sir."

He left, and I gathered my things to go home as well, but I stopped on the third floor to give Miss Kelly the message first.

"Interesting," she said.

"Why's that?"

"Never you mind. Between you and me, Myrtle isn't coming back. We'll do interviews later this week." She looked up at me. "Unless he likes you enough to keep you."

I didn't appreciate being referred to like I was a stray dog he had found on the street. "What if I don't want to be his secretary?"

Once again, a hint of amusement crossed her face. "Somehow, I believe you could pull off being incompetent if that were to be the case. Though I think this could be a chance for you to get closer to your goal."

I was less sure of that as I clearly already had two strikes with Mr. Pullman between being a woman and being Jewish. But if he liked me, *maybe* he would be willing to take a chance on me writing once I earned his trust.

"I'll think about it," I told Miss Kelly.

"I'll need an answer by the end of business Wednesday if he doesn't send you back before then."

"Yes, Miss Kelly."

But as I rode the bus home, I thought about Mr. Pullman's eyes wandering over my frame when he first saw me. I might keep that letter opener on me this week after all.

13

Tuesday saw me fending off more irate phone callers, and I began to realize why the *Tell everyone Mr. Pullman isn't available* rule was created. Literally everyone who called was either shouting or cursing.

It also became apparent that Myrtle had likely left by choice. I didn't know how many days of being screamed at for things I didn't know anything about I had in me either. But taking to heart Miss Kelly's musing that this could get me closer to writing, I had Mr. Pullman's coffee brewed before he arrived and a cup on his desk within a minute of him sitting down.

At the end of the day, when he went to leave, he turned around again. "It was Judy, wasn't it?"

"Yes, sir."

"Hmph. Good work today."

The elevator doors closed with him inside, and I gathered my things to leave as well, thinking I would stop by Miss Kelly's office to tell her I would take the job. Even if Mr. Pullman never let me write, at least my fingers wouldn't be a gnarled mess of arthritis from typing all day by the time I was twenty-five.

The phone rang in Mr. Pullman's office. I didn't know he had a direct line. I squinted at the clock—it was six minutes after five. I was officially off the clock.

And I had no idea if I was supposed to answer Mr. Pullman's private phone or not.

But if I wanted to get ahead, sacrifices had to be made. He would clearly appreciate a message from whoever it was if they were important enough to call him directly. Wouldn't he?

"*Washington Digest*, Mr. Pullman's office," I said.

"Put Pullman on," a man's voice with an accent said. Was that Russian? German? I couldn't tell. One of those guttural-sounding languages for sure.

"Mr. Pullman isn't available at the moment, but I'd be happy to give him a message for you."

There was a muffled sound, as if he had covered his end of the receiver and was speaking to someone else. And while I strained to make out what was being said, I had the distinct impression it wasn't English.

"You are his secretary?"

Officially no. But this week, I was. So I said yes.

More muffled speech. Definitely not English.

"Tell him Havana is with Texas, mass goal in sight."

"Havana with Texas," I said as I wrote it out. "Mass goal in sight. And who may I tell him left this message?"

"He will know," the voice said. Except *will* came out as *vill.*

The line went dead.

I stood there holding the phone, looking out over the nation's capital, and a chill ran down my spine. Havana. A Russian accent.

I thought back to the article I had typed for Fields. The failed Bay of Pigs invasion last year had made major headlines, but things had seemed largely quiet since then. No, we weren't allowed to travel to Cuba anymore, and even the cigars were taboo under the trade embargoes, but I had never even been on an airplane, nor had I smoked a cigar, so neither situation directly affected me.

But a line in Fields's article played back in my head. An unnamed source had said the president's office was "concerned" about the new friendship between the Soviet Union and Cuba, which had blossomed in the wake of the Bay of Pigs and the resulting embargoes.

I had hidden under my desk enough times in school to know we didn't want a country that was only ninety miles off our shore friendly with the Soviets. And a Russian accent—I was more and more convinced that it was Russian—discussing Havana boded ill.

Havana is with Texas. With Texas. Had the city of Havana turned against Castro? But if so, what did Texas have to do with it? Wouldn't he have said Havana is with Washington? What on earth did Texas have to do with Havana?

Mass goal in sight.

Were we invading and trying again to remove Castro from power to keep the USSR from having a foothold so close to us? The CIA had sent Cuban expats last time to try to seize power. Were they sending a group of Texas soldiers now? No, they hadn't managed to defend the Alamo, but that *was* a long time ago now.

Then again, why would a Russian be alerting a Washington newspaper editor about a military maneuver? Seemed unlikely. Unless . . .

I looked around Mr. Pullman's office. What if he was actually working for the government? A newspaper would kind of be perfect for that, wouldn't it? He would have access to all kinds of information. And as managing editor, he was able to control what the public knew and what they didn't.

It was all very curious and exciting.

I sat in Mr. Pullman's chair, trying to puzzle it out. What strange wording though. *Mass goal.* Why not just *Goal in sight*? Was that a translation issue from Russian?

Not that any of this was my business. But it had to mean something. I knew it did. The call to the direct line. The accent. The cryptic message. The refusal to leave a name. The muffled side conversation.

Whatever this was, it sounded important.

I put the message slip on his desk, centered on the blotter. He would see it immediately, but I would still tell him to look when he arrived the following morning.

What about the overnight cleaning crew though? This felt too significant to leave lying around for others to see. I tugged on a drawer, but it was locked. They all were.

My eyes landed on a framed photograph of Mr. Pullman with an attractive woman, who, based on the looks of the two children flanking them, a boy and girl who appeared to be in their early twenties, was his wife.

I made a wry face. Bet she didn't know he was ogling his secretary, who was their daughter's age, while at work. Then again, maybe she did and didn't care. She wouldn't be the first wife to look the other way in order to preserve a way of life.

There was always my desk to leave it in. But it wasn't *my* desk, was it? I didn't have a key, and Myrtle's son or boyfriend still stared at me from his picture frame each day.

Which left my handbag. I would keep the message safe overnight and bring it back before Mr. Pullman arrived in the morning, handing it to him with a cup of coffee as soon as he arrived. That was the answer. Surely Miss Kelly would approve.

Miss Kelly. I looked at the clock ticking on Mr. Pullman's desk. It was a quarter past five. Hopefully she was still downstairs. I pocketed the message and rushed back to my desk for my things, hoping to catch Miss Kelly to tell her I would take the job. It had just gotten infinitely more interesting after all.

As I rode the elevator down to the third floor, I wondered briefly if I should tell her about the message. Surely she would have a way to reach him at home if this was actually a matter of national security.

Then I realized how foolish I would sound suggesting that Mr. Pullman was a spy of some kind. And how much worse it would be if he actually *was* a spy and I outed him. No, I would keep the message safe until it went to Mr. Pullman.

But as I lay in bed that night, a new thought crossed my mind—what if Mr. Pullman wasn't an *American* spy? The man's voice *had* sounded distinctly Russian after all.

Havana is with Texas, he said in my head. *Mass goal in sight.*

No. That was crazy. And in all likelihood, it was a tip for a story, not a military plan. The simplest explanation was most likely the correct one after all.

14

The following morning, I was the one hurrying my father out the door.

We got into the car, and as soon as we were on Sixteenth Street, he turned his head toward me. "You got a story, didn't you?"

"What?"

"Judy. I've never seen anyone this excited to go to work. They're letting you write today?"

My shoulders sagged. "No. Not yet."

"Then what's this about?"

I explained about being moved to the managing editor's desk, but didn't tell my father about the cryptic message I had taken the evening before.

"So a secretary, then?" His brow furrowed. "Why the rush?"

"If I impress him enough, Miss Kelly—she's the one who runs the typing pool—she thought I might have a better chance. Eventually."

"Why not just keep applying at some of the local women's sections?" he asked. "Then at least you'd be writing."

"Because that section is all cooking and cleaning and fashion." I knew I sounded petulant, but I didn't care. "I want to write actual news. I want to write about the government and uncover scandals and—"

"Muckrake?"

"No." He glanced over, saw my wounded face, and patted my shoulder awkwardly. "I want to write stories that matter."

"But wouldn't a women's section be a stepping—"

"It's a death sentence is what it is. No one leaves the women's section."

"No one has *yet*. They haven't met Judy Greenberg."

"Thanks, Daddy."

We rode in silence past Rock Creek Park as I periodically checked my bag to make sure the message was still there. Not that it mattered—I could have rewritten it from memory. *Mass goal in sight.* What could that mean?

We pulled up in front of *The Digest*, and my father stopped me before I got out of the car. "You'll make this work," he said. "I believe in you."

I smiled, then hurried into the building, anxious to make sure Mr. Pullman saw how trustworthy and savvy I was.

I brewed the coffee immediately, waiting to pour him a cup to ensure it would be hot. The elevator dinged, and the secretaries flowed out in their colored dresses, bobbed hairdos, and Chanel No 5. I had the dress and the perfume, but my hair was still longer than theirs. They looked like a line of paper dolls, practically impossible to distinguish from one another, and infinitely more glamorous than the typing pool.

The editors would be arriving next. I went to get Mr. Pullman's coffee.

The next time the elevator bell sounded, he stepped out, surrounded by the male equivalent of paper dolls, all in suits and ties, three in spectacles, two without, clean shaven, and smelling of Aramis. Mr. Pullman nodded at me as he passed, and I followed him into his office before he could shut the door.

He turned around, surprised. "Yes, Judy?"

I shut the door behind me, forgetting Florence's warning, and he began to smile lasciviously. He thought I—no, I needed to relieve him of that assumption and quickly.

"Your coffee," I said, holding out the cup. He took it and turned back to me. "And this." I handed him the slip of paper. "Your phone rang after you left yesterday—I took a message. I thought it sounded important."

A cloud crossed his face, and he practically snatched the message from my hand. "Your job is to answer the phone out there, not in here. Understood?"

I swallowed. This wasn't going how I expected at all. "Yes, sir. I just didn't want you to miss anything important."

He read the message, then ripped the paper into tiny shreds, which he pocketed instead of tossing it in the wastepaper basket.

"It was nothing," he said. "Not worth the effort of entering my office."

"It didn't seem like nothing," I said, hating how high my voice sounded. "The man on the phone insisted you would know who he was. He—he had a Russian accent."

"I said it was nothing. Forget you ever answered my phone."

The words slipped out before I could stop myself. "But Havana is with Texas—is there an invas—"

"I SAID FORGET IT," he roared.

"Yes, sir," I said meekly, doubting I would forget that message as long as I lived. If it were nothing, he wouldn't care this much.

"Do your actual job, or you won't have one any longer. Am I clear?"

"Yes, sir, Mr. Pullman."

Grumpily, he sat in his desk chair. "That'll be all, Miss Greenberg."

He had called me Judy the previous two days. None of the editors called their secretaries by their last name. This was bad.

~

After lunch, Florence approached me. "Mr. Davis says Mr. Pullman is madder than hell. What happened?"

"I answered the phone in his office after he left last night."

She sat on the edge of my desk, pulled a pack of cigarettes from her pocket, removed one, and lit it. "Was it a mistress? Or did his wife think that's who you were?"

"Neither. It was a man. I just took a message and gave it to Mr. Pullman this morning."

"Huh," she said. "You'd think he'd thank you."

"That's what I thought too. But he was mad." I thought for a moment. "Does Mr. Davis lock his desk when he leaves for the day?"

She looked at me like I was crazy. "No. Why would he do that?"

"Just curious."

"What was the message anyway?"

I thought of Mr. Pullman's face when I suggested an invasion. "I don't even remember," I lied. "That's why I wrote it down."

She shrugged. "Story tip maybe?"

"If so, it was in code. I couldn't make heads or tails of it. And the man wouldn't leave his name. Said Mr. Pullman would know who it was."

"Curiouser and curiouser," she said. Then she stood up. "Probably nothing though. If he doesn't like you answering that phone, don't do it again and you'll be fine."

I hoped she was right.

At the end of the day, Patricia rode the elevator up from the third floor to tell me that Miss Kelly wanted to see me when my shift was done. I swore quietly. She hadn't been in her office when I stopped by the previous afternoon to tell her I wanted the job. And she had said she needed to know by today. After the morning I'd had, I didn't *actually* want it. Getting yelled at by the same man who made a comment about my being Jewish wasn't exactly appealing. But whatever that tip was yesterday, it had awakened every journalistic nerve in my body, and I wanted to investigate. I wanted to pick the lock on his desk with a hairpin and find all the mysteries this newspaper held.

Okay, I wasn't going to do that last part. If I landed myself in jail for stealing company secrets, the only newspaper I would be writing for was a prison one.

Still, I could win Mr. Pullman's trust. I knew it. And so when he left at the end of the day, without even looking at me, I took the elevator down to three.

I crossed the room and rapped on Miss Kelly's open door. "Miss Kelly? Patricia said you wanted to see me?"

She shook her head. "So you didn't want the job, then."

I was confused. "No, I do actually—I meant to tell you yesterday that—"

"Then you should have been more competent. Mr. Pullman told me to find him a 'real secretary.'"

"Oh," I said, deflating entirely. It wasn't an unfair criticism. But I had just talked myself into wanting it. Returning to the typing pool meant friends, but no extra money and no leads that hadn't already been written about. "I understand."

"Close the door."

I did as she told me and then she gestured for me to sit. She steepled her fingers and stared at me for an awkwardly long time before speaking. "What happened?"

I hesitated. Lying to Miss Kelly would surely have consequences. But so would telling her when Mr. Pullman had told me to forget I had answered his phone.

"I think—I think it was just what he said. He wants a real secretary."

She studied me again, but I maintained eye contact, unsure if I was being demoted back to the typing pool or fired.

But eventually she nodded. "You'll go back to your desk on this floor tomorrow. A girl with secretarial training will take over for the rest of the week until we hire someone." She scrawled a note on a legal pad in front of her, then looked up and seemed surprised to see me still sitting there. "You're dismissed." She waved a hand airily in my direction.

I rose to leave, then stopped. "Miss Kelly?"

"Hm?" She didn't look up.

"What happened to Myrtle?"

That got her attention. "Excuse me?"

"You said she's not coming back. But her things are still at her desk—she's got a picture of a young man, and—"

"Family emergency," she said brusquely. "Now if you'll excuse me, I would eventually like to be able to go home too."

I apologized and left, dejected at having failed and extremely confused about why that message had relegated me back to the typing pool, but hadn't gotten me fired.

15

"You can't go out on Friday nights, can you?" Patricia asked me on Thursday.

I shook my head. "If Jewish boys did, it wouldn't be as hard a sell to my mother, but no. The nice Jewish boys are home with their families." Or at my table after my mother promised them me on a platter, if last week was any indicator of what I had to look forward to.

"Shame," Patricia said. She lowered her voice to say, "We're going to Off the Record tomorrow night."

"What's Off the Record?"

"Shh." She perched on the edge of my desk. Then, lowering her voice further: "It's the bar in the basement of the Hay-Adams Hotel."

The Manger Hay-Adams was a swanky hotel a few blocks away, known for being the closest hotel to the White House.

"Oh. Yeah, my mother would *definitely* disown me if I went to a bar, let alone a *hotel* bar. Like sitting shivah and everything."

Patricia grinned wickedly. "You sure you can't sneak out?"

"Not on a Friday night." I looked at her more carefully. "What's so special about that bar?"

Leaning in closer, she said, "It's where the president and vice president pick up girls."

It was no secret that our young president had a wandering eye. Well—maybe it was a secret to the first lady. But everyone else in DC had heard the rumors. And the vice president, though less young and attractive, was no better. Then again, most of Capitol Hill had mistresses. Which meant the first lady likely did know and just turned a blind eye—who wouldn't, to be the envy of every other woman in the country?

But the two most powerful men in the free world going to a bar?

"Is there an underground tunnel, or do they just walk out of the White House to—you know?"

Patricia laughed. "*They* don't go there. But they have men they send out to find the girls. Gladys's cousin's friend's sister supposedly went to the White House from there."

A tenuous source at best. No journalist worth his salt would take that lead.

I shook my head. "You go have fun. Tell me what happens."

"Spoilsport," she said. "You're going to have to get out from Mama's skirts someday, you know."

That *was* of course the plan. But even when I managed to move out, I didn't doubt that those Shabbat dinners would remain nonnegotiable. Saturdays, on the other hand . . . I imagined a future where I slipped on a slinky dress and sipped cocktails with the girls from the office—in the daydream, I was a reporter by then, but I would stay friends with the girls in the typing pool, of course—fending off advances from the most powerful men in the world.

Hey, if I was going to fantasize, might as well make it count.

"Break time is over, Miss Holloway," Miss Kelly said.

Patricia immediately stood. "Yes, Miss Kelly." She waited until Miss Kelly had moved on to chastise another typist, then rolled her eyes at me. I smiled back. But it faded quickly as I realized the article I was about to start was a Jack Fields piece.

Miss Kelly was still stalking around the newsroom like a panther, so I couldn't very well return it to the board and grab a different one, which I would have likely done had she been in her office, so I began to type.

His leads really were weak. This one only had three of the five *W*'s and one *H*. I had been taught to use at least four and always start with *who* or *what.* He started with *when.* If we were strictly following the inverted pyramid, *when* was never the most important information.

I looked around again. Out of all the girls in the typing pool, he wouldn't know who typed his. And he'd have the least grounds to say anything about edits after the stunt he had pulled.

While I disliked the idea of helping him, especially because he *would* get credit for solid writing, I was bored. It was only my second week at the newspaper, I had done two separate jobs now, and I was already tearing my hair out. My fingers itched to fix the article. To make it sparkle. Miss Kelly walked past me on her way back to her office and shut the door forcefully.

Why not? I thought. It was a healthier way to pass the time than smoking.

I pulled the sheet of paper from the roller, inserted a new one, and began again.

"Soviet premier Nikita Khrushchev announced yesterday that . . ."

I finished the article, took the last sheet from the typewriter, and read through my handiwork. *Much better,* I thought. I had rewritten the lead, tightened up several weak paragraphs, and rearranged a couple of quotes to better fit the inverted pyramid and improve flow. He would know it was me, and I didn't *really* want him hanging around again. But for fifteen minutes, at least I wasn't bored.

After walking it to the box to go upstairs, I selected another article from the board. I skimmed it on the way back to my desk. Insanely dry. The vice president had given a speech about the space program, and he wasn't the dynamic speaker that the president was.

Sitting back at my desk, I rolled a new sheet into the typewriter, and my fingers began to fly across the keys, transforming the editors' markings into print-ready copy.

Then I stopped. A line in the article jumped out at me.

The Texas Democrat.

Texas.

Havana is with Texas.

What if that wasn't a *place* but a person? Had the vice president secretly gone to Cuba? After the Bay of Pigs debacle last year, it seemed unlikely that he would be welcomed there, but maybe there was a peace deal in the works? Was it possible that Castro could be swayed to the side of the United States and not the Soviets?

No. That was too far-fetched even for fiction, let alone a newsroom.

But I had a feeling I was close. There were plenty of Texas politicians, but the vice president was the most prominent of them. What could the "mass goal" be if it *wasn't* fixing the situation with Cuba?

Then again, the voice had sounded Russian. Their version of fixing things seemed to be a lot different from mine.

"You in there?" Carol asked, breaking my train of thought.

"I'm sorry—what?"

"Lunch," she said. "I asked you twice."

I squinted at the clock across the room. "Yes." I left the article on my desk. "Where do you want to go today?"

16

I had thought ahead to wear my own dress to work on Friday—even if it was less fashionable than Betty's clothes—so while I did have to race upstairs as soon as I got home to get the typewriter ink off my fingers, I didn't have to change. I did, however, sneak a peek into the living room on my way upstairs. If there was a visitor as unpleasant as Cantor Levy, I would throw on dungarees and an old blouse to look as unappealing as possible.

Granted, then I would need to swipe a black dress from Betty for the funeral—my mother would surely die if I pulled something like that.

Thankfully, it was just family. My mother had yet to recover from the shock of finding that stain on her white sofa where Cantor Levy had sat. My grandmother definitely didn't discourage her from thinking it was something other than chocolate—even going so far as to suggest that her cooking hadn't agreed with the poor man. I had never seen my mother go so pale.

We sat at the table, my mother covering her eyes to say the blessing over the candles, and my father led us in a quick, far less melodic rendering of the motzi before we began to eat.

My grandmother winked at me from across the table. "It's so nice when it's just family. Isn't it, Edna?"

My mother pursed her lips at her mother-in-law but said nothing. If I were my grandmother, I'd take it a little easy on my mother—she didn't *have* to let her live here. But torturing her daughter-in-law seemed to be my grandmother's main hobby these days—other than her frequent canasta, bridge, and mahjong games—and I got the impression my mother thrived on their sparring too.

"Mother," my father said warningly.

"What?" Grandma Sylvia asked innocently. "He looked like the frog in that book I used to read to the children when they were little."

I stifled a laugh. She meant Toad from *The Wind in the Willows*. The resemblance was quite remarkable.

"Yes, well, he didn't exactly want to come back after whatever you and Judy said to him."

"Maybe he was embarrassed," my grandmother said. "I would be if—"

"How was work this week, Judy?" my father asked, desperate to change the subject before his wife and mother started a brawl at the table.

I didn't know how to answer that after the roller coaster of becoming a managing editor's secretary, only to lose the position within three days. "Interesting," I said, opting for a half-truth. "I'm learning a lot." Mostly gossip about the typing pool's dating life, but I *was* learning. Besides, I now knew where the Oval Office staff met women. I hadn't known that at the start of the week.

"Speaking of work," my mother said as she speared herself a piece of brisket and placed it on her plate. "Do you know a Jacob Feldstein?"

I assumed she was talking to my father, and I looked to him as I chewed a bite of potato. But my mother was talking to me. I swallowed. "Never heard of him."

"His mother said he worked at *The Digest*. Or maybe it was *The Evening Star*?"

Unlikely to be *The Digest*, considering how Mr. Pullman had responded to my last name. I wondered briefly if Patricia, good Irish girl that she was, would have been sent back to the typing pool for answering his personal phone. But over the course of a week and a half typing articles, I had seen a lot of reporters' names, and that one hadn't come up.

I shrugged. "Must be *The Evening Star*."

"Could be a good match. You'd have someone to talk about journalism with over dinner."

I glanced involuntarily at Betty. She was right where she had always wanted to be—a wife and mother. Life would be so much easier if I could be like her. But I wasn't. The idea of having to listen to a male journalist talk about his day in the newsroom while I scrubbed toilets, diapered babies, and cooked every meal? If hell existed, that was my own personal version of it. I knew my mother meant well, but she didn't understand that I wanted a different life for myself.

"I had a friend, a long time ago," my grandmother said. "She became a very successful matchmaker—lived in Philadelphia for many years. And she'd call that logic a load of horse manure."

"Grandma!" Betty said as my mother set her jaw.

"What? Common interests are a dime a dozen. You need common values. Judy wants to *be* a journalist, not marry one."

I smiled at my grandmother, touched beyond words that she understood me.

"So you need to find her a doctor or wealthy businessman—someone who can afford to hire help when she wants to write a story." My shoulders sank. "Or—wasn't the Wainwright girl's father Jewish? Does she have any sons?"

"The father was Jewish, but the mother wasn't," my mother said. "So she's not Jewish, and her kids aren't."

"Pity. If you married into a journalism dynasty, that would be the best of both worlds."

Leave it to my mother and grandmother—the one thing they had in common was they could recite the Jewish lineage of literally anyone in town, whether they knew them or not.

"It's a shame Joseph Pulitzer died over fifty years ago—I could have just married him. Jewish *and* a newspaper tycoon."

"Does he have grandsons?" my mother asked, entirely serious.

I pushed my chair back and stood up. "I'm full. Anyone mind if I go to bed early?"

"Sit," my grandmother said, pointing down toward my chair. "We're just teasing you. Aren't we, Edna?"

I snuck a glance at my mother, who definitely was *not* teasing me and would likely be asking her network of yentas if there were any remaining unmarried Pulitzers running around, but I did as my grandmother asked, and thankfully she steered the conversation toward speculating whether Betty would have another boy or another girl.

"Whatever it is," Betty said, rubbing at her lower back as I had seen her doing more and more frequently, "carrying this one is much harder than before."

"That's because you have two other kids to take care of this time," my mother said.

Betty sighed. "That's what the doctor said too. I guess you're right."

"Probably just a big head," my grandmother added. "They get that from their father's side."

Reuben *did* have a big head. But I saw Betty grimace in pain as she sat down. I didn't know how a baby with a big head would cause back pain. Then again, what did I know about pregnancy and babies?

17

"You *have* to come next time," Patricia said.

I felt a pang of jealousy. While my family was assessing me for potential suitors like a piece of meat at the (kosher) butcher shop, Patricia and the girls from the typing pool were sipping martinis and mingling with the city's elite.

"Go any other night," I said. "I just can't do Fridays."

"But Friday is the best night. Everyone is looking to unwind after the workweek."

Another twinge of envy. I leaned forward, an elbow on my desk. "Tell me everything."

"Well, *technically*, you're not supposed to talk about what happens there—that's why it's called Off the Record." She grinned wickedly. "But I suppose, as long as you promise to come with me sometime—"

"I do," I said too quickly.

She laughed, then sat on my desk. "Robert McNamara was there!" She leaned closer and, lowering her voice, she added, "and the French ambassador."

I had no idea who the second man was and couldn't have picked him out of a lineup. "Who even is that?"

"I don't know, but Gladys said he was." Gladys could have pointed to literally any man in the place and said that. Her need to feel important frequently outweighed the truth, as I had learned. But if McNamara was there, anything was possible.

"No White House trips?"

"No." Patricia shook her head. "But that's probably for the best. I mean, I wouldn't say *no*, but I'd feel guilty. I like the first lady."

It was on the tip of my tongue to ask if she would have minded if she *didn't* like the first lady, but the fact that she had said she wouldn't say no was a clue.

My mother would pull me out of this job by the hair if she knew the type of friends I was making.

But my curiosity about the evening was stronger than any moral outrage I was supposed to feel. "What do you wear to a place like that?"

"A cocktail dress."

I had nothing resembling cocktail attire. Even Betty only had one dress that could possibly fit the bill, and it was still in her closet. Any plans to go with Patricia would have to wait until I could afford something to wear.

Apparently my dismay showed on my face. "Don't worry," Patricia said. "You can always borrow a dress."

I looked at Patricia's long frame. A short dress on her would be ankle length on me.

She laughed, reading my mind. "The girl who rents the room next door to mine is about your size. She won't mind. Just don't spill anything on yourself."

Miss Kelly came out of her office to stalk through the typing pool looking for infractions, and we busied ourselves with articles until the door to her office was shut firmly again with her inside it, then Patricia was back at my desk, this time with Carol.

"Are you coming to the Bohemian Caverns with us Thursday night?" Carol asked.

"The what?"

The two of them exchanged a look and smiled at each other. "Fresh off the farm," Patricia murmured, the corners of her eyes crinkling.

"It's a jazz club on U Street," Carol explained. "We met this night-club singer from Cuba at Off the Record Friday night, and she invited us to her show."

Cuba again.

I looked up sharply, the article I had been typing completely forgotten, as a thought began to form. "Where in Cuba is she from?"

Carol shrugged, and Patricia said, "Havana, I think she said. She was a favorite of Batista's and had to leave during the revolution." She looked at Carol. "I ran into her in the bathroom. She was there with a senator—I don't remember which one—but we talked for a while. She was gorgeous."

A nightclub singer from Havana. With a senator. At Off the Record.

It's where the president and vice president pick up girls, Patricia said again in my head.

Texas Democrat.

Havana is with Texas. Not Cuba. Havana specifically.

It was flimsy, but it was a lead. And one that I was itching to follow.

"Do—" I paused and lowered my voice. "Do the president and vice president's—" What did you call a man who procures girls other than a pimp? "Do they send people to this Bohemian place too?"

Patricia and Carol both looked at me curiously. "I don't think so," Carol said slowly. "I've never heard that anyway. It's too far from the White House and just a jazz club. But they get all kinds of other famous people there."

So that club wasn't anything special. But a woman from Havana was at the bar where the most prominent Texan picked up women . . . Okay, it was a long shot. There had been an influx of Cuban refugees three years ago when the revolution happened, but they had primarily settled in Florida. It was too much of a coincidence, coming just days after that phone call. Instinct told me there was something there. And I wanted to see it for myself.

"What would you think of going to Off the Record tonight?"

"Tonight?" they both asked, incredulous. It was a Monday after all. "Why?"

"Because I could get away with it," I said. It wasn't the whole truth—especially because I would have to get dressed at Patricia's apartment to avoid arousing my mother's suspicion. And I had no idea how I would explain coming home late from a bar. If she smelled so much as a hint of liquor on me, I was done for, twenty-two or not. But my gut was telling me I had to be in that room and see if my hunch was correct.

"How about tomorrow?" Patricia asked. "I kind of have a date tonight."

"Kind of?" Carol asked. A slow grin spread across Patricia's face, and Carol started to laugh. "You don't mean—?"

"Shh," Patricia said. She glanced at me. "He's a congressman. I'll tell you who he is if it turns into anything."

"You're *terrible*," Carol said. "Teach me your ways!"

I laughed, and Miss Kelly came striding over as the other two girls scattered.

My output for the rest of the day was miserable. I kept making mistakes as I typed, trying to figure out *Texas is with Havana, mass goal in sight.* Something in the back of my brain was tingling, telling me that I was onto something with Off the Record, the vice president, and this singer from Havana. I just didn't know what yet.

But, I reminded myself, all of that assumed she had told Patricia the truth. Or was the senator whom the singer was with from Texas? Was this all just a scandal about a senator cheating on his wife with a foreign singer?

If so, why did someone with a Russian accent care? And what was the "mass goal," then?

There was a more-than-decent chance that I was chasing shadows here. But I couldn't shake the feeling that this mattered. The Russian accent. Havana. And a bar where the most powerful men in the country picked up women. If Patricia had gotten a date with a congressman, how hard would it be for a Cuban spy to cozy up to someone even more influential?

Or I was insane. That was always a possibility.

"Where *is* your head today, Miss Greenberg?" Miss Kelly said as she gestured toward my now-overflowing wastepaper basket. "If you've been fraternizing with any of the men upstairs—"

"No fraternization here," I interrupted her. She looked at me in surprise. "Miss Kelly, I am the *last* girl you need to worry about with that. I promise." She looked unconvinced. "My mother and grandmother would take care of me before you could if I was fooling around with someone who wasn't Jewish. And I'd put good money on that leaving very few options here."

The third hint of a smile I had seen from Miss Kelly appeared. "You would win that bet," she said. "But that 99 percent typing accuracy seems to have been a gross overstatement today."

"Yes, Miss Kelly. I'll fix that right away."

"See that you do," she said. Then she left me alone for the rest of the day while I alternated between trying to solve this puzzle and trying to figure out the much more complicated question of what I would tell my mother so that I could get to Off the Record Tuesday night.

18

On the bus home from work, I tried to think of an excuse for my mother that wouldn't make my life more difficult.

The best choice would obviously be to say I had a date with a Jewish man. But then she would expect him to come to the house and meet her and my father, and I had no one to parade through their living room.

I blew out an exasperated breath, and the woman with two rambunctious daughters and an infant next to me looked over. "Sorry," I said. "It's not about you—or them."

She offered me a smile. "Boy troubles?"

"What? No."

The smile turned indulgent. "Parents?"

I looked at her more closely. How did she know that? I nodded.

"I'm an expert on both sides now," she said. "Come on. Spill it."

I obviously couldn't tell her about the lead I was following, but I found myself explaining that I wanted to go to a bar with the girls from work and my parents were overprotective and would lose their minds if they knew the truth.

"I understand," she said, shifting the baby to her other shoulder. "Believe it or not, I spent plenty of time getting around my parents before all this." She gestured to the kids. She held out a hand. "Evelyn Gold."

"Judy Greenberg."

She looked me over appraisingly. "So you can't say it's a date or they'd want to meet him—right?" I stared at her. "Do you have any male friends?" I shook my head. "That worked for me once. Then again, I wound up marrying him." She grinned. "Okay, here's what you do: You tell them you're meeting up with a girlfriend on a double date. When they argue that they want to meet him, you tell them that's too awkward when you and your girlfriend are going on the date together."

"Won't they eventually want to meet him?"

"Not if you come home mad. Slam some doors, stomp around, say *The nerve!* and things like that."

"You might just be a genius," I said.

"I'm sure these three will pay me back when they get bigger," she said, ruffling the middle child's hair. "Especially this one. Won't you, Joanie?"

~

And somehow, my parents bought it. I originally said I would be going out after work with Patricia—though I told my parents she was named Paula Hoffman to avoid conflict—but my mother didn't like the idea of me taking the bus home alone late at night and convinced my father to let me take the car. "Invite this Paula for Shabbat dinner sometime," she said. "I'd love to meet her."

She had yet to ask about a single work friend I had mentioned. But give one a Jewish last name and she was invited to Friday night dinner.

"I will," I promised. "But her family has their own Shabbat dinners every week, so I don't know if she'll be able to make it."

"Of course," my mother said reverently. "Maybe a Saturday afternoon?"

I thought quickly. "Oh, she doesn't drive on Shabbat." My mother opened her mouth, and I cut her off. "Very pious. And she goes to visit her grandmother every Sunday in Baltimore. But I'll extend the invitation nonetheless."

My mother patted my arm. "She sounds like such a good girl. And a good influence! And these boys . . . ?"

"Jewish," I assured her. "They—uh—they're down from Baltimore for the night too."

My mother looked concerned. "That's awfully far."

"Well, they may be moving to the District for work, so we'll see what happens."

~

The following evening, outfitted in a dress of Betty's that my mother sanctioned my wearing without permission, I found myself driving down Sixteenth Street toward Patricia's apartment. My nerves were humming with excitement. My gut told me I was onto something—and perhaps even more likely to encounter a clue on a weeknight than a weekend. If the vice president was smart, he *wouldn't* try to find girls on a weekend, when more people were there.

I stopped at a red light and shook my head. In all likelihood, this would just be a trip to a bar with friends from work. The odds of stumbling into a major story were slim at best, and my boredom in the typing pool had me grasping at straws. Deep down, I knew that. But it never hurt to keep your eyes open in Washington. And maybe, even if this turned out to be a dead end, I would see *something* I could take upstairs to Editorial eventually.

I parked in front of the imposing boardinghouse on Second Street on Capitol Hill where Patricia lived, knocked at the large front door, and told the woman who let me in that I was there for Patricia Holloway. She directed me to a parlor on the left, where Patricia sat smoking in a form-fitting blue dress.

"Judy!" she cried, standing up. "Come on. Let's find you something to wear."

I had assumed that Betty's dress would be appropriate for a weeknight, but apparently I was mistaken. Patricia brought me upstairs, explaining that men weren't allowed anywhere except in the parlor. She rapped smartly on a door on the third floor, and a petite girl of about my size answered. "This is Judy," she said. "Judy, meet Roberta. We need to borrow a cocktail dress."

"And I thought I was the one girl here who was safe from all that," Roberta said, but she was smiling. "Come on in. We'll find you something."

Patricia ushered me into the room and immediately began digging through Roberta's closet. "Anything off limits?"

"Nah," she said. "I've worn all of them a million times. Besides, I think Ted is going to propose soon. Hopefully I won't need them much longer!"

Patricia turned around. "Really?" Roberta nodded. "Good work bagging that one! Isn't his family loaded?"

"They are." She looked at me. "I can donate all these to you when we get married."

I thanked her for the generous offer.

After I had tried on three, Patricia and Roberta agreed that the little black sheath with a high neck and low back would be just the thing. I felt naked. Most of Betty's dresses that I borrowed were a year or two old and still flared at the hem somewhat, and all of them were easily worn with a brassiere. This one, I'd have to go without, or it would be visible in back.

"Honestly, you can pull that off," Patricia said. "I could never." Which was true but still stung slightly. I would never have curves like she did.

"*Very* Audrey Hepburn," Roberta agreed.

I looked in the mirror, and for a moment, I *felt* very Audrey Hepburn. Touching the ends of my hair, I wondered if it was time for a bob. There was still a slight schoolgirlish air to me, and the hair would correct that. "Thank you," I told Roberta. "I'll take good care of it."

"Do you want to come with us?" Patricia asked.

"And risk jeopardizing things with Ted? No. He thinks I'm a good little girl who stays home except to go out with him." She winked. Then she looked me over again. "You need more makeup."

"I'll take care of that," Patricia said, pulling me by the arm as I gathered up my clothes.

She took me to the room next door, which was hopelessly messy, with clothes covering the twin bed and half the floor. A dresser held a cosmetics case, open, with a lipstick-smeared tissue next to it. Patricia cleared off a chair and sat me in it, putting wings on my eyes with kohl and finishing it off with red lipstick. "Perfection," she said, handing me a mirror.

I hardly recognized the glamorous woman in the reflection. "Wow."

"I know," Patricia said. "Come on. We'll take a cab."

"I have my father's car."

She grinned. "Even better."

So off we went. As we drove through the nation's capital, I debated telling Patricia why we were really going to the bar. She was so much more worldly than I was and could likely spot connections that I wouldn't know to make.

But she also talked too much. And if I told her, there was no guarantee half the typing pool wouldn't join in hunting for clues, and suddenly my lead would have vanished into smoke.

As would my job, most likely.

No, I thought, as she prattled on about her date the night before. I needed to play this one close to the vest until I knew if I needed help or not.

19

I found a spot across Sixteenth Street from the Hay-Adams Hotel and only struggled briefly with pulling my father's beast of a 1958 Buick into the parallel spot. Yes, it was moderately crooked, but it would do.

Only Lafayette Square separated us from the White House. A four-minute walk at most. Maybe five in heels, stumbling, tipsy, on the arm of the president's man.

I swallowed, feeling none of Patricia's bubbly joy. Either I would find nothing and be stuck in the typing pool indefinitely, or I was about to uncover something that would change everything.

The former was obviously far more likely.

But on the sidewalk, I couldn't help but pause as I looked up at the historic building. Did my career as a journalist start here tonight?

Patricia elbowed me. "You've got to land a big fish to wind up in one of *those* rooms," she said with a wicked grin. Then she nodded toward the White House. "Or one of those."

"Patricia!"

She laughed. "Fresh off the farm. Would you really say no to the most powerful man in the world?"

Yes, I thought primly. I had no interest in an affair, even if it was with someone who could launch a nuclear war or declare me the journalist laureate of the nation—a title he would have to create specifically for me. Okay, if he was willing to do *that*, then maybe.

"Hard to say," I said to appease her. She linked her arm through mine, and we walked arm in arm under the portico, where a sharply dressed bellman in a red coat and buttons so polished that they sparkled opened the door for us. Our heels clacked on the marble floor, and I felt my breath catch as I looked around the archways of the lobby, lit from beneath. The only hotels I had ever spent time in were a Catskills resort, where we shared a bungalow for a week with my aunt and uncle's family, and a small hotel on the Jersey shore that had sand in the bedsheets when we arrived. Nothing like this.

"Don't stare," Patricia whispered. "Act like you come to places like this all the time."

"But I've never *seen* a place like this," I whispered back.

"Look bored," she instructed. "Almost disdainful. Like you spend the night in fancier hotels all the time."

"There are fancier hotels than this?"

She chuckled. "Loads. In town alone, there's the Mayflower and the Willard, not to mention the Georgetown ones."

I shook my head. This was a world I hadn't even truly considered. And if I was working as a journalist, I could be reporting on the happenings at places like this one.

Patricia directed me to a small staircase leading down into the basement of the hotel. The walls were painted red, and the tufted leather chairs matched, with wooden legs that complemented the polished wood flooring. Small windows placed high on the walls reminded us that we were below ground, and framed caricatures of politicians of old hung as decor. A huge marble fireplace took up much of one wall, opposite a mahogany bar.

It wasn't crowded, with pockets of suited men and well-dressed women sitting around tables laughing, and men sitting alone at the bar nursing drinks.

Part of me instinctively wanted to leave. This was so far outside the world I inhabited. What was I doing in a swanky hotel bar? My father had a drink before dinner. Wine at Passover was all I'd had. But this? I wouldn't know how to begin to fit in, let alone look for a Cuban woman who was implicated with a Texan. I was way out of my depth here, and I was sure that everyone who even glanced my way would see it instantly.

And the more I thought about it, the more ridiculous this was. A Cuban nightclub singer had a drink here Friday night, and I thought I had found a story lead? Mr. Pullman was right. The typing pool was where I belonged. My confidence slipped away. Maybe my mother was right and I should be looking for a husband, not story leads that would ultimately lead *me* nowhere. This whole thing was foolish. I wanted to go home, but it was too late to do so without Patricia getting upset with me.

"Let's get a drink," Patricia said, guiding me toward the bar. "Better yet, let's find someone to buy us drinks."

I looked at her askance. "Won't they get ideas, then?"

She winked. "Men can have any sort of ideas they want. We're modern women—we get to decide which ideas are good ones." Then her posture straightened, and she turned around. "How's my lipstick?"

"Perfect. Why?"

"Remember the congressman I went out with last night? I kind of . . . may have . . . told him we'd be here tonight."

I looked at the far wall, where a man with gray hair and an unmistakable wedding ring sat at a table. He looked vaguely familiar, but I could place neither a name nor the state that he represented. And I fought to keep my shoulders from dropping. No, I hadn't told Patricia the real reason I wanted to come tonight, but I had thought I would have some backup at least. This was definitely a mistake.

The man raised his drink at us, and Patricia sauntered over, her hips swinging like she was Marilyn Monroe. He stood to greet her, and she let him kiss her cheek. She gestured toward me, and he waved me over. The last thing I wanted to do was be a third wheel on Patricia's date with a married man. But to avoid being rude, I went to the table.

"Darling, this is my dear friend Judy. Judy, this is Cong—"

"Phil," he said, cutting her off smoothly and holding out his hand. *Phil,* my brain repeated over and over until it clicked. *Phillip Clement. South Carolina.* There had been some scandal a few years back. Something with a girl. I couldn't remember what, but it clearly hadn't had much of an impact on his career or his marriage. I just hoped Patricia was wise enough to not become the next tabloid headline. "So nice to meet you." His accent told me I was correct about his identity.

"Likewise," I said guardedly.

"Let me get you ladies a drink."

"A martini for me," Patricia said. She looked at me.

I had no idea what one ordered at a bar. And I doubted they had kosher wine back there, which was the one thing I knew.

I swallowed again. "I'll have the same."

"But just one for Judy," Patricia trilled. "She drove me here tonight."

"I'll go get those drinks," he said, winking at Patricia.

When he got to the bar, I put a hand on Patricia's arm. "Isn't he the one—"

"Shh," she said. "It was all a misunderstanding. The baby wasn't his. He explained it all on Saturday. Total frame-up to get money, you know?"

I did not know. And if he was now on a date with Patricia, I didn't buy that for one second. "Just be careful."

She mimed crossing her heart. "I'm practically a safety patrol." She leaned closer. "Besides, I'm protected."

Against babies, I thought. *Not against reporters with grudges or jealous wives.*

Congressman Phil returned to the table, two drinks in hand. They were clear, with an olive on a toothpick in each one. Didn't look so bad. And I liked olives. He handed us each a drink, and Patricia held hers out, clinking it to mine. "Cheers," she said merrily.

I almost replied, *L'chaim,* but, looking around, I was likely the only Jew in the establishment that night—possibly ever. As I brought the glass to my lips, I spotted a familiar face watching me from a booth, his back against the wall.

Jack Fields raised his glass to eye level, then brought it to his lips as I took my first sip.

I started coughing as soon as the gin hit my throat. Patricia gave me a few whacks on the back, and suddenly Fields was beside me. "Are you all right?" he asked.

Patricia rolled her eyes. "She's fine, Fields. What are you doing here anyway?"

He ignored her, crouching down so our faces were level. I managed a nod, wishing I had a glass of water instead of whatever that olive was marinating in.

"Let me get you some water," he said, as if reading my mind. A moment later, he reappeared with another glass, which he shoved into my hands. "Here. This'll help."

I took a slow sip and was finally able to respond. "Thank you," I said. "Just a little—stronger—than I'm used to."

"Listen, I—" He looked up to see Patricia and Phil watching him. "I—uh—do you mind if I borrow Miss Greenberg for a couple minutes? I wanted to say I'm—I wanted to talk to her."

"She's a big girl," Patricia said frostily. "Judy, do you *want* to talk to Fields?"

Not really, no. I was embarrassed about choking on a drink in front of him, and I wasn't proud of how rude I had been when he apologized. But it was preferable to watching Patricia and the congressman make eyes at each other, so I stood, picked up my martini, and excused myself.

Fields nodded. "Patricia. Congressman Clement." The congressman blanched at the use of his title and last name, and I suppressed a grin as Fields led me to his table.

20

"What are you doing here?" Fields asked as soon as I sat down on the leather bench across from him in the booth.

When he had said he wanted to talk to me, it sounded like he wanted to apologize again, and after his quickness in grabbing me a water, I was inclined to accept this time. But if he was going to act like my father, then no.

"Is that your business?"

He leaned back slightly. "I meant with Clement. He's bad news."

I sighed. "I know. Patricia met him here Friday, and apparently this is their second date. I didn't know who it was until we got here."

"He's the one who—"

"Patricia said that was a frame-up."

He leaned forward again. "Does Patricia know the girl died in an"—he hooked his fingers into quotation marks—"'accident' not long after that?"

My eyes widened. "She did?"

He nodded. "Don't let her leave with him. She doesn't like me, but she'll listen to you."

I turned slightly, looking at the two of them over my shoulder. He had moved his chair closer to hers, and their hands were entwined as she laughed at something he said that I doubted was funny. I wasn't so sure she would listen to me. I would have to lie and say I left something

I needed in her room. I very much regretted suggesting we come here. I wanted to follow my (admittedly flimsy) lead, not break up an affair.

"I'll figure it out. Thanks." I pushed my chair back to leave, but he reached for my arm.

"Listen, Judy—I really am sorry about all . . . that."

I looked at him in the dim light of the bar. Under other circumstances, I might have found him handsome. But I wasn't working at *The Digest* to be distracted by a pair of kind eyes and a dimple when he smiled. I was here to make a name for myself.

"Water under the bridge."

He smiled. "How about another drink—something easier this time?"

I took another look at Patricia and the congressman. She wasn't going to be willing to leave soon from the looks of things. Resigned, I turned back to Fields. "I don't suppose they have Manischewitz here?"

He let out a hearty laugh. "No. I doubt they'd know what that was. A Shirley Temple maybe? Or do you want to try a real drink?"

"I'm not twelve years old," I said, bristling at the Shirley Temple remark.

He looked confused. "I wasn't trying to insult you."

I closed my eyes and counted to three. We needed to reset a bit here. "Is there anything . . . softer . . . than a martini?"

The right side of his mouth curled up. "Let me see what I can do." He stood and strode to the bar. I took the opportunity to look around the room. There were a handful of familiar faces from Capitol Hill, but no obviously Cuban women, and no sign of the vice president. This was lunacy. Besides, how would I even spot someone from Cuba? All I knew was Ricky from *I Love Lucy*, cigars, and Castro. I shook my head, annoyed at myself.

When Fields returned, he held a coupe glass filled with a carbonated yellow liquid.

"Try this," he said. "The bartender said it's on the house if you don't like it though, so maybe make a face when you take a sip."

I chuckled. "You're a terrible date, Jack Fields."

He looked at me carefully. "Is this a date?"

"Absolutely not." I took the glass from him. "What's in it?"

"It's a champagne cocktail. Champagne, sugar, and bitters."

I took a small sip. "It's sweet. But almost . . . dry . . . at the same time." I actually liked it. But I turned toward the bartender and scrunched up my nose for effect. He shrugged at Fields, and I turned back around.

"Thanks for that. Champagne is a lot on my salary."

"Then why—"

"I owe you," he said quietly. "That wasn't right. I just—Louise didn't want to write. And your work was so much better than hers. I didn't think about how it would make you feel."

I took another sip. "Thank you for *that*."

"I—uh—did you work on my article from yesterday?"

"Maybe. I don't know. I type a lot of articles."

He turned his head, looking at me from the corner of his eye. "I know your style."

"Fine. It's boring just typing all day. And I figured you couldn't complain without getting yourself in trouble."

"For the record, I'm never going to complain about you helping me. You're really good."

"I know I am," I said. Then I gestured around us. "Funny choice of words here though. Why *is* the bar called Off the Record?"

He smiled. "It was a speakeasy during Prohibition. So you know, keep it off the record that you're drinking here. But it's always been a haunt for politicians. And where politicians go, journalists follow."

"Is that why you're here?"

He nodded. "You never know who's going to walk in and drop a story in your lap."

I felt a tingling in my stomach that I doubted was the champagne. "Have you gotten any leads here?"

"Plenty." He leaned in closer, then lowered his voice: "Can you keep a secret?" This time I nodded. "The vice president keeps a room upstairs."

My mouth dropped open. Texas.

"Fields," I said, suddenly deadly earnest. "Is there a Cuban woman?"

"I'd assume there are a lot of them or there would be no Cuban babies."

"No, I mean—is there a Cuban woman he's involved with?"

Fields's eyes narrowed as he tried to work out what I was getting at. "The vice president?" I nodded. "Not that I know of. Why?"

I pressed my lips together. This was my lead, and he covered the White House. I didn't want to be the person who dropped a story in his lap; I wanted to be the person uncovering and writing it myself. If I told him my suspicions, he would have to follow it—any journalist would, myself included. And Mr. Pullman was likely smart enough to put two and two together about how he had gotten the story, which would mean I'd be out of even the typing pool.

"No reason."

He leaned back in his seat, studying me. "You have a lead, don't you?"

I wanted to ask how he knew that. He couldn't know that. "No."

"Judy."

"Fields." We stared at each other, neither flinching.

"Look," he said eventually. "I can help you. This is my job."

"Yes. And I want it to be mine. I'm not handing you anything."

For a full minute, no one spoke.

"How big is it?" Then he shook his head. "You're asking about the vice president, so it's big, right?"

I chewed the inside of my lip. I might have already given too much up. If he went digging for information on the vice president and a Cuban woman, well, he'd probably solve this whole thing faster than I could. He had credentials and access that I could only dream of. Better to work *with* him and make my intentions known. Or so I hoped.

"I don't know," I said. "It could be nothing."

His gaze locked on mine. "It's why you're here, isn't it? You don't strike me as the bar type."

Part of me wanted to ask what type he thought I was. But this was more important. "I want to write it if it's anything."

He thought about this for a moment. "*The Digest* would never take it from you."

That stung, but he wasn't wrong. "Cowrite, then. Double byline. And you refuse to give it to *The Digest* if they won't run it with my name too."

"That's a hard bargain to make without knowing what it is. I could lose my job if they say no."

"Those are my terms. Take them or leave them."

Another moment of silence. Then Fields extended his right arm, his hand straight toward me. "Deal."

I shook his hand, my heart racing. I knew he could double-cross me, but something in his face told me he wasn't going to make that mistake.

21

"So what's the lead?" Fields asked.

I glanced over my shoulder. Patricia was deep in conversation with her congressman. I didn't exist any longer.

"You *swear* I'll be on the byline? And Mr. Pullman will never find out where you learned about this?"

Fields's brow furrowed. "Pullman?"

"Swear it."

"I swear on my life," he said solemnly. "And my mother's."

"That doesn't mean anything to me. Your mother could already be dead. Or awful."

He chuckled. "I assure you my mother is alive and well. And I love her very much."

I studied him for any tells that he wasn't serious but saw none. If he was lying, he was good at it. I turned and looked around the room again. I did need help. I didn't know what I was looking at on my own. He clearly did. Especially if he knew about that room upstairs.

But suddenly I was nervous. It wasn't much more than a hunch. If he laughed at me—I bit the inside of my lip and looked down at my drink. The napkin it sat on had a quote on it, "With great risk comes great reward," attributed to Thomas Jefferson.

Buoyed, I took a deep breath and leaned forward. In a low voice I said, "Mr. Pullman's secretary left suddenly last week. Miss Kelly had me fill in."

"Myrtle?" he asked. "Where did she go?"

"I don't know. Miss Kelly said she won't be back though."

His brows came together as he thought about this. "Louise and Myrtle in the same week. That seems—"

"Do you want to know about the lead or not?"

"Go on." He leaned back against the booth, amused.

"Anyway, Miss Kelly had me fill in, and after Mr. Pullman left on Tuesday, the phone in his office rang."

Fields sat up straighter. "Pullman never takes calls."

"Well clearly sometimes he does, because I took a message from that phone, and it landed me back in the typing pool."

"What was the message?"

"This is where it gets weird—the man had a Russian accent. And he said to tell Mr. Pullman, 'Havana is with Texas, mass goal in sight.'"

He repeated the phrase to himself, his lips moving silently.

"The man said he will know what it means. Except it was definitely a Russian accent. He *vill know vhat it means.* And he made sure I was his secretary before telling me. Does that mean anything to you?"

He shook his head. "What happened when you gave Pullman the message?"

I sighed. "He dressed me down for going into his office, then he read it, ripped the paper into tiny pieces, and pocketed them. Then told me it was nothing. When I mentioned the Russian accent, he yelled at me. By the end of the day, I was back in the typing pool."

Fields scratched his forehead. "Sure doesn't sound like nothing if he reacted like that."

"That's what I thought too. But I can't make heads or tails of it. Originally I wondered if it might mean something about an invasion—"

"Not after how the Bay of Pigs ended," he said, leaning forward. "Between you and me, they've moved on to smaller-scale attempts on Castro himself. But if you tell anyone I told you that, I'll deny it." He thought for a moment. "Why would Pullman know anything about an invasion anyway? We should assume it's a journalism tip, not national security."

"It could be both. What if the Russian is giving Mr. Pullman the scoop on a huge national security story?"

"Maybe. But why a Russian accent?"

"Double agent?" It sounded stupid once it came out of my mouth.

But Fields didn't laugh at me. He shook his head, his brow furrowed. "Something doesn't add up there. Not with giving it to a newspaper."

"What if it's a misdirect? We publish something wrong, and it gives incorrect information to the enemy?"

"But Pullman said it was nothing. He wouldn't even throw the pieces away. He doesn't want this to run, whatever it is, or you'd still be answering his phones. Unless you made his coffee wrong or something like that?"

"I can make a cup of coffee competently," I said, wounded. He didn't need to know that another secretary had to teach me how.

"Okay," he said, moving on. "So why do you think it's the vice president?"

"Patricia and some of the other girls said the president and vice president pick up girls here. And they came Friday night and met a nightclub singer from Havana and . . . I don't know. It just felt like too much of a coincidence to not mean something."

Fields wasn't sold. "I think that might be too much of a reach," he said gently.

"Fine," I said, standing, hoping I could get away before he saw the ashamed blush rising in my cheeks. "I'll solve this myself. Thank you for nothing, Mr. Fields."

"Smooth your ruffled feathers," he said. "I'm still on board. I just want to make sure we're not missing something else."

I sat back down, arms crossed.

"You look like I tugged your pigtails when you make that face," he said, but he was smiling. "And if we're going to be partners, you should probably call me Jack. Now tell me about this singer."

"I wasn't here. But the girls said she invited them to come see her sing at the Bohemian Caverns."

He nodded. "Okay, so she's a real singer if she's performing there. I think I'd have heard whispers if the vice president was involved with someone high profile though. Don't get me wrong—he's a dog. He goes after women of high and low rank equally. But the well-known liaisons are more talked about for obvious reasons." He thought for a moment. "You're not off base about him using the bar though. His secretary comes down here hunting frequently. And he *has* had mistresses wait at the bar while he finished other meetings in the past. I just don't think he would do that with someone well known."

"It might not be *her* specifically. I just started thinking that maybe the Texas and Havana parts were people, not places."

"Not a bad idea," he conceded and took a sip of his own drink, which was brown liquor in a low glass. "What's the mass goal, then?" His eyes were on mine.

"I don't know. I can't figure that part out. It's strange wording, isn't it?"

His head tilted. "Maybe. Language barrier?"

"Could be. But it sounds foreboding. Like mass graves."

Fields shook his head again. "I can't see the vice president doing anything nefarious. He's not who I'd choose for president, but I can't see him working against the United States. He's a patriot."

"Or a good actor?"

"No," Fields said. "I'd need a lot more evidence to get behind that one. But I'm with you on it being a woman. That does fit his character to a T."

"So a Cuban woman, trying to get information out of him for some bigger goal?"

He leaned back. "Hell of a story if so. We'd need evidence." He swirled his drink, looking into it. "But we have a bigger problem if it's true."

"What's that?"

"Pullman, who has to give us the go-ahead to run it, is implicated."

I hadn't thought about that part. And I swore loudly enough for a neighboring patron to turn his head.

"You can say that again."

I mouthed an apology to the man two tables over. "I'd rather not. What do we do, then?"

Fields finished his drink. "We go over his head. Or we take it to *The Washington Post.* Hell, if we get enough evidence that he's in on something like this, we give him to the FBI."

"You know people in the FBI?"

He grinned. "You do too. You just don't know it yet." I stared at him as he held up his hand to the bartender for another drink. "Welcome to Washington, Judy Greenberg. You have a lot to learn."

22

The vice president wasn't in residence that night, Fields told me. He paid a maid to let him know when he was.

"What good does that do?"

He shrugged. "Never hurts to know who's going up there with him. It's not always women." My mouth dropped open, and Fields started to laugh. "Not like *that*. At least I don't think so. But he's taken some interesting meetings. And then you know who to follow up with."

I thought about this. "So if this is what you do, what does the senior White House correspondent do?"

The corners of his mouth turned down. "Sit in press conferences and take credit for anything juicy. But my turn will come."

"Well, you're halfway there."

He laughed. "Hey now. I apologized for that."

"I know, I'm teasing," I said. My cheeks felt warm. I hadn't finished my drink, but I pushed it away. That was enough.

"Didn't you learn to drink in college?"

I shook my head. "I lived at home. Strict parents and no money for room and board."

"And they let you out in a dress like that?"

"It's borrowed," I admitted. "They think I'm on a double date."

"You almost were," he said, nodding toward Patricia and the congressman.

"Is there anyone in Washington who doesn't cheat on his wife?"

"They are few and far between," he agreed. "But I don't think we're finding anything tonight."

"Why's that?"

He gestured around the room. "No visibly Cuban women present. You're the only brunette."

I turned around. He was right. It was a sparse crowd, and of the four women present, three were blond—though I suspected that Patricia's came from a bottle. And all were engaged at tables with men. "Hair color can be changed," I said, nodding toward Patricia. "What happens next, then?"

"I come here a lot. I'll keep an eye out for our mystery woman from Havana and see what happens."

I looked at him sharply. "Like hell you will."

His eyebrows rose in surprise.

"I'm coming with you. This is my lead. I'm not letting you steal it out from under me."

"I wouldn't—"

I held up a hand. "Apologies are well and good, but trust has to be earned, Jack Fields."

He shrugged, then lifted his glass to me. "To our partnership, then."

I picked up my glass and met his, then took another small sip.

"Tomorrow night?"

I had no idea how I was going to swing two nights in a row, let alone another dress. I had to hope Roberta would be okay with another loan. I agreed that I would be there the next night.

"What time is it?" I asked.

"Ten."

I pushed my chair back quickly and stood. It would take me nearly an hour to get home by the time I dropped Patricia off, and if I wasn't home by eleven, I would have a lot more explaining to do. "I should go. I'll see you tomorrow night."

"Same time, same station," he said, quoting Jack Benny.

I smiled at him and made my way to Patricia, whose hands were clasped in the congressman's. "Patricia? I need to get home."

She glanced up, surprised, as if she had forgotten I was there. "Oh." Her face fell. "Phil, darling, I suppose I need to leave too."

"I can take you home," he said. "Later."

"I don't mind driving you," I told her.

She looked from me, to him, to me again. "It's fine. I'll see you tomorrow."

"What about Roberta's dress?"

She waved a hand. "She won't even notice. You could probably keep it."

I didn't like leaving her. Judging from the number of empty martini glasses on their table, she had obviously had a few drinks, and Fields's words about the girl Clement had been involved with rang in my ears. If Patricia didn't make it home, it would be my fault.

"I—uh—I don't want to walk out by myself," I said, trying to figure out how to get her alone to warn her. "Walk me to the car at least?"

"Can't Fields do that? You two looked awfully cozy."

Great. That was going to be the rumor going around the office tomorrow. I would be sacked for fraternization by Friday.

"Patricia," I said plaintively. "Please."

She looked up at me again, then pushed her chair back and stood, the slightest wobble in her step. "I'll be right back," she told the congressman. "Don't you go falling in love with someone else while I'm gone."

He reached for her hand and kissed it. "Never."

I wondered what the etiquette involved in vomiting on a congressman was, because he was *married* and this was disgusting. But I held my tongue until we got upstairs, crossed the lobby, and made it out into the muggy June night air.

"Do I need to walk you across the street too? Or is seeing your car good enough?"

I turned to Patricia. "Don't stay with him."

She laughed. "Oh, honey, I can take care of myself."

"Fields told me—"

"Fields talks too much. It was a shakedown. I told you. He already explained it."

"Did he explain that the girl had an 'accident' right after that? She's dead."

Patricia studied me, her expression thawing slowly. She bit the inside of her lip. "Well—that does put a—damper on things—if it wasn't a real accident, that is." Then she straightened her posture and fluffed the ends of her hair. "I'll be careful."

"Don't you want someone who isn't married?"

Her face was sad. "Happy endings only happen in fairy tales—and even then they're only for the princess in the story, not the girl from the farm." She gave me a playful little shove. "Go on home, princess. I'll see you tomorrow." She turned to walk back into the hotel. "And we'll be talking about the way Fields was looking at you tomorrow too."

I had done the best I could—I just hoped that was enough.

Thankfully, I had left my own dress in the car. I did have to pull over on a side street and shimmy out of Roberta's dress and into mine, but I managed decently without being seen.

The front light was on, but the living room lights were off, and I breathed a sigh of relief as I let myself into the house. It was so much easier if my parents were asleep and I didn't have to tell them about the supposed date—I couldn't exactly say he had been a louse if I needed to go out again the next night, and I didn't feel up to waltzing in pretending to be all starry-eyed to convince my parents I was falling in love.

I took my shoes off at the front door and tiptoed up the stairs toward my room.

I flipped on the light and—

—let out a shriek of surprise to find my grandmother sitting in my desk chair with a cup of tea.

"What are you doing in here?" I asked, clutching my chest and trying to steady my breathing.

"I wanted to know how your date went."

"So you sat in the dark?"

She shrugged. "You would have washed your face first if you knew I was in here. And your parents may believe that tall tale you told, but I know better. Where did you *really* go all dolled up like that? I won't tell."

Historically that had been true—at least when it came to keeping any misdeeds I committed from my parents. But the fewer people who knew about this, the better. And Sylvia Greenberg's tongue had a tendency to wag at the beauty parlor or mahjong with her friends.

However, she also saw through me immediately when I lied. And if I wasn't honest, I ran the risk of her asking leading questions in front of my parents. "I'm working on a story."

She raised an eyebrow. "Is it taking place on a street corner with that lipstick?"

"What? No! But there's a lead I'm following at a bar. With another reporter. It's all aboveboard, I promise."

She stood up and crossed the room toward me, putting a hand on my cheek. "I know, *bubbelah*. But you're going to have to produce a young man soon if you want to keep using that excuse on your parents. Unless you want me to dig one up for you? I'm not so sure Miriam Rivkin's grandson likes girls. He might work."

"Grandma!"

"What?" she asked. "You think I was always such a good girl when I was young? No, you get this from me, not that mother of yours." She shuffled to the door. "Wash your face before bed. It ages your skin to sleep in makeup." She patted her own cheeks. "That's why I look so young."

I shook my head as she closed the door behind her. She was too much. But it felt good knowing I had help in my corner.

23

Fields came by my desk first thing the next morning with an article.

"We're back to that, are we?" I felt a little awkward around him—and not just because he had seen me in a cocktail dress without a brassiere the night before. We had a secret now. This was definitely fraternization territory.

He leaned in close, and I glanced over my shoulder to make sure Miss Kelly was nowhere nearby. "The story is just for cover," he whispered. "I wanted to tell you the vice president is in California until Saturday."

My shoulders dropped. So much could happen between now and Saturday. The mass goal could occur before we found out what it was. Someone else could scoop us. "So we just wait until he's back, then go sit at Off the Record until we see something?"

"Actually," he said, then straightened and said in a louder voice: "News needs this by eleven." His tone was strictly professional. "And you're the fastest typist."

I looked at him, confused, then saw Miss Kelly cross behind him, clearly listening. "Right away, Mr. Fields," I said. "Does it need edits, or have you figured out how to write an effective lead?"

Her lips twitched, though she didn't actually smile, as she headed toward the elevators.

"Ouch," he said, lower.

"Start with *who* or *what*. *Where*, *when*, *why*, and *how* aren't the most important information. You're losing interest before readers even find out who's involved."

He blinked three times. "That's—"

"What they teach in introductory journalism—unless you missed that day?"

He grinned sardonically. "Thanks, professor."

"You're welcome." I lowered my voice: "Now what were you saying?"

"Are you sure you're done ripping apart my writing style?"

"No, but the other conversation is more interesting."

Fields shook his head. "You're quite annoying, do you know that?"

"I prefer *tenacious*."

"That too," he said, then glanced over his shoulder as the door of the elevator closed, Miss Kelly inside it. He knelt down to my desk. "We should go see the nightclub singer."

My skin began to prickle with the excitement—and potential danger—of the situation. "Do you think she's the one who—"

"I don't have any idea. Probably not, actually, if it's anything big. The higher profile the affair, the less likely it is to be anything secretive."

He had a point. A movie star had serenaded the president for his birthday a month earlier, and the rumors were flying about their involvement.

"Say, speaking of that, are the president and—"

"Off the record," Fields interrupted, knowing where I was going with my question. "Yes. But you didn't hear that from me."

I looked at him, surprised. "Why wouldn't you write it, then? That's a huge story."

He sighed, but he sounded annoyed. "I know. But the paper won't touch it. Partially because of national security. Partially because the feds are going to want to know sources, and then I lose access to people who have information on much more important stories. Better to let the scandalous but unimportant one go to catch a bigger fish."

"What could be a bigger fish than the most famous woman in the world?" He said nothing but looked at me as I worked it out. "You don't mean . . ." Then, in a low voice: "Havana, do you?"

"Anything the Soviets are doing that actually affects millions of lives is more important than who someone is sleeping with. Even if one of those someones is the most powerful man in the world and the other is the most beautiful woman. And we know the Soviets are in bed with Castro—pun intended."

A chill ran down my spine. The Soviets partnering with a country within missile range of the US couldn't mean anything good. For any of us. Was it *really* possible I had found a key to unlocking that story though?

"But if you don't think this singer is our Havana lead, why go see her?"

"She may know something. She may not, but it doesn't hurt to try. We're fumbling in the dark here to see if this lead of yours means anything, which means we should explore any possible connections we can find."

I felt like I was vibrating with excitement—he believed I could be onto something. Enough to really explore it.

The Bohemian Caverns show was going to be tricky though—it did make it easier if I didn't have to make up an excuse every night. But the girls from the typing pool would be there, and it was going to raise suspicions if I arrived with Fields. Patricia didn't like him, but would anyone actually turn me in to Miss Kelly for fraternization if they thought we were dating?

Speaking of Patricia, her desk was empty. I squinted at the clock. I had gotten in early, thanks to my father driving me to work. She still had a minute before it was time to worry.

But I was a Jewish woman, so no clock was going to stop me from worrying early.

I was about to ask Fields if he thought she was okay when the elevator door opened, and Patricia walked out. I exhaled.

"The typing pool girls who met her last weekend are going to her show Thursday night. How do we deal with them?"

He looked over his shoulder and saw Patricia rolling her eyes at me over him being at my desk. "We—uh—might have to pretend to be . . . friendly. Or something."

I shook my head. "What about the no-fraternization rule?"

Fields grinned. "That's at the office. Do you really think there's no funny business going on after hours?"

I looked at him sharply. "Is there?"

"Are you kidding?" He used a finger to count girls around the room. "Eight of them are dating reporters."

"But they know I don't like you. I mean that I didn't. You know what I mean."

He held a hand to his heart, pretending to be wounded. Then he winked at me. "Isn't that how the best love stories start? Romeo and Juliet? Beatrice and Benedick? Darcy and Elizabeth? Rhett and Scarlett?"

I laughed loudly enough for several girls to look over, including Patricia. "Don't go expecting a happy ending from me, Fields."

"Jack," he reminded me.

"At work, Fields. And we're working off the clock too."

"Fair. But in front of people, you may need to pretend." He hesitated. "So should I pick you up Thursday, or . . . ?"

"No," I said quickly. "My parents—"

"Right. I forgot you live with them."

My grandmother's words from the night before rang in my head. I *was* eventually going to need to produce a man. And Fields could pass for Jewish, if we Yiddished up his name some.

"I'll go with the girls, and then you 'happen' to be there."

"Like Clement last night?"

"Exactly. Although hopefully with less of a scandalous past."

He smiled, and it struck me that my mother was going to love him as long as she didn't find out what we were playing at. Or that he wasn't Jewish. "I'm practically a Boy Scout."

I rolled my eyes. "Get out of here before Miss Kelly comes back. I'll see you tomorrow night at the Bohemian Caverns." He started to take the paper on my desk back. "I can type that."

"You don't have to." His tone was sheepish. "I was just making an excuse for Miss Kelly."

"It'll look bad if she comes back, and it's on the board. Besides, *someone* has to clean up your leads."

Fields looked at me for a few seconds, then shook his head. "You're going to keep me on my toes, aren't you?"

I shrugged. "It's only fair. I had to wear heels to even see over the bar last night."

His laughter rang through the typing pool as he walked away.

Patricia was at my desk before he was even in the elevator. "You two seem . . . *cozy*."

I was a little miffed about how she abandoned me the night before. "Well, we had a lot of time to talk last night." She colored slightly, and I felt bad. No, I didn't approve. And I was worried about her safety. But the way she had called me the princess and what she said about happy endings made my heart ache. "He's not so bad. You won't tell Miss Kelly on me, will you?"

She looked hurt. "Of course not."

"Thank you," I said, and her demeanor softened. "What happened last night after I left?"

Her lips stretched into a sly smile. "Let's just say the rooms at the Hay-Adams don't have coin-operated beds."

"Patricia!"

"What? A girl's got to have some fun." She leaned closer. "I did hear you last night though. I'm not getting attached."

"Good." Though I wondered how much fun a man old enough to be her father could really be. "Think I can tag along to that singer's show tomorrow night?"

"Of course. Do you want to pick me up again? We can snag you another dress."

24

"Two dates with him, and we haven't met him yet?" my mother asked. "No. He should come here first."

"His car is in the shop," I said, thinking quickly. I glanced at my grandmother, who was crocheting a blanket for Betty's new baby in the corner, an idea forming. "His—uh—his grandmother borrowed his car to pay a shivah call and crashed it."

"Is she all right?" my mother asked, instantly invested. Which meant she was buying my story, but my grandmother had looked up, her lips pursed wryly.

"She's fine—it wasn't a bad accident, but his car isn't ready yet."

"Whose shivah was she going to?" my grandmother asked innocently. Her eyes were shrewd though, watching me.

"One of her friends," I said, staring her down. "You know how it goes. At your age."

She chuckled. "Why don't you have his friend bring him here, and we'll meet both of them? Decide which one we like better?"

I was going to throw out her favorite crochet hook the next time she wasn't looking. Yes, she had saved me from the cantor, but this was spiteful. She knew I was lying. I knew she knew I was lying, and she knew that I knew that she knew I was lying. Why torture me and risk my mother finding out?

"Because they're already driving down to DC from Baltimore to Pat—Paula's house, and we're far out of the way."

"Are we?"

I maintained eye contact. "If they're taking Route 1, yes."

"Mother, stop interrogating the poor girl," my father said. "She returned my car without a scratch." He turned back to me. "It's fine. But we would like to meet him."

"I think—" my mother said, but my grandmother cut her off.

"Yes, have him come by when his car is fixed." She winked at me. "And maybe this Pat—Paula too."

Once my parents were back engaged in their reading, I scrunched up my face at my grandmother, who blew me a kiss in return. She had never made anything easy. I doubted she would start now.

~

Outfitted in a red dress that Roberta assured me was perfect for the Bohemian Caverns, I drove with Patricia up to U Street—an area that I had definitely never traversed before. Located near Howard University, this part of the city was technically integrated, but mostly in the sense that white people sometimes ventured there for entertainment purposes.

Patricia, however, seemed not to notice that we were getting stares at stoplights, and so I decided to follow her lead.

"Have you been to this place before?"

"Once," she said. "It's fun."

Her idea of fun and mine clearly differed, but I wasn't there for a good time, I reminded myself. I was there to follow a lead. And this singer was the only Havana lead we had right now.

We entered through an intricately carved door, and then went down a narrow staircase decorated with stucco to look like we were in a cave, with faces peering out from crevices. The staircase opened up into a large room with a low ceiling, stalagmites and stalactites protruding up and down at us. You had to watch where you were walking, and a tall man wouldn't last long.

"What *is* this place?" I asked loudly over the music.

Patricia grinned. “I told you it was fun!”

I looked around the semidark room, my eyes adjusting. It was a mixed crowd—a little over half of the patrons were white, which seemed high based on the neighborhood. From the framed posters on the wall showcasing recent acts, this was clearly a place where famous people performed when in the nation’s capital.

The girls from the office waved us over to their table. I chose a seat where I could see the stairs, keeping my eyes open for Fields, who walked in just as we got our first round of drinks. He spotted me quickly and began making his way through the crowd.

“Incoming,” Gladys said, and every head swiveled. I was glad no one noticed my reaction because I was sure my cheeks were as red as the dress I had on, which I now desperately wished was a little higher cut.

“Ladies,” Fields said, then nodded to me. “Hey, Judy.”

Then everyone turned to look at me, and I hoped the darkness of the club hid my flush.

“Jack,” I said, his first name feeling foreign on my lips. I didn’t look at my friends, but I could feel their eyes on me.

“Mind if I steal Judy for a bit?” he asked.

Patricia exhaled loudly. “She’s here with us.”

I looked around the table as they waited to see what I did next. “I—um—I kind of invited him tonight.”

“Why?” Patricia’s tone was incredulous.

I thought fast and then shrugged. “What was it you said? A girl’s got to have some fun.”

Patricia laughed. “I meant with *someone* actually fun. But whatever makes you happy, doll.” Something caught her eye, and I looked in the direction her head was turned. The congressman had just walked in. “Speaking of which . . .” She stood up.

So much for not getting attached.

Fields offered me his hand, and I took it, following him to an empty table tucked in a corner, with a clear view of the stage. “Well that worked out,” he said.

"I don't trust that man."

"Nor should you. But for all her faults, Patricia has a good head on her shoulders. I think she'll be okay."

"She wouldn't give you such high praise."

"Yeah, well, maybe she's just too mean to get herself into any real trouble."

I laughed but smacked his arm lightly. "That's my friend you're talking about."

"A friend who would have ditched you two nights in a row if we hadn't had other plans." He had a point there.

The lights dimmed, and a voice announced over a microphone, "Ladies and gentlemen, the Bohemian Caverns is proud to present, straight from Havana, Cuba, home of the mambo, the queen of Morro Castle herself, Señorita Maricela."

A woman in a long, form-fitting silver dress appeared in a spotlight at a microphone. She was the most beautiful woman I had ever seen, with long, dark hair that fell in curls to just above her waist and a tropical flower over her ear. Her tanned skin glistened in the club's lighting, and her dark eyes shone with a mischievous glint. She opened her mouth, and a soulful soprano voice rose in a mournful Spanish song. I couldn't understand the words, but it was impossible to take my eyes off her. Impossible to not feel the pain of whatever loss she sang about. And even I, who had suffered so little, felt tears welling up as she held the final note.

"Let's have a little fun now," she said in a lilting accent over the thunderous applause that echoed off the walls of the aptly named caverns. The lights illuminated the band behind her as they began a more upbeat song, and her hips swayed seductively as she sang, again in Spanish, but this time a clear dance number. Couples rose from their tables and came together on the floor in front of her.

"Want to dance?" Fields asked in my ear.

I shook my head, cupping my hands around his ear to be heard over the music. "I don't know how to dance to this."

"Neither do most of them," he said, pointing toward the floor. It was true. While a handful of people were doing variations of the mambo, most were just moving to the music as they saw fit.

I looked back at Fields, tearing my eyes from Maricela. I wondered how she commanded a room like that. I had never seen a woman so powerful, so imperious, so comfortable in her own skin, and it awakened something in me that I hadn't known existed.

We were there to work. And I had no intention of falling for this man or any other who was just going to get in the way of me becoming the reporter I wanted to be. But, if we *were* onto something, he was the man who was going to help me achieve my goals.

And more than that, my feet, my legs, my hips ached to move to this irrepressible Latin beat.

I stood up and turned toward the dance floor, looking back at Fields over my shoulder. "You coming or not?" I asked loudly.

He grinned, taking my hand and following me onto the crowded floor.

25

We copied couples around us, swaying and twirling, pressed closer and closer together by the ever-expanding crowd of dancers as Maricela switched between mambo numbers and poignant ballads that made me long for a homeland that wasn't mine and that I had never laid eyes on.

I lost count of how many songs we danced to, stopping only when Maricela took a break, promising she would return in a few minutes.

"Let's get a drink," Fields said as she retreated off stage.

"We have to talk to her." I could tell my eyes were starry, and quite honestly, I wasn't sure if I was more interested in whether she was our Havana lead or whether I just wanted to know more about her.

"After the show," Fields said. "We won't get anything now."

"How do you know that?"

He nodded toward a man who was making his way backstage, and my eyes widened. It was a very well-known and prominent senator. But not a Texan.

"Patricia said she was with a senator the other night."

"He's from Missouri. And he's a Republican who hates this administration with a passion," Fields said. "If they have anything going on, she's definitely not our girl in Havana."

"What if she's working with him to get to the vice president?"

Fields shook his head. "No. He wouldn't do anything underhanded. It's more about filibustering and braggadocio."

My shoulders dropped. "Then this was all pointless."

"Not necessarily," he said. "I still think we talk to her. She could be a good resource." He nudged me with his shoulder. "And that was fun, wasn't it?"

It was. But I wasn't about to admit that.

"I *could* use some water," I conceded, flushed. All that dancing and the heat of the crowd. That's all it was.

"Not a champagne cocktail tonight?" He had a hint of a smile on his face, and I was tempted. But no. We were working.

"Clear heads," I said. "You may be used to working with a drink or two in you, but I'm not."

"Water it is." He led me back to our table, where he left me while he went to the bar, then returned with two glasses. I drank half of mine in one long gulp. "How ladylike."

"This isn't a date," I reminded him.

"Of course," he said. "I cowrite with Bob Jenkins all the time, and we *always* dance that close."

"What you and Bob Jenkins do in your spare time is no concern of mine. We"—I gestured between us—"need to keep up appearances."

"In that case, look a little more like you actually want to flirt with me. The typing pool girls are looking."

I scowled at him for a couple of seconds, then threw my head back in a laugh, placing a hand on his arm. "Better?"

He leaned close. "Better."

Something fluttered in my stomach, but I ignored it.

Then the lights dimmed, and Maricela reappeared. Fields offered me a hand, and I joined him again on the dance floor as she sang her way effortlessly through a second set.

I had been to dances before, but nothing like this, with no chaperones, a man's arm around my waist, our bodies close in the darkness as other couples pressed even closer, forgetting that anyone else was there at all. I looked at Fields in the dim club lighting at one point, forcing myself to remember that none of this was real. It was just the music, the lighting, the atmosphere, making my eyes drift to his mouth. Nothing more.

Besides, I reminded myself, as soon as he *opened* that mouth, he was quite annoying.

Usually.

"We have a special guest tonight," Maricela said breathlessly. "In DC for one night only, ladies and gentlemen, from my home country, Mr. Desi Arnaz!"

My eyes widened as the man who had spent so many evenings in black-and-white in my living room took the stage next to this magnificent woman, and the band behind them launched into Mr. Arnaz's hit "Cuban Pete," Maricela taking the Lucille Ball part of the song. Fields spun me around, holding me close as I watched the two of them together on stage. He looked older than he did in his *I Love Lucy* days, a little sadder and more tired now that he, in real life, no longer loved Lucy. But the energy of the song was infectious as they danced a samba together onstage.

He dipped her low at the end of the song, and the two of them took a bow, retreating together. I searched the crowd for the senator but didn't see him. I wondered if he had left earlier or if seeing Maricela with the television star had been too much.

I looked back at Fields. "What now?"

He chewed his lower lip for a second. "We try to get to her backstage."

I shook my head. "They'll never let us back there."

Fields grinned at me. "Sure they will." He reached into a pocket and pulled out a laminated ID card from *The Washington Digest* with his picture on it. I needed to remind Miss Kelly that I still didn't have one of those—even if mine was just for the typing pool. "We tell them we're writing a profile on her."

"But you cover the White House."

"*You* know that. I doubt *she* does."

"What happens when there's no profile?"

He shrugged. "We worry about that later. If she even notices. She may not read her reviews." He took my hand, leading me through the crowd, most of which were going the other direction, toward the bar, the tables, or the exit. I glanced back over my shoulder, and the girls from the office were heading toward their table. Patricia was nowhere to be seen.

We reached the door to backstage, where a burly man stood, arms crossed, shaking his head at men with flowers. "No," he said as soon as he noticed us.

Fields pulled out the badge. "Jack Fields, *Washington Digest*," he said confidently. "I'm writing a piece on Señorita Maricela's performance tonight. I wanted to confirm a few things for it."

The man studied it for so long that I wondered whether he could read.

Finally, he opened the door behind him with one arm. "Just him," he said to me as Fields entered.

"She's my stenographer," Fields said. "No article if I don't have her."

"Where's her badge?"

"They don't waste them on the women," he said with an eye roll. I knew what he was doing, but his tone still made me want to stomp on his foot with my high heel.

"Where's her notepad, then?"

I reached into my purse and produced one. A good reporter always had paper and a pencil on her. He stared me down for a moment, then grudgingly let me pass.

"Glad you had that," Fields said with a nod.

"Stenographer." I rolled my eyes.

"Hey, it worked, didn't it?"

I did have to give him that.

We walked down the narrow hallway. A room to the right had a faded star on the door, with a handwritten paper taped to it reading "Maricela."

"Not so glamorous back here," I murmured.

"Ready?"

I put a hand on his arm. "What's our plan? We can't just come out and ask her if she's working for the Russians."

"No," he said quietly. "We start with some general questions and feel her out."

I nodded, and he knocked on the door. "Miss Maricela? Jack Fields, *Washington Digest*."

"Come in," she called, and Fields opened the door.

She had stripped out of the silver number she had worn onstage and was in a pink satin dressing gown, feathered at the neck, sleeves, and hem, but her makeup was still on. Flowers from admirers adorned the small makeup vanity as well as the coffee table that sat in front of a sagging loveseat. But the dingy dressing room was barely noticeable as Maricela's stage presence extended offstage as well.

"I hope you enjoyed the show," she said, waving a manicured hand toward the sofa, indicating that we should sit. "It is, of course, a smaller crowd than I was used to back home, but"—she smiled sadly—"circumstances have changed."

I followed Fields's lead, sitting on the sofa. It was small, and our legs just touched. I tugged awkwardly at my dress.

"Yes," Fields said earnestly. "Allow me to introduce my associate, Miss Judy Greenberg."

She nodded to me, and I offered a smile.

"That's what I do love about this country," she said. "So many more opportunities for women."

Hah, I thought. I would have loved to set her straight. But that wasn't what we were there for. I opened my notebook. "We just have a few questions," I said. "Can you spell Maricela for us?"

She complied.

"And your last name?"

"Just Maricela. Of course, that's just my stage name. I was born Anamaria Castilla."

Fields and I exchanged a glance. Either this wasn't a spy, or she was giving us a fake name.

I wrote that down. "And you're from Havana?"

She laughed. "Didn't you hear the announcer? The queen of Morro Castle." We shared another look. "No. I was born in a town called Banes. My parents were poor until I became famous enough to help them." She sighed sadly. "I got out when the revolution came. My parents weren't so lucky."

She had said *were*. "Are they—?" She shook her head.

"They weren't political. But they knew Batista back when he was still Rubén Zaldívar. If I hadn't been so well known . . ." Her voice trailed off. "But that's done now."

My eyes threatened to well up as I imagined feeling responsible for a loss like that. If this was true, no, she definitely wasn't working for Castro's government in any capacity. But we did have to be sure before we could ask anything else.

"Let's speak of happier things," she said, the sadness disappearing behind a mask. "How did you like the show tonight? My guest should make for quite a headline."

"How *did* you get Desi Arnaz?" Fields asked.

She smiled. "He was passing through town, spending the night on the way from New York to Miami. My agent called in a favor."

"So you didn't know him from Cuba?"

Maricela laughed. "No. His family left in the 1933 revolution. Nobility, you know? I wasn't born yet. He's practically as American as you are."

I didn't know much more than him telling Lucy she had some *'splaining* to do. And I realized most of what I knew about Cuba, aside from recent headlines, I had learned from a man playing up stereotypes of a country he left as a teenager.

"Full of promises that one. Swears he'll put me in a show. I doubt I'll hear from him. You don't get far in this business believing men like that."

I thought of Patricia and her congressman. Our worlds may not have been that different after all.

"Tell us more about leaving—I heard you were a favorite of Batista's?"

She smiled wryly. "That's one way to put it." She leaned forward, and there was a heaviness in her face. "He wasn't a good man—not for the people. Not for Cuba. But I wanted to be the most famous singer in all of Cuba. I did what I had to in order to make that happen. And when the revolution came, they weren't interested in what you actually believed." She looked straight at me. "I think with a last name like Greenberg, you understand that better than Mr. Fields here."

My breath caught. Yes. I understood what she meant. My family had been here during the war, but so many others hadn't been so lucky. I found myself nodding.

Then she shook her head, and the heaviness was gone again. "It was an honor performing with a man such as Desi," she said. "You write that down. I shouldn't have spoken so freely of him before. Forgive me."

Fields started to speak, but I put a hand on his arm. I couldn't explain it, but I trusted this woman who could shift faces so quickly it could give a person whiplash. "Maricela," I said softly. "Have you ever been to Texas?"

"Texas? No. Miami and New York mostly."

"Have you spent time with anyone from Texas?"

She looked at me curiously. "No, not that I know of. Though I suppose if they don't wear those big hats and speak like in the movies, maybe."

"Judy," Fields said warningly.

"That senator," I said. She sat up straighter, looking like she was going to object. "He's married, you know."

"I don't know what—"

"They don't leave their wives for singers. Or girls from the typing pool at a newspaper."

She chuckled, shaking her head. "I know. I'm not so green as that. But men in power are good protection. Old habits and such I suppose."

"We're not actually writing about you," I said suddenly.

She looked alarmed, and Fields said my name again, louder this time.

"We need your help."

"Can I have a minute with my . . . associate?" Fields said, rising.

"Fields. She's not the one we're looking for. But I like her. She can help us." He stared at me. "Sit. Please."

He sat down, and I turned back toward Maricela.

"I take it you're not a fan of the current leadership in Cuba?"

She turned her face toward the door, looking at me from the side of her eye, like she was ready to call for security. "Who are you?"

"We told you our real names. And we do work for *The Washington Digest*. But we're following a lead, and I think you might be able to help us crack this one."

She shook her head again. "I'm just a singer. I don't know about anything else."

I leaned forward. "I think you know more than you realize. Do you think you could spot someone else from Cuba? If they were pretending to be American?"

"Maybe?"

"Judy!" Fields said again, more insistently. "What are you playing at?"

I looked at him. "We take her to the bar with us. See if she can find who we're looking for."

"I don't think this is a good idea."

"And I don't think we have any other options if we want to figure this out!"

For a long moment, he held my gaze. Then he turned toward Maricela. "Would you be willing to go to the Hay-Adams Hotel with us? To try to find a woman from Havana?"

"I'm not going to a hotel with you," she said, standing up. "I don't know what the two of you want from me, but I think this has gone on long enough."

"Not the hotel," I said quickly. "Off the Record. The bar. In the basement. We think a woman is meeting someone important there."

"Judy!"

Maricela blinked a few times, looking at me. "A Cuban woman? You mean a spy?"

"We don't know exactly. But—"

"They are here," Maricela said quietly.

Fields's mouth dropped open. I felt a chill run down my spine at the certainty of her statement. *They are here*. Were we too late?

"They?" I asked.

"Castro's people," she said. "I don't know who they are. I got a message—in code—from a friend at home telling me to be careful. Not to trust anyone from Cuba if I didn't know them already."

I tried to imagine how that must feel. What if any other Jewish person I met could be gathering information at best, trying to kill me at worst? "Will you help us?" I asked.

She didn't reply, staring past me, and I was sure she was going to say no. It was too dangerous for her, and I had pressed too hard. Fields was right. I should have kept my mouth shut.

"Yes," she said finally, so quietly it took me a moment to register that she had spoken at all. "I will help you."

26

Back in the hall outside Maricela's dressing room, armed with the name of the hotel she was staying at to arrange a time to meet, I was elated. Fields less so.

I started toward the door guarded by the bouncer, ready to rejoin the girls from the typing pool, but Fields grabbed my arm.

"What are you doing?"

I looked at him, surprised by his tone. "We already knew she wasn't the one we were looking for. What are you upset about? She's going to help us."

"We don't know this woman. For all we know, she's working with the Texas one."

I shook my head. "She's not. I trust her."

He made a scoffing noise. "What do you know about trusting people?"

I hated my height. I wanted to be able to tower over him as he was doing to me. But all I could do was put my hands on my hips and maintain eye contact until he backed down. "I knew enough to trust you to help me—unless that was a mistake?"

His posture shifted as he relented some, and he shook his head. "You'd better be right. This isn't a game. A cornered spy will kill people to get away."

The room spun slightly, but I stayed steady on my feet and took several deep breaths. "I know that," I lied. It had never once occurred to me that the message I had taken in Mr. Pullman's office could end my life. Was that why he had been so secretive with it? Was he keeping me safe? Or himself?

"Maybe—" He swallowed visibly and tried again. "Maybe you let me do this."

I scowled at him. "Are you *protecting* me?" I asked, mockingly. "Or just trying to get all the glory for yourself? Because I am *not* some damsel in distress, and this was *my* lead. Maybe *I* should do it *myself*."

I turned and walked toward the door, but Fields stopped me with a hand on my arm. "I've spent a few years around politicians now. Some of them are less savory than others. This is your first story, and she acknowledged Cuba has spies here. I don't want anything to happen to you."

I rolled my eyes. "Got a little crush on me, Fields? Well, get over it. We're partners on this story, and that's it."

He barked out a short laugh. "Trust me. You're not my type."

"Yeah, well, you're not mine either," I said. It wasn't a total lie—my parents would sit shivah for me if I came home with a boy who wasn't Jewish.

"Just—promise me you'll be more careful," he said, his eyes softer. "For both of us—and for the story. Whatever this 'mass goal' is, we could be saving a lot of people if we get it right."

He had a point there. And I *had* gone in guns blazing, based on nothing more than a hunch, which was a reckless gamble.

But I wasn't about to admit I had been wrong either.

"Fine," I said, with much more attitude than he deserved. "I need to find Patricia. What time is it anyway?"

"Time for you to get a watch," he said. "What reporter doesn't have a watch?"

"I have one," I lied. "It just doesn't go with my outfit." I grabbed his wrist and checked the time. If I didn't get back soon, my nights of investigating were going to be over before they really got started. "I need to get home."

"I can take you."

"I drove myself," I said over my shoulder as I started toward the door again. "Like I said, I'm not some damsel in distress, and I don't need a white knight rescuing me."

I tossed my hair over my shoulder as I reached the door, loving that I was leaving him on such a strong parting line—like Katharine

Hepburn sweeping out of a room—when the door swung open, flinging me into Fields like a rag doll, knocking us both to the ground.

As we lay there stunned, a well-dressed man walked past us with hardly a second look. I started to laugh as Fields helped me up. "I should have picked a different actress," I said.

He looked at me like I was crazy. "Actress?"

"I thought I was making a Katharine Hepburn exit. And I was. But the movie turned out to be *Summertime*. You know—the one where she fell in the canal."

"You are one strange cookie, Greenberg."

I shrugged as the bouncer held the door for me. "That's part of my charm, Fields."

~

Only Carol and Gladys remained at the table where the girls from the typing pool had been sitting. "Have you seen Patricia?" I asked.

They looked surprised to see me. "She thought you left with Fields," Carol said. "So she left with her new fella."

"Where *did* you two disappear to?" Gladys asked, leaning forward, her elbow on the table. "Please tell me you didn't sneak out to a car. You deserve a room at least."

My mouth fell open. They both started to laugh, and Gladys passed Carol a dollar. "Told you," Carol said. "She still lives with her parents. She's not doing all that."

"Yet," Gladys said. "I'll earn that one back in another week or two."

~

For the second time, I drove myself home from the city alone. My mind wandered back to our interaction with Maricela. Had I been rash? Was Fields right?

Maybe. If she *had* been connected to whoever we were looking for, the Texas question could have ended very differently. I imagined her pulling a dagger from a concealed pocket in her dressing gown.

Then again, real life wasn't like the movies. She just would have declined to help us if she knew anything.

Or she would *agree*, just as she had, to find out what we knew.

I thought of the warning she'd received not to trust anyone from Cuba she didn't know. We certainly didn't know her. But something in my gut told me she was on our side. I couldn't explain it. But just like how instinct had led me to take the typing pool job, to not forget about that message like Mr. Pullman had told me to, and to trust Fields to work with me, I trusted her to help us. And honestly, that was a better lead than anything else we had found so far.

I thought about what she had said about Batista though. *He wasn't a good man—not for the people. Not for Cuba.* I always thought the US supported Batista. We certainly weren't fans of Castro. I would have to ask Fields about that.

I took a quick detour down a side street to change back into my own dress before arriving home. I wasn't going to risk my grandmother sitting in the dark in my room again. Her knowing I was out chasing a story was one thing. Seeing me in a dress like this was a whole other story.

And it was a good thing I did, because she stopped me from the living room this time, nearly giving me a heart attack once again.

"Are you just going to hide in a different room every time I go out?" I asked her.

She clucked her tongue. "You act like I didn't raise four children of my own. And I know full well you changed out of that other dress before you walked in," she said, indicating the flash of red under my arm. I felt my cheeks warming but didn't bother denying it. I could talk my way out of trouble with my parents, but not with her. Namely because I was never actually *in* trouble with my grandmother, but also because she had seen right through me since the day I was born. Sometimes I thought that was why she moved in with us instead of one of her other three children. There was certainly no love lost between her and my mother, but none of my cousins were much trouble—or much fun.

"Now," she said, "the real question is: Is Pat-Paula short for Patrick or Patricia?"

"Grandma!"

"I wasn't born yesterday. And while I don't mind you having a bit of excitement, I don't have any intention of sitting shivah over a wedding to an Irish boy."

I stared at her for a few seconds, then gave in. "Patricia. She's a girl from work. We just went out downtown. There's no boy." She studied me, and I fought to keep her gaze and willed my cheeks to keep from changing colors. Besides, Fields wasn't a boy like *that.* I wasn't lying—just not telling the whole truth either.

"Mmhmm," she said finally. "Well, make sure whoever this boy *isn't* that he looks Jewish enough when you bring him home the next time you go out. And best not slip on the name again. Your mother is sharper than you think she is."

Lord, I hoped that wasn't true. But I was confident Fields could stand the scrutiny as long as I prepared him with the name of a temple to say his parents belonged to in Baltimore.

My grandmother stood up, her back creaking as she did, and stretched. "Start getting home earlier. My bones are too old for these late nights." She tucked something into my hand as she passed me on her way to the stairs.

I looked down, and in my palm was a silver marcasite watch that I had seen on her own wrist. Fancy enough to wear with a cocktail dress but still appropriate for work.

"For me?" I asked.

She turned around at the top of the stairs and grinned in the dim light rising from the living room. "Like I said, I have no intention of sitting shivah. Besides, I look terrible in black. And if you don't start getting home on time, I'm going to be forced to wear it."

I smiled as I shut off the living room light and felt my way up the stairs. *Take that, Fields,* I thought. I *was* a real reporter. Watch and all.

27

I wanted to march into the newsroom and find Fields first thing the next morning. If the vice president was returning on Saturday, we needed to make plans for this weekend.

It also didn't escape my notice that I had yet to even *see* the newsroom at *The Digest*. The men up there should get used to my face. I hoped they would be seeing a lot of it before too long.

But that was a quick way to wind up out on my behind because there would be no hiding the fraternization, which, while not actually the type Miss Kelly meant, would be apparent the second I walked across the newsroom floor.

So I waited for him to approach me. As I typed, mistyped, and retyped, waiting, I determined I was going to get his phone number, whether he thought that was forward or not. Of course, I would have to walk half a mile to the gas station on Grubb Road to use the pay phone if I wanted to call him without my mother listening to every word and quite possibly picking up the other extension to hear both sides.

Sure enough, Fields stepped out of the elevator around ten, papers in hand. I wondered how he had time to still be writing news stories when he was out until all hours with me. But however he was doing it, it kept our cover for now. "They need this right away," he said, tossing the pages onto my desk.

"Fields," I said, confused—and maybe just a little hurt—as he turned to walk away.

"I don't have all day to spend in the typing pool," he said coolly. "And you have work to do. I've heard my leads aren't up to snuff."

I was debating chasing after him when I saw Miss Kelly observing me. I narrowed my eyes at his back and shook my head, then worked to steady my breathing. It was an act to keep me out of trouble. That was all. But we did need to talk, and I had to get that message to him somehow.

I looked down at the pages in front of me. They were paper clipped at the top, as always, but there was another clip at the bottom of the second page. I flipped to it and saw a scrap of paper. "Duke Zeibert's. Noon," was written on it in blocky, penciled letters. I quickly pocketed the paper, keeping my face neutral, and got to work polishing his article until it sparkled. Not that it was a date, of course. Just a place to talk. Like the two journalists that we were.

Carol asked about lunch at 11:30, but I said I had plans.

"Make sure Fields pays," she said with a wink. I looked around, but Miss Kelly was nowhere to be seen.

I spoke quietly anyway. "Have you ever dated a reporter?"

"Honey," she said, "everyone in here has. What Miss Kelly doesn't know won't hurt her."

"What about Fields?"

"What about him? I wouldn't guess reporters were his style."

I rolled my eyes. "I mean, does he usually date girls in the typing pool?"

"*Fields?* No, never. I mean, Patricia thought he had a thing for Louise, but"—she made a round gesture over her stomach to indicate pregnancy—"that definitely wasn't him."

"Who was it?" I asked, my voice low.

She smiled slyly. "All I know is she spent some time on the seventh floor, and things changed after that."

The seventh floor. "Did she work for Mr. Pullman?"

Carol looked confused. "I don't think so, but I don't know for sure. Why?"

"No reason," I said quickly. But it seemed awfully coincidental that Fields preferred she type his articles, she wound up on seven, and then she got the axe. Had she stumbled onto something too?

I found myself fidgeting as I walked over to Duke Zeibert's. It was bad enough that the typing pool was all gossiping about me and Fields, but Duke knew my father and uncle. All I needed was for him to mention that I was there with a man who wasn't Jewish, and I was sunk. Duke made it his business to know *everyone* who ate at his restaurant.

Which became even more apparent when I arrived, and I told the host I was meeting someone. He directed me immediately to a back corner near the kitchen, without my even having to say who. And sure enough, Fields was sitting there and waved to me, his normal smile back in place. No one would notice us back here at least.

He stood as I approached, pulling out my chair for me. "This isn't a date," I reminded him as I sat down.

"Trust me, I know. But I can still be a gentleman. Besides, Duke wouldn't let me in again if he saw me being rude to a lady. Even if the lady in question is well . . . you."

I laughed. It was hard to be mad at someone who could dish it out as well as he could take it.

"Isn't this awfully public? I don't want to get canned."

"I told you, that's just in the office. This is cover."

"Cover?"

"If someone sees us together at Off the Record—or if anyone saw us dancing last night—we're a couple, remember? Professional at work, dating off the clock."

He wasn't wrong. But—"Duke knows my father and uncle," I blurted out.

"Duke knows everyone's uncle. What are you so worried about?"

I didn't have it in me to play coy, especially not with Fields for some reason. "Why did Louise get fired? The real reason."

Fields shrugged, picking up his menu. "I have no idea. I got the same gossip everyone else did."

"But you and she—"

He lowered his menu and looked me right in the eye. "Absolutely nothing was happening with me and Louise. You're the first girl I've even pretended to date at *The Digest*."

"Why?" It came out before I could stop myself.

He shifted in his seat. "I don't know . . . I—why didn't you get married straight out of college like most girls do?"

"Because I didn't want to. I wanted to be a journalist."

"Yeah, well, so do I."

"But you can do that married."

"So could you, if your husband wasn't a caveman."

He was so clueless. No man wanted a woman who was going to be out all day instead of keeping house. Sure, plenty said they would be fine with it—until dinner wasn't on the table by six. Or until kids came along. And there was a big difference between accepting something and supporting it.

"Right," I said dismissively, picking up my own menu.

"Why are you so defensive today?"

I wasn't going to tell him the real reason, which was that I didn't like how he talked to me that morning, even though it was a ruse for Miss Kelly. I was being ridiculous, and I knew it. But even though I understood we had to sneak around and pretend we both were and weren't a couple, this was *my* lead. *I* got Maricela on board. No, I didn't have an in at the Hay-Adams like he did, and no, they wouldn't run an article without his name on it, but this was my story. And I wanted to feel my part in it was just as important—if not more so—than his.

I was saved by Duke himself, stopping by our table. "Judy Greenberg!" he said immediately. I looked up, surprised that he remembered my first name, not just the connection to my father and uncle. "Your uncle was in here just the other day." I blanched.

But Duke laughed. "He's all bark, no bite that one. But I won't tell him I saw you with anyone." He winked at me.

Uncle Gil certainly had a lot of bark, but I had felt some of the bite as well, and it wasn't as harmless as Duke thought.

"And Jack Fields," he said warmly. "What are you two doing all the way back here? I'm going to tell them to move you up toward the front."

"No, I asked for this table," Fields said. "We're uh . . . keeping this quiet for now."

Duke smiled knowingly. "Then I *definitely* won't tell your uncle I saw you. Don't you two lovebirds worry. Your secret is safe with me." He put a hand on Fields's shoulder and winked at me. "We'll skip the onion rolls for today though. I'll send over some potato knishes instead. Better breath."

He moved on to another table, and I was ready to hide under ours out of embarrassment. "Well that was—"

"Mortifying," I finished.

Fields looked amused. "Am I that bad?"

"We need to talk about that."

"About how bad I am?"

"No, about the fact that you aren't Jewish. My parents want to meet you—well, not *you*, but the guy I made up who I said I went out with the last two times we saw each other. And Duke knows your real name, so if he tells my uncle . . ."

"He does know my real name," Fields said with a hint of an amused smile. "But Duke is discreet. If he says he won't say anything, then he'll take it to the grave."

I was less confident of that than Fields was, but I didn't have another course of action than to trust him.

"So," he continued, menu in front of his face. "Your parents want to meet me?"

"For better or worse, I'm still living there until I can afford a women's boardinghouse, and they can make my life a lot harder if they don't approve. And the clock is ticking."

"It is," he said. "That's why I asked you here. I think we should go to Off the Record Sunday night."

"Why Sunday? You said the vice—" I lowered my voice: "You said the Texan would be back Saturday."

"He spends his first night back with the sec—with his wife." The restaurant was buzzing loudly enough, but it was better we didn't use titles that would attract attention.

"Always?"

"Always," Fields confirmed. "If he's our man, we won't see anything happen until Sunday. And not before eight. He has dinner at home most nights."

"Okay. If it was *tonight*, I'd be in trouble."

"Why's that?"

"My family does Shabbat dinner—that's the Jewish sabbath—every Friday night. I can't miss it."

"I'm familiar with the concept," he said, setting the menu aside. "Is that when they want to meet me?"

"No," I said quickly. I definitely didn't have time to teach him the motzi or anything else he would be expected to know before dinner that night. "But . . . I think you should pick me up Sunday." I studied him. I had been right before. He could pass with his coloring. He had a good nose, but so did I, and that was often a stereotype anyway. One sometimes rooted in truth, but it wasn't the telltale sign that many people believed it to be. "Your name won't work though."

"What's wrong with my name?"

"It's not Jewish. Jack is fine—plenty of Jacobs go by Jack. But Fields won't do."

"What do you suggest?"

Normally I would keep it close, but my mother had mentioned a Jacob Feldstein, so better to keep it far enough from that to avoid awkward questions. I thought for a moment, going down a list of my parents' known friends for names to avoid. "Fleishman," I said finally.

"Jack Fleishman," he repeated. "Not the same ring as Fields, but I suppose I can remember it. Anything else I need to know?"

There was a lot. But if I could get him in and out in under ten minutes, we would probably be okay.

"We need names for your parents."

"And their real ones won't do?"

"Ethel and David," I said decisively. "You have a sister named Frannie."

"Frannie Fleishman?"

"She's married, so it's Frannie Weisman now."

"I feel like I should be writing this down."

I pulled my notebook and pencil from my purse and shoved it across the table. "My grandmother lives with us. Her name is Sylvia and she's sharp. Too sharp. But she won't tell on us. Mention your grandmother. Call her your *bubbe*. That'll be enough for my mother."

"And your father?"

"Act like a gentleman and he'll be fine. You're from Baltimore. You grew up at Temple O'seh Tefillah. It's not real so they won't know anyone there. Orthodox, but your family isn't. Oh, and your grandmother—your bubbe—she crashed your car going to a shivah call. That's like a Jewish wake with less drinking. That's why you didn't come to meet them sooner."

Fields looked at me sideways. "You're picturing quite the interrogation, aren't you?"

"No." I shook my head. "That's the first three minutes at the outside."

He chuckled. "So basically, you learned interview skills from your parents and didn't need to go to journalism school."

"Don't be ridiculous. If I hadn't gone to journalism school, I'd write leads like you do."

He held a hand to his heart, miming a wound. "I've had Jewish friends before. I can do this."

I hoped he was right.

"Pick me up at seven," I said, taking the notebook back. "I'm writing down my address. And my phone number. I need yours too. If you need to reach me, call and . . ." I didn't know what to tell him to say. "Talk in a high-pitched voice and pretend you're a girl named Paula. Say you have a cold and can't go out. Then I'll walk to the gas station and call you back from the pay phone. I need your number for that."

"If I'm coming to pick you up, why can't I call you?"

"Because my mother will listen in. If nothing changes, don't call."

"You have an awful lot of rules, you know that?"

I glared at him until the waiter came to take our order.

"I'll call Maricela's hotel and tell her to meet us at Off the Record," he said after.

"She shouldn't sit with us." Fields looked at me quizzically. "It'd look suspicious. What are we doing on a date with a Cuban nightclub singer? Have her sit at the bar and keep an eye out. She and I can meet in the bathroom to debrief."

"Smart," Fields said.

"Don't act so surprised." I ripped the notes he had taken from the notebook and passed them across the table to him. "And make sure you study these. Like I said, my grandmother in particular is sharp. No slips here."

"Yes, ma'am," Fields said. "I have no intention of landing on your bad side."

"Good," I said. But as I watched him read over his notes, I hoped he could pull this off. I would really hate to be sidelined over him mispronouncing his new last name.

28

Under the guise of bringing over a frozen kugel that my mother had made in anticipation of another bris, I'd stolen the closest thing to a cocktail dress that Betty had on Saturday afternoon. Emerald green and sleeveless, belted with a slim fan skirt—paired with heels, it could pass. While I had zero qualms about Fields seeing me in a repeated dress, I shyly didn't want someone as glamorous as Maricela thinking I only had the one dress.

I tried to see if I could wear the green dress under a regular dress, but none of my dresses were big enough to hide it. So I was going to have to figure out a way to smuggle it out of the house and then change in the car, and Fields was just going to have to avert his eyes. The perils of being an investigative reporter and all that. Nellie Bly had gotten herself committed to an asylum to write a story after all. I could change clothes behind Jack Fields.

But by Sunday evening, I *was* nervous. If he couldn't keep his cover with my parents, this was going to be the world's quickest ending to a career. And I hated relying on other people. I was a firm believer in *If you want a job done right, you do it yourself.* As I brushed my hair, I cursed the society that wouldn't let me, as a woman, prevail without a man's help. It wasn't fair. But I would prove them all wrong yet. We were going to figure this one out and write the best story possible. And my name would be on it.

That was worth everything.

I checked my new watch repeatedly, knowing full well my mother was stationed by the living room window watching for Fields.

"Fleishman," I reminded myself out loud. If I slipped and called him Fields, we were sunk. "Jack."

Why did his first name feel so strange to say? If I liked him romantically, I would want to use it. But I didn't. That's why, I told myself.

Then I heard a commotion downstairs, and my mother called, "He's here! Leonard! Judy! Sylvia! He's here!"

I came rushing down the stairs, afraid to leave him alone with my parents—and especially my grandmother. My mother and father might not question my story, but my grandmother certainly would. I stopped short at the sight of my mother holding the lamp from the living room end table.

"What on earth—?"

"What?" she asked, panicked. "Do I have something in my teeth?"

"You're holding a lamp. Are you planning to bludgeon him?"

She looked at her hand, then set the lamp down and grinned at me sheepishly. "I knocked it over when I got up."

"Mom. Calm down. You're not going on the date. I am." She came over to me and smoothed my hair, then pinched my cheeks, hard. "Ow!"

"Gives you a little more color," she said.

"I have blush on."

"Well maybe not enough."

"Edna," my father said warningly as a knock sounded at the front door. "Leave the poor girl alone. She's already been on two dates with this young man. He knows what her cheeks look like." Then my father opened the door.

To his credit, Fields was wearing a jacket and tie and had brushed his typically unruly hair. He did look quite presentable. And he held a bouquet of flowers.

"Mr. Greenberg," he said with a nod. "Mrs. Greenberg." He held out the flowers, and I was surprised. They were for my mother, not me. Then he smiled at me. "Judy."

"Come in, come in," my mother said, fawning over him and the flowers and practically tripping over her own feet.

"Mom, Dad, meet Jack Fl—"

"Feldstein," he said. "Jacob, actually, but everyone calls me Jack."

"Jacob Feldstein!" my mother exclaimed. "And you work at *The Digest* with Judy?" He nodded. "I know your mother!" She turned to me. "Judy! You said you didn't know him!"

I was going to murder him. We had a plan. Why would he change the name? He couldn't have known my mother knew the mother of a Jacob Feldstein, but this was going to blow up when she called her, which was likely happening the second we left. I knew I couldn't trust him. This was a disaster.

"You know how Judy loves a surprise," he said with a smile. "My mother sends her love and says she'll see you for mahjong on Tuesday."

My mother held a hand to her heart. "This is such a perfect *shidduch*. I'm *kvelling*."

"It's a third date, Edna," my father reminded her. "Unless you've been hiding this for longer with that Baltimore nonsense," he said with a sidelong look at me. I realized my mouth was open and closed it, then shook my head. "Judy isn't exactly known for accurate storytelling," he told Fields—Feldstein—Jacob. I was so confused.

"I don't know about that," whatever-his-name-was said. "She's doing a great job at *The Digest*. I don't want anyone else typing my stories." He leaned closer to both of them. "I think she's got a tremendous future in journalism."

"No, no, no," my mother said. "She'll make a much better wife."

"Mom!" If she wanted my cheeks redder, she was getting it.

"What? I'll love your in-laws. So much better than Betty's."

"We should be going," I said quickly. "We have a reservation, right, *Jacob*?"

My grandmother chose that moment to wake up from where she had been sleeping—or pretending to—on the sofa.

"So this is the mysterious Jack," she said suddenly. I jumped.

"Not mysterious," I said.

"Well he's kept you out all hours while making you drive to meet him without meeting your parents."

If the earth opened up and swallowed me whole right then and there, no one would hear me complaining.

"That was all Judy," Fields said. He was still *Fields* to me. "I wanted to do things properly, but because you and my mother know each other, she felt there was too much pressure until we knew we really liked each other."

"That doesn't sound like Judy," my grandmother said. I couldn't decide whom I hated more in that moment, her or him.

"She *has* been awfully secretive about dates in the past," my mother said. Then she realized her gaffe. "Not that she's dated a lot. I mean, she's been on dates, of course, but no one serious until this, you know. She just—"

Fields looked like he was trying desperately not to laugh. At least one of us was amused. I glanced at my grandmother. Correction. *Two* of us were amused.

"You must be Judy's bubbe," Fields said, crossing to her on the sofa.

She offered a hand, palm down as if she expected him to kiss it. "I like this one," she said to my parents. Then back to him, "You may call me Sylvia."

He looked from her to my parents, then back. "I'm going to go with *Mrs. Greenberg*, unless I'm guessing incorrectly."

"You are not. What a gentleman."

He was a liar and a lout was what he was. I closed my eyes and counted to five. The story mattered most. I would deal with letting my mother down after the story came out. Until then, she could make whatever wedding plans she wanted. My grandmother knew full well this was a sham, and I would see her eventually in hell, if it existed, for the extra hoops she was making us jump through right now. I had no doubt she would be running the place by the time I got there anyway.

"Judy's right," Fields said, with the gall to look disappointed. "We do have a reservation. But it was so nice to—finally—meet you all." He looked to me. "Are you ready?"

The green dress was hidden under my skirt. I had spent Saturday night sewing—badly—a makeshift pocket into the dress I was now wearing. I could rip it out easily when it was no longer needed without doing any damage. Which was fortunate, because both dresses were technically Betty's.

And I had additional makeup in my purse—I had taken the bus to the drugstore especially to buy it.

"I am," I said, trying to keep the iciness out of my tone. But oh was he getting an earful when I got him alone!

"Leonard," my mother said, putting a hand on my father's arm. "Give him your keys."

My father looked at her like she had grown a second head. "Why?"

"They should take your car."

"Why? He has a car. Doesn't he?" He peered around my mother to look out the window.

"Yes, but did you see it? They should take yours."

Fields and I exchanged another look. "Mom—*he can hear you*."

"Well I'm sure he knows what his car looks like."

I grabbed Fields's arm and practically dragged him out the door. "We're leaving. Don't wait up."

"So nice to meet you," he called again helplessly as my parents watched from the doorway.

29

"What was *that*?" I asked as soon as we were in the car. Which admittedly *was* a late forties Plymouth that had seen better days.

"What?" he asked innocently.

"Who are you? For real?"

"You know who I am."

"Well my mother is calling Jacob Feldstein's mother right now and if that's *not* your mother, I'm about to be in a world of trouble."

He smiled in the dark car. "That's my real name."

"What do you mean *real name*? Are you a spy or something?"

"Yes. A spy investigating a spy to write a story on the other spy. Very logical, Greenberg." He glanced over at me. "How many Jews have you counted at *The Digest*?"

I was definitely the only one in the typing pool. And I hadn't actually seen a single Jewish name in bylines I had typed, now that I thought about it.

"They don't hire Jews?"

"I mean, clearly they *can* because they hired you. But I got turned down at enough places without even getting an interview as Jacob Feldstein that I tried Jack Fields. And wouldn't you know? Suddenly I was a good hire."

It made sense. I thought about Frank, passing for Italian. And I wondered, if I had been Judith Graham, if I would be writing legitimately instead of in the typing pool.

Not at *The Digest*. There were no women in the newsroom. But would *The Post* or *The Evening Star* have looked at me twice if I had goy-ified my name?

Either way, I hadn't and they hadn't. And I liked being Judy Greenberg, even if I did get asked periodically if I had horns.

"Why didn't you tell me?"

He shrugged. "You never asked."

"I literally gave you a Jewish last name the other day. That was the time to say, 'Hey, by the way, I'm actually Jacob Feldstein, and I know all of this already.'"

He looked over again, a devilish grin forming this time. "It's not easy to get your goat. You get mine all the time. I saw my chance, and I took it."

I smacked his arm, probably more forcefully than necessary. "If I hadn't played that off, I'd be off this story right now—they'd lock me in my room."

"I have a feeling you'd find a way out. You strike me as a girl who knows how to climb out a window when she needs to."

He had a point there.

"Speaking of which, pull over—preferably on a side street."

"Why?"

"I need to change."

"Change what?"

"My clothes. I can't wear this to Off the Record."

He looked at my dress. "Why not?"

I sighed heavily. "Everyone there is in cocktail dresses. This is a regular dress."

"You look fine to me."

"You're a man—I can't expect you to understand fashion. Now pull over." I pointed. "There's good. I don't know anyone on that street."

He turned and pulled over at the end, away from the houses. I climbed into the back seat. "You're changing in the car?"

"Do you want me to do it in the street?"

"I mean no—I just—I—uh—what if—"

I laughed. "Flustered, Fields?"

"Feldstein. And no."

"You're still Fields to me. Just close your eyes."

"I—um—I'm just gonna look straight ahead. In case a cop comes or—something . . ."

"Don't you have a sister or know any girls?"

"I have a sister, but she hasn't changed in front of me since I was probably four."

"Well I'm not your sister, and I'm behind you. You'll be fine."

He shook his head, but dutifully kept his eyes straight ahead without so much as a peek in the rearview mirror. "If you say so."

I shimmied into the green dress but then realized I needed help. "I need a zip," I said. He reached an arm back without turning around and accidentally knocked me in the head. "You can turn around," I said, exasperated.

"Are you decent?"

"What would you do if I wasn't? Can you just zip me up already? You're being a child." He turned around and stared at me. "What?"

"Where did you get that dress?"

"I had it hidden under the skirt of the one I was wearing."

He shook his head. "Being a woman sounds exhausting."

"It is," I agreed, turning around and pulling my hair up for him to zip the dress. He pulled the zipper gingerly up my back, grazing the skin above my brassiere slightly as he did. I tried my best not to flinch but felt something fluttering in my stomach. This was strangely intimate—more so than I expected. *Just business,* I reminded myself. "Can you do the hook too? If not, I can probably reach."

He turned all the way around to use both hands and threaded the hook through the eye at my mid-back, his fingers brushing bare skin again. "There."

I turned around again. "See? Better, right?"

He swallowed. "Yeah. I see what you mean."

I climbed into the front seat and slipped my shoes on. "Don't go yet. I need to put some more makeup on, and I don't want to mess it up if you hit a bump."

He watched as I used a mirror compact to apply eyeliner and red lipstick. I blotted with a tissue from my purse, then told him I was ready to go.

"Fields," I said, remembering my question for him as we drove past Rock Creek Park, "what did Maricela mean when she said Batista was bad for Cuba and bad for the people? I thought he was good?"

Fields shook his head. "He was a dictator too. The US government just supported him because he hated Communism."

"We supported a dictator?"

He looked over, amused. "We've supported plenty of them as long as they were somewhat on our side."

I thought about this. "So if Maricela worked for him . . . ?"

"She's likely done some unsavory things."

"Can we trust her, then?"

He shrugged. "You know the old saying 'The enemy of my enemy is my friend'?" I nodded. "That's half of American policy. And it's the best we've got right now."

30

I thought Maricela would either already be at the bar or walk in later, but she was sitting in the hotel lobby, smoking a cigarette, when we arrived. She stood up when she saw us and inclined her head toward the restrooms. Then she turned and walked into the ladies' room.

I looked to Jack. "I think she wants me to follow her."

He didn't seem to know what was going on any more than I did. "See what she says?" he murmured.

Shoulders back and head held high with a confidence I did *not* feel right then, I followed, only to see an empty room. The door closed and clicked shut behind me, and I felt a chill run down my back.

Maricela had turned the lock on the door.

For a split second, I thought Maricela was the person we had been looking for after all, and I was in real trouble. But she smiled, leaned in to embrace me, and kissed both of my cheeks.

"Amor," she said warmly. I knew no Spanish, but from her tone, I could tell it was a term of endearment. "You look beautiful."

I felt my shoulders relax. "Not compared to you."

She smiled and touched the ends of my hair. "What's the expression? Apples and oranges." Then she leaned in closer. "Now listen—we cannot be seen together. You go and pretend you're on a date. But look around the room. Notice everyone. When I leave, wait five minutes and meet me in here again." Her face darkened. "If I can spot your

Cubana, she can almost definitely spot me. I was well known . . . in certain circles."

"And our cover is blown if she sees us with you."

"If you want to get close to her, yes. And I didn't escape by lying in the smuggling hold of a fishing boat overnight to be killed now."

I swallowed. "You think—?"

"Whoever she is, she's not here for the weather. Trust me. That's better in Cuba." She saw the fear in my face and put a hand on my arm. "We'll try to figure it out. But remember—she may not be the only agent in the room." She shook her head. "I'll see what I can find out. You go out first and get a table where you have a good view of the room. I'll follow."

I looked at her, wondering what this woman had been through. "Be safe," I told her.

"Ten cuidado," she said. "You too."

Ten cuidado, I repeated in my head as I unlocked the door and went back into the lobby. I didn't know what it meant, but the way she had said it sounded musical. My grandparents had traveled to Havana once, when I was small, and I wondered if relations between our countries would ever warm enough for me to see Maricela's homeland as well. Or if she would ever be able to see it again.

Fields was waiting, perched on the arm of a chair, and rose quickly when he saw me. I smiled, though I was quite honestly still annoyed at him about the name stunt, and took his arm, leaning up to kiss his cheek. He looked down at me in surprise.

"Pretend we're on a date," I whispered, glancing around to make sure we were unobserved. A man in a suit walked past us without a second look.

"Are your parents here?" He looked around.

I reached up and turned his head back toward mine, feeling the smoothness of his recently shaved cheek. "Maricela said if she can spot a Cuban"—*Cubana,* I thought—"they can likely spot her. We leave five minutes after she does, and she tells me what she saw."

He nodded slowly. "That makes sense. Should we head in?" He took a step forward, but I didn't move yet.

"Fields," I said quietly. "She said our Cuban woman may not be there alone. We need to play this off well."

"I should take you home," he said decisively. "This was a mistake."

My eyes narrowed. "Easy there, Lancelot. I told you, I don't need a knight. This is my story."

"Judy—"

"Fields, you can come with me, or I'm going alone. But I'm not going home until we know something."

He stared at me, and finally his shoulders dropped in defeat, then he took my hand. "So your mother doesn't approve of my car, huh?"

I looked at him with an eyebrow raised. What did *that* matter?

"Play along," he whispered. "We're on a date."

"Do *you* approve of your car?"

He laughed, and it only sounded a little forced as we walked toward the staircase that would take us to the subterranean bar. "When I get promoted to senior White House correspondent, I'll upgrade."

"Yes, but my mother is on the phone with yours right now asking about your ability to support me."

"Is she really?"

"Either that or telling her we can live with my parents when we get married."

Fields laughed, shaking his head. "Jewish mothers."

We selected a corner table, and I slid into the booth, unwilling to give up my view of the room. Fields sat beside me, surprising me at first, our legs pressed together under the table. I inched slightly away. It wasn't a real date after all. But sitting together, we could both see the room and could talk more quietly than we could have across from each other.

"I'll get us drinks," he said suddenly. "Did you like what you had the other night?"

I shook my head. "Water. We need clear heads."

"You'll look conspicuous not drinking at a bar—why wouldn't we go to a restaurant instead? You should have a drink, even if you nurse one all night."

I sighed. "Fine. That again."

"I'll be right back."

He went to the bar, and I took the opportunity to look around. Several couples sat in booths like we did. A group of women clustered together at a bigger table, glancing frequently at the door. A handful of men sat at the bar, seemingly alone, and two men talked to elegantly dressed women at the bar. No one stood out to me as Latin. But other than stereotypically darker hair, skin, and eyes, I didn't know what would give them away.

Fields returned quickly and handed me a coupe glass. I noticed his glass held brown liquor, ice, an orange slice, and two cherries on a stick. "What are you drinking?"

"An old-fashioned."

"What is that?"

He pushed his untouched glass toward me. "Try it."

I took a small sip, making a face as it went down. "Not for me."

He shrugged, taking the glass back. I reached over when he put it down and took the stick, sliding one of the cherries into my mouth.

"Rude," he said mildly. "But sexy."

I flushed. "Not a real date," I reminded him quietly. "We're working."

"Right. But we do need to play the part." He took a much longer drink, letting his eyes wander the room as Maricela walked in. Most people turned to look at her, I noticed. I wondered what that felt like—I was pretty enough, but no one was going to use the words *glamorous* or *buxom* to describe me.

I sipped the champagne cocktail, the bubbles tickling my throat. "I think we can rule out the table of girls."

"I agree."

I looked at him quizzically. "Why do *you* say that?"

"They're watching the door. They're hoping for one of the president's or vice president's staffers." He glanced over at me. "I come here a lot. Remember?"

I wondered if he had ever picked up one of the girls who didn't make it to the White House or a room upstairs. Not that it was my business. I looked their table over, trying to figure out which one would be his type.

Then I realized he had said something, and I'd missed it. "Sorry?"

"Why did *you* say it's not them?"

"Their dresses are cheap. See that lump in the back of the redhead's? She kept the tag in—she's returning it tomorrow, buying another, and trying again. And they're being too obvious that they're watching the door. If we're looking for a professional, she's going to pretend not to care who's here."

"That leaves the women on dates or the two at the bar."

"If our girl is here."

"If we're right about Texas, tonight is a good bet," Fields said.

A man left the bar and approached Maricela, where she had sat alone at a table, across the room from us. She smiled, her head tilted, and said something to him. He decamped to the bar, returning with a glass of champagne for her. He started to sit, but she shook her head, offering her hand instead, palm down, like my grandmother had. He kissed it, then returned to the bar. She caught my eye and winked, then quickly looked away, taking a sip of champagne.

"The brunette," I said, watching a woman pick up a cigarette at the bar. "She looks like she could be Cuban."

Fields shook his head. "That's why I don't think it's her. It's too obvious."

Another woman got up unsteadily from a table where she had been sitting with a man and left the room. "Her?" I asked. "She could be going upstairs."

"Bathroom, more likely," Fields said. "Besides, she's here with a congressman from Georgia."

I squinted at the man's profile, recognizing him. "Seriously, is there anyone in Washington who doesn't cheat on his wife?"

Fields chuckled. "You're sitting with him."

"You don't *have* a wife."

"Yet. A *shidduch* made in heaven," he said, mimicking my mother in a falsetto.

I smacked him lightly with the back of my hand. "That was your own fault. If you'd used *Fleishman*, like I said, she wouldn't be out renting a *chuppah* right now."

"Is the rabbi going to be there with a *ketubah* when I drop you off?"

"Possibly."

"Would that be the end of the world?"

I had taken a sip of my drink and started to choke on it. Fields whacked me on the back apologetically. "I'm considering that as an attempt on my life," I wheezed when I could speak.

He laughed, and the woman I had suspected returned to the congressman's table.

For over an hour, we watched people come and go, sometimes arriving together and leaving together, sometimes arriving alone and leaving together, sometimes leaving as alone as they had arrived. But we saw nothing we could tie to our lead.

And then, Maricela stood up from her table, leaving a half-finished drink, and made her way to the door, not sparing us a glance.

"That's our signal," I said to Fields, excited. "She saw something."

"How do you know?"

"She told me to wait five minutes when she left, then meet her back in the bathroom." I turned to him. "Is anyone watching her go?"

"Everyone is watching her go," he said, confused. "Why?"

"In case Havana isn't alone."

Fields shook his head. "I don't know what I'm looking for."

I glanced around the room, then down at my watch, marking the time. "Look at me then. In case anyone is watching."

He leaned in close until our foreheads were nearly touching, and I felt my breath catch.

I had finished my drink. I hadn't meant to. But that was all the light-headed feeling was. And the excitement.

Our legs were touching—I didn't know when the distance between us had closed again, and my palm was in his, his other hand lightly tracing the lines of mine. I took my hand back, making a big show of looking at my watch.

"We should be getting back," I said loudly. "My parents will worry if we're too late."

Fields's lips twitched in a smile. "We'll tell them my car broke down."

"Your car might just do that," I shot back, and he laughed. "Better get that promotion soon, Fields."

"Or we'll just take your father's car next time. *Leonard, give him your keys.*" His impression of my mother *was* good.

He took my hand and placed it in the crook of his arm as we stood up, and together we climbed the stairs to the lobby.

31

I looked around before going into the bathroom, but the lobby was mostly deserted, and only Fields was watching me. Maricela was on a small sofa in the mirrored lounge area, smoking a cigarette, but she shook her head at me as I heard a flush. I nodded to her and entered a stall.

Water ran from the sink, and I heard a clicking that I assumed was the sound of a powder compact opening, then closing. I stayed in the stall, not wanting to risk being seen in the same room as Maricela. Eventually, the outer door shut, and Maricela told me it was clear. I flushed, washed and dried my hands, then joined her on the sofa.

"The blonde in the purple satin," Maricela said decisively, taking a long drag on her cigarette.

"You're sure?"

She nodded. *"Absolutamente."*

That one I could understand. "How do you know?" I had seen the woman she was referencing sitting at the bar, but with her alabaster skin and a far more natural-looking head of dirty-blond hair than Patricia's, we had discounted her.

The mask dropped away from her face entirely, and she looked younger, almost afraid. "Because I've seen her before."

A chill ran down my spine at the way she said it. "Who is she?"

"La diabla," she said, almost in a whisper. I could have figured out what that one meant from her tone alone. "Her name is Alejandra de Bernal. She fought with Che Guevara's troops."

"Women fought in the revolution?"

The hint of a smile crossed her lips, then was gone. "Cuban women are strong. But this one . . ." She shook her head.

"You know her." It wasn't a question.

"No," Maricela said. "Not—not like you think." She stopped talking, and I waited, hoping she would tell me more. Eventually, she spoke again. "I wasn't a 'favorite' of Batista's. I worked for him." I could tell she didn't mean singing. "I'm not proud of the things I've done, but doing them meant I could make a better life for my family. Until I couldn't. When he fled—in the night, like a coward—he left us all for the revolutionaries. They held trials, but they were a joke—what's the expression? A kangaroo court?" I nodded. "We were all declared traitors. They started executing people. Castro and Guevara said to spare the women, but she . . ." Maricela shook her head, and I waited again.

It took her a while to continue. "One of Cienfuegos's men took pity on me and got me out before she could kill me. A fishing boat took me to Miami in the night." I had seen coverage of Cienfuegos's alleged death—he had ranked high in Castro's army but disappeared a few months after the revolution.

"But this Alejandra de Bernal knows who you are?"

Maricela nodded.

"Then you aren't safe here. You need to leave. Tonight."

A steeliness returned to her eyes. "I don't think she saw me. Besides, I'm a civilian now. And a famous one. She wouldn't risk being exposed over me." Then her shoulders dropped and she stubbed out her cigarette. "But yes."

"Where will you go?" I asked, reaching for her hand.

"It's better for both of us if you don't know that." Her eyes fixed on a point over my shoulder, seeing some past that I couldn't imagine. "Though if she wants to find me, she will."

I shivered involuntarily, then squared my shoulders. If Fields and I figured out what she was after and broke the story, we could remove the threat. I squeezed her hand. "I'm sorry. But thank you for your help, Maricela. I—we—really appreciate it."

"Carmen."

I looked at her, confused. Had she forgotten my name?

She smiled. "You didn't think I was naive enough to use my real name the other night, did you? I spent four years gathering secrets for a dictator. I'm no one's fool."

"No," I agreed. "You're not. But promise me you'll be careful?"

"*Por supuesto*. Of course, I will. And you, *ten cuidado.*"

I tried to picture her hiding in the hold of a fishing boat, running for her life, while revolutionaries executed her family and friends. I knew the stories of the survivors in my own community who had made it here. The war was over for them at least. For her, it might never be. I wouldn't have given a real name the other night either.

I just hoped we weren't making things worse for her as I unlocked the bathroom door.

Fields was sitting in a lobby chair, watching anxiously for me, and he sprang up as soon as I came out. "Well?" he asked as I reached him.

"I should be getting home," I said, louder than I needed to. There were a few men in the lobby, and I remembered Maricela's—Carmen's—warning that the woman we were looking for may not be alone. "My parents will worry."

For a second, Fields looked confused, then he nodded and offered me his arm. "We wouldn't want that."

I wanted to go back downstairs to watch this Alejandra woman and see what she did. But it would be too conspicuous after we had left. And besides, a glance at my watch told me we *did* need to get me home if I wanted the freedom to come back another night.

When we were safely back in his car, Fields turned to look at me. I shook my head. A man had followed us outside and was leaning against the exterior of the hotel, lighting a cigarette. It was impossible to tell if he was watching us in the darkness. "Drive," I said, inclining my head ever so slightly toward the building.

Fields glanced over at the building and laughed. "That's the deputy director of the FBI. If he's working for Castro, we're all in trouble."

"Oh," I said sheepishly as he put the car in drive. "Then why did he follow us?"

"I don't think he did. He always smokes outside."

I looked over at Fields, illuminated only by the streetlamps we passed under. He did know far more about the important players in this town than I did. "The blonde in the purple satin," I said. "Maricela recognized her—although her real name is Carmen."

"The blonde's name?"

"No, Maricela's. She lied to us the other night."

"And you trust her now?"

"I do. The blonde is named Alejandra de Bernal. Carmen called her *la diabla*."

"The devil," Fields said.

I nodded. "She fought alongside Che Guevara's troops to overthrow Batista and put Castro in. Carmen wasn't a singer—that was her cover. She worked for Batista—it sounds like as a spy for him. And this Alejandra woman was going to kill her, but a soldier took pity on her and helped her escape."

"That's . . . a lot."

"Yeah. Have you seen her here before?"

Fields tilted his head, still focused on the road. "Maybe? I don't know." His eyes darted in my direction. "If I'm being honest, I'm usually only paying attention to the women if they come in with someone interesting. Or leave with someone more interesting."

"But you noticed me," I blurted out. Then I wished I could sink into the sagging bench seat and disappear.

"You're hard not to notice. You were choking. Loudly. Remember?"

I did, and I was glad he couldn't see me blushing. "Martinis and I don't get along," I said much more nonchalantly than I felt.

"Apparently not."

For a few minutes, neither of us spoke. "What do we do next?" I asked.

"We check the vice president's schedule and go back when he's free. And then we try to follow her up to the second floor to be sure." Fields stopped at a red light.

"And then what?"

A muscle in his jaw tightened. "And then, if she does go up there, we have to figure out this 'mass goal.' And why a Russian is involved."

I thought for a minute. "How do we get the vice president's schedule?"

Fields smiled as I studied his profile. "That one's easy. I call his press secretary and ask for it. Being the junior press secretary who is known for asking for annoying details does have its perks sometimes." He paused. "Did this Alejandra recognize Carmen?"

"She didn't think so. But she's leaving tonight just in case."

His eyes narrowed. "If this woman at the bar is that dangerous—"

"Don't even say it," I interrupted. "I'm not afraid." It wasn't entirely true. What Carmen had told me definitely rattled me. But the excitement at my hunch being right, at uncovering something—even if we didn't fully know what it was yet—overshadowed that. And there was no way I was backing down.

He exhaled audibly but didn't reply.

When we got to Silver Spring, I had Fields pull over on a side street again so I could change back into the dress I had left in. He didn't protest when I asked him to unzip me, though I thought I caught his eyes darting to the rearview mirror once. But it was dark and hard to tell. I climbed back into the front seat and pulled a tissue from my purse to wipe the red lipstick away. There wasn't much I could do with the additional eyeliner, but I doubted my mother would look that closely.

I directed Fields back to the house, where he pulled into the driveway and cut the engine. "They'll ask me when I'm seeing you again."

He thought for a second. "Tell them I have to check my work schedule, but definitely this week."

"Okay," I said. I knew I should get out of the car. Especially when I saw a flutter at one of the living room curtains. But part of me was looking for a reason to stay. "Did you know that women fought in the revolution in Cuba?"

"It wasn't a lot of them, but yes." He was looking at me, our hands close on the bench seat. I hadn't been on a lot of dates, but I had been on enough of them to know that look. "I guess they weren't afraid either."

"I should go," I said quickly, then I pointed toward the front window. "That's either my mom or my grandmother watching us. Or both."

"My money is on your grandmother," he said. "She seems like fun."

"That's one way to put it. Good night, Fields."

"Good night," he said. But he stayed in the driveway until I was safely inside. Which I knew, because I glanced back when I reached the door.

My grandmother was on the sofa, snoring lightly when I shut the door.

I flipped on the light. "You can stop pretending. I saw you watching us."

She sat up. "You should have kissed him. What if your mother had been the one watching?"

"Good night, Grandma," I said sharply as I started up the stairs.

"Where *did* I go wrong with that girl?" she asked herself.

I shook my head.

But as I lay in bed that night, I remembered Fields saying he had noticed me that first night at Off the Record because I had been choking. Except that wasn't true. He had raised a glass to me when he saw me walk in and only came over when I choked.

32

"Do you think Roberta would lend me a couple more dresses?" I asked Patricia at work on Monday.

"Actually, yes," Patricia said. "She got engaged this weekend. Why don't you come home with me after work today, and we'll remind her that she said she'd give you a few of the dresses she won't need anymore."

As appealing as that sounded, where was I going to keep them? I could get away with Betty's dresses because my mother knew I was "storing" them for her. But a slew of cocktail dresses was going to raise questions.

The elevator doors opened, and Fields walked toward us, smiling at me until he saw Miss Kelly.

He put two sheets of paper on my desk, his hand covering them as she passed by. "This one definitely needs edits."

"Fields," I whispered as Miss Kelly chided Gladys for some unseen infraction. "You have to help me with something."

"Shh," he said. "Put it in the article."

"Huh?"

"How long will it take?" he asked loudly. "I'll come back for it. This one probably needs a few drafts."

I bristled. My work didn't need multiple drafts, and he knew it. I opened my mouth to respond tartly, but he turned and walked away. He really was the most irritating man.

Thoroughly annoyed, I slid a fresh sheet of paper into my typewriter and looked down at his pages, then stopped myself. It wasn't an article at all.

"VP is presiding over the Senate all week, so he's in town. State dinner for a French diplomat tonight—try again tomorrow night?"

The rest of the document was nonsense.

That gave me time to get dresses this evening. But . . .

I started to type.

"Tomorrow should work. But I need you to take me to Patricia's building after work. Or at least pick me up there. I need more dresses, and I can't take them home." I filled the rest with gibberish.

Fifteen minutes later, he came back into the typing pool. Miss Kelly was nowhere to be seen, and he crouched down by my desk. Patricia and Gladys were observing us with great interest as he read what I had written. "What am I supposed to do with dresses?" he asked quietly.

"Preferably hang them in a closet so they don't get wrinkled—unless you live with your parents too?" He rolled his eyes but looked amused. "Good. Can you take me over there?"

He shrugged. "Meet me downstairs after work? We can make a plan then."

Miss Kelly came out of the elevator, a pencil behind her ear and about a dozen newspapers in her arms. She frowned when she saw Fields, and I spoke loudly to make sure she heard. "I think those are all the changes you need."

He looked confused, then turned around, saw Miss Kelly, and stood up. "Right. I'll have another draft to you this afternoon."

"We do have an editorial department for a reason, Mr. Fields," Miss Kelly said icily. "Miss Greenberg isn't being paid to work there."

He smiled ingratiatingly, which changed nothing on her face. "You and I both know that's only because the top brass upstairs is afraid women—like you—will take their jobs." He nodded to me. "Miss Greenberg."

Miss Kelly stood by my desk until he was safely in the elevator. "Say the word, and I'll ban him from this floor."

"I don't mind," I said, and she looked at me sharply. "Not like that. I just like getting to use my degree a little."

"See that that's all you're using with him," she said. She left a newspaper on my desk, and I started to call after her to tell her she had dropped one, but the picture caught my eye and stopped me.

It was the arts section of Sunday's *Evening Star*, and Maricela was on the front page from her show Thursday night at the Bohemian Caverns. In it, her arm was outstretched over the dance floor as she sang. And just barely visible, at the bottom right of the photograph, was my face in profile, Fields in front of me.

I turned around quickly as Miss Kelly walked into her office without sparing me a second glance.

It was a coincidence, right? She hadn't left that on my desk on purpose, had she?

And if she had, was it a warning about Fields, about Maricela, or about the lead we were chasing?

I looked at her closed office door for a long time, wondering what warning I should be taking from this. It could be nothing. I could be about to get fired for disobeying both her and Mr. Pullman. I was in it now though, come hell or high water.

But Fields and I were going to have to be more careful around Miss Kelly now. I doubted there was much she did that wasn't intentional.

33

"I think we need to take a field trip tomorrow," Fields said as we pulled away from Patricia's building to fight rush hour traffic up to Silver Spring.

I looked at him askance. "We are. We're going to Off the Record."

"No, I mean during business hours."

"Is the bar even open then?"

He shook his head. "No. We need to go to the library."

I was confused. "Why?"

"I want to verify Maricela's information if we can."

"How would we do that at the library?"

"Newspaper archives. If we go through Cuban newspapers from before and during the revolution, we can make sure Maricela is who she says she is and—if we're lucky—find something on this Alejandra de Bernal."

He wasn't wrong. We couldn't run a story based on one woman's word—especially if we didn't know she was a rock-solid source. I trusted her. And I believed her reaction to seeing the woman she called *la diabla* was genuine. But Fields's assertion that if she worked for Batista, she had done unsavory things—which she had basically admitted to me as well—did make her story slightly shakier.

But there was no way I was going to be able to go to the library with him during business hours without losing my job.

"Can't we do it after work? Or at lunch?"

"It'll take longer than a lunch break. And the library is closed after work."

“What library closes at five?”

He smiled. “This one does.”

“Then I can’t go. Miss Kelly will fire me.”

Fields glanced over at me and laughed. “Stop pouting. I have a plan.”

“I’m not *pouting*.” Okay, I had been. But only because it wasn’t fair. This was *my* story. And because I was a woman, I didn’t have the freedom to leave during the day and research it like he did.

~

The next morning, I was working my way through the edits on an article about the Alcatraz escape—debris had been found that was believed to be from the prisoners, but no bodies had been recovered yet—when Fields strode through the typing pool, a paper in hand.

I sat up a little straighter, only to see him walk right past my desk and to Miss Kelly, who was lecturing Helen over something I couldn’t quite make out.

“Good morning,” he said to her jovially. I had to strain to hear over the clacking typewriters.

“What do you want today, Mr. Fields?” she asked.

“I need someone to take notes on some research.”

“No.”

He held out the paper in his hand. She pushed her glasses up onto the bridge of her nose and looked it over, then scowled. “My girls shouldn’t have to work harder just because you don’t warrant a secretary.”

He shrugged. “Take it up with upstairs. I wouldn’t object to a secretary.”

She glared over her glasses. “You can take Gladys.”

My shoulders dropped. Gladys had the biggest mouth. She would tell everyone what he was researching.

But Fields shook his head. “I need Judy.”

Miss Kelly crossed her arms. “I just bet you do. Well, you’re not getting her.”

"Miss Kelly, you and I both know Judy is the fastest typist you have. With the highest accuracy. I need both of those today."

"Which is exactly why I need her here if I'm going to be down a girl. Besides, she doesn't know shorthand."

"Yes, I do," I volunteered from across the room. Then I bit my lip. It didn't help that I had clearly been listening in.

"Since when?"

"I had to learn it in college."

"It wasn't on your résumé."

"I—didn't think I was applying to be a secretary." She stared at me for several seconds, but I kept my expression neutral.

Finally Miss Kelly handed the paper back to Fields, then pointed a finger at him. "If I find out there's any funny business going on here—"

Fields mimed crossing his heart. "No funny business at all. Just good old-fashioned investigative research."

She shook her head. "In my day, reporters got their own hands dirty," she muttered. But then she turned in my direction. "I want you back here before the day ends."

"Yes, Miss Kelly," I said, pulling my handbag from my desk drawer. She resumed berating Helen on whatever the poor girl had done wrong, and I headed toward the elevators.

"Hope you called my doctor," Patricia whispered as I passed her desk. I made a face at her.

Safely downstairs, I warned Fields that Miss Kelly would be watching us like a hawk now.

"Let her."

"She put that newspaper with our picture on my desk yesterday. She thinks we're up to something."

He leaned in conspiratorially. "We *are* up to something."

"You know what I mean."

"I do. But as long as you don't wind up like Louise, we'll be okay."

I could feel my cheeks coloring as I followed Fields toward his car.

~

My mouth dropped open when I looked up at the library he had meant. "The Library of Congress?"

"I doubt the one on Colesville Road has Cuban newspapers on microfiche."

I had never been inside the Library of Congress, and I looked around in awe as we walked into its hallowed halls. No, this was nothing like the library where I had finally come off the waiting list for Marilyn Kleinman's novel, which was *still* on all the bestseller lists six months after publication. The palatial-looking reading room had a huge domed ceiling, with desks arranged in a circle, and archways all around the surrounding walls, going up multiple levels to balconies where people walked with the important air of researchers.

What were we *doing* here?

Fields strode confidently up to a librarian, who directed us to a much smaller room downstairs, where an older man wearing Coke-bottle glasses sat at a desk.

"Help you?" he asked.

Fields introduced himself and then me. "We're looking for Cuban newspapers from 1957 through 1959." The man went to the card catalog behind him, opened a drawer decisively, and removed a stack of cards for us.

"You'll want to take these next door, and they'll pull the films for you. Then you can look through them at a reader in the microfilm room. Make sure you bring them back when you're done."

We followed his directions to another librarian, who asked if we wanted English only or English and Spanish, then pulled the reels we had requested, explaining which newspaper was on which reel. He then showed us how the reader worked, instructing us to call him if we had any questions.

"Is there a way to make a copy of anything if we need it?" Fields asked.

"There is," the librarian said, his face lighting up. "Used to be much harder. But we got one of those new Xerox printers. Makes a copy go real quick."

I wasn't sure what that meant, but it was good to know regardless.

Fields offered me the chair at the screen, then fed a different reel into the reader next to mine. "Faster if we split the job," he said.

I agreed and began scrolling. But it was going to be a long process. "What exactly am I hoping to find here? This is a needle in a haystack."

"Not necessarily," Fields said. "Maricela said she was famous in Cuba. Look for either a headline that mentions a singer, or pictures that could have her in them. We just need to look in the front and entertainment sections—she's only going to appear before the revolution really got going, so I think 1957 is our best bet. Let's confirm she's who she said she was first. Then we look for revolutionaries."

We scrolled in silence for nearly an hour. It was an effort to keep my eyes from blurring, and it began to feel hopeless. Every issue had multiple articles on Batista, but nothing stood out. Then suddenly—"Fields! I found her!"

He came around to my screen. "You found more than that." He tapped the screen. "She's with Batista."

"Then she was telling the truth."

"Looks that way. Let's see what the article says." We moved the image on the screen to read the article, which said she was a frequent performer at the presidential palace. "We should print this."

He started to stand up to get the librarian, but I put a hand on his arm and shook my head. "Don't print this one."

"Why not?"

"It's not worth it. We can't name her in the article."

"She didn't tell us anything was off the record."

"She didn't have to," I argued. "If we name her, we put a massive target on her back. You didn't see her face when she talked about this Alejandra. She was scared of her."

He looked at me for several seconds, then eventually nodded. "Fine. *But* be aware that we could get interrogated on this one."

"By who?"

Fields shrugged. "I doubt it goes to court. They won't want the publicity. But I wouldn't be surprised if the Secret Service or FBI wanted our source."

"Do we have to give it to them?" The rules were clear when it came to being subpoenaed to reveal a source. Any reporter worth their salt would refuse to name names, then either pay a fine or spend a night in jail for contempt of court, both of which won you bragging rights. If you named a source who had been promised anonymity, you would never work in journalism again. But I had no idea what happened if you refused the FBI or Secret Service. Was there an American version of a gulag that we would get thrown into?

"Legally, no. And the courts have upheld that. But federal agencies don't always go through the legal channels. And with the Cold War . . ."

"We're in uncharted waters."

"Exactly."

I thought about the reading room we had passed through to get down here, just behind the US Capitol, and took a deep breath, exhaling loudly. "I believe in the First Amendment," I said. "We protect our source."

He shook his head slightly but was smiling. "You might just be a journalist yet, Greenberg."

He hadn't used my last name unless he was mad or there were other people around. But I recognized it as a badge of journalistic honor that he referred to me as he would to a male reporter.

"I told you I was."

Fields rolled his eyes. "Don't go getting cocky on me. We still need to find this devil. Let's skip to the late 1958 and early 1959 films. That's when we'll find articles on the revolutionaries."

"Maricela said she was with Che Guevara's troops."

"Then we look for those stories. They're the ones who took Havana on New Year's in 1959. Castro took a few days to arrive."

He pulled the film from my machine first and loaded a new reel, then took care of his own. And we went back to work.

This one was harder, as when we did find pictures of revolutionaries, we had to scan every grainy face to find one that we had only seen in passing Sunday night. Neither of us spoke for a long time as my eyes grew tired and practically crossed from the constant scrolling.

I went through two reels, Fields through three. "This is hopeless," he said, standing up and stretching out a crick in his back. "They probably sent her here because she doesn't exist on paper."

I thought for a minute. "What about *Life* magazine?"

"What about it?"

"There was a spread after the revolution, wasn't there? I think I remember that some American photographer flew down to Cuba that day." I scrunched up my face trying to remember. A journalism professor had talked about it. "Burt something."

"Glinn," Fields said, his eyes wide. "I remember that. He heard the revolution was happening and hopped on a plane—got the best pictures of Havana falling."

He got up, heading for the librarian's desk. The librarian pointed upstairs and Fields returned. "Come on. They have paper copies."

"Don't we have to return the microfilms?"

Fields grinned. "He said he'd take care of it. I may have made it sound like I was going to mess everything up."

"You're incorrigible."

He took a bow, pretending to sweep off a hat. "At your service. Now come on."

We went upstairs and talked to another librarian, who brought out a bound volume of *Life* magazines from 1959. Walking back into the rotunda of the reading room, we sat at a desk, our heads together, flipping pages until we got to the issue from mid-January 1959 that covered the events of two weeks earlier, the newly installed dictator, who was too young to actually be president, speaking passionately into a microphone on the cover.

Turning to the section on Cuba, we pored over pages and pages of photographs together. Then I gasped. "There." I touched the page in front of us. "That's her!"

Fields squinted. She had dark hair then, the bottom of her face slightly obscured by a man's arm. But there was no denying it. She wore fatigues and had a rifle pointed at someone off camera. There was no identifying information, no way to find her name. And she appeared in no other photographs that we could find. But it was her.

"I'll be damned," Fields said. "You found her."

"*We* found her. I wouldn't have thought to come here." I gestured to the grand space we inhabited.

Fields pulled a notebook and pen from his pocket, writing down the issue number, date, page, and photographer's name. "I don't know Glinn, but someone at the newspaper will be able to get permission to reprint this. Hell, he may have more of her that didn't run."

"Should we ask him?"

"Let the editors worry about that. They're more connected than we are. Besides, we have enough evidence that she's a Cuban revolutionary now."

I thought of Pullman. Some of them were more connected than we knew. "So tonight we try to confirm she's having an affair with the vice president?"

"We do."

I looked again at her picture. The ferocity in her face as she pointed that gun. We were dealing with a dangerous woman.

But it was going to make a hell of a story.

I smiled. "Lay on, Macduff."

34

"Twice in three nights?" my mother asked, adjusting the neckline of my dress to show more cleavage.

"Mom!" I said, pulling my dress back up to a respectable level. Then again, I would be shedding it in the back of Fields's car for one of Roberta's numbers soon enough anyway.

"What? I'm not saying *do* anything inappropriate. You just want to make sure he stays interested."

"And my sparkling personality isn't enough for that?"

"We're doomed," she deadpanned. She reached for my face, and I ducked away from her.

"No more pinching. Or pulling. Or any of that," I said. "And no planning a wedding."

"Who's planning anything?"

"Fi—Jack told me you called his mother."

"I shouldn't call my friends? Fine. I'll sit here at home all day, alone like a dog."

"You have Grandma," I reminded her. "And I'd never even heard of a Mrs. Feldstein until last week. She's hardly your best friend."

"What would you know about my friends? You're never home anymore."

I turned to look at her. "You want me to stay home tonight?" I was bluffing of course. I knew she couldn't turn down a date with a Jewish man. I took out an earring as her mouth dropped open in horror.

She snatched it up and practically stabbed it back through my ear. "No no no, you go on your date," she said. "Just maybe be a little less . . ."

"Less what?"

"Less you. At least until you have a ring on your finger."

She was exhausting. I wondered if she had pretended to be less *her* to catch my father. That was worth asking my grandmother about. Though I couldn't imagine my grandmother being less *anything* and she had turned down marriage proposals. Her own mother practically had a heart attack over that, she had said. Then again, she lied.

A knock at the front door told me I was being saved. And although I had told Fields that I didn't need a knight to rescue me, right now I would take what I could get.

"I hate to break it to you, Mom. But he doesn't want less of me." Then I ran down the stairs and flung the front door open before my parents could interrogate him further. "Let's go," I said, shutting the door firmly behind me. "Quick."

"I shouldn't come in?"

"Do you want my mother to pull the ring off her own finger and hand it to you to propose with?" I was already down the front steps and halfway to his car. He followed me, starting toward my side, but I opened my own door and got in.

Fields pulled onto the same side street for me to change without me telling him to this time, and I climbed into the back seat. "Say," I asked as I pulled on the turquoise dress that I had told him to bring for me. "How do we follow this woman upstairs without being seen?"

"We can't," Fields said, his eyes drifting toward the rearview mirror. They met mine, and he looked straight ahead again, caught.

"Then what do we do?"

"We have to be seen."

I leaned forward, resting my arms on the back of the front seat. "Then won't—"

He didn't look at me, but I saw him swallow. "We—uh—probably—have to pretend we're—going to a room too."

I digested this, a funny feeling in the pit of my stomach. "Together."

"It looks less suspicious than one of us staying at the hotel alone when we're at the bar so often. If anyone follows either of us home, it's obvious we would have no reason to rent a room alone."

"But we have to rent a room, then?"

"It's . . . safer that way."

For whom? I thought wryly. If my parents caught wind of this, I was a goner.

It was a toss-up whether I would rather be caught by my mother or a dangerous Cuban revolutionary in this situation.

"How do we guarantee we get a room on the right floor?"

Fields offered me a half smile. "You say you're afraid of heights."

"Why can't you be the one afraid of heights?"

"I—uh—I think you'd be more convincing to a male concierge."

I rolled my eyes. He wasn't wrong. But I hated even pretending to be afraid of things. "In for a penny, in for a pound," I sighed. "Zip me up, will you? *Darling*."

He chuckled as he turned to pull the zipper up to my mid-back, placing the hook through the eye without me needing to ask. "Anything for you—but maybe try to sound less sarcastic, *dear*."

I climbed back into the front seat. "We should have taken my mother's ring after all. At least I'd look more respectable going into a room with you."

"Your honor is safe with me," Fields said.

"Is that with Jack Fields or with Jacob Feldstein?"

"Both."

We would see about that.

35

A simper and some fluttering eyelashes was all it took to convince the man at the desk that I didn't want to be higher than the second floor. We were lucky, he told us—if it had been the night before, the delegation from France had the whole second floor.

But it was difficult to keep my eyes from bulging when he told Fields the rate for a night. It was more than I made in a week. He reached into his pocket like that amount was nothing, and I had to excuse myself to the ladies' room to avoid asking where he got that kind of money.

When I returned, Fields was waiting for me, and he flashed me a discreet thumbs-up. I shook my head but took his arm, and together we went down to the bar. The blonde was nowhere to be seen.

"What if she's not here? You just wasted all that money."

"Occupational hazard," he said.

"If you have that kind of money, why are you driving that car?" I clapped my hand over my mouth. "Sorry. I—"

Fields laughed. "I told you—I'm not getting a new car until I get promoted. But my big expenses are rent and having a drink here while I listen for gossip a few nights a week. And I've been working for four years now."

"But you told me to pretend I didn't like the champagne cocktail so it would be free."

He shrugged. "A free drink is a free drink."

I wanted to ask if he ever took girls out. If he had rented a hotel room before. If he knew nothing was going to be happening in that room he had just paid for. But when I opened my mouth, he spoke instead. "Nine o'clock."

I glanced down at my watch. It was only eight. But Fields angled his head to the left, and I looked past him to see our blonde walking in.

"Drinks," I said suddenly as she took a seat at the bar. He started to stand up, but I put a hand on his arm. "I'll get them this time—my treat. You just spent enough."

"I can—"

I shook my head and walked toward the bar. "An old-fashioned, right, darling?" I called back over my shoulder. He nodded, looking at me bewildered.

I had absolutely no plan. Carmen had told me this woman was dangerous. A soldier. But I went right for the empty seat beside her, narrowly beating out a man in a suit who tried to sit next to her. She glanced in my direction disinterestedly as the bartender brought her a martini. I hadn't seen her order, which meant he knew what she drank.

The bartender looked me over. "You old enough to be in here?" he asked with a smirk.

"Yes," I said, looking him right in the eye. "But I can go grab my driver's license if you want."

"Good thing there's no height requirement," he said, shaking his head. "What can I getcha?"

He may have thought he was being cute, but there would be no tip at this rate. "An old-fashioned and a champagne cocktail."

"Your fella's not paying tonight?"

I shrugged. "Lost a bet."

"If you say so, short stack," he said, then turned to make the drinks.

Alejandra de Bernal hadn't looked over during the exchange, and I needed to figure out something to say to her quickly or I was going to lose my chance. I couldn't ask if she came here often, because she could have noticed us two nights earlier. Or the first time we were here. Just because I hadn't seen her didn't mean she hadn't seen me. Especially if she was a spy working the vice president for something.

She sipped her drink.

"How are the martinis here?" My heart was racing, and I wasn't sure I would be able to hear a reply over the sound of blood rushing in my ears.

She set the drink down. "Better than Old Ebbitt's. Not as good as the Willard's." Her English was flawless. Nothing like Carmen's. Nothing like mine. She sounded like she had been to boarding school, and for the first time in my life, I understood F. Scott Fitzgerald's description of Daisy Buchanan's voice sounding like money.

But there was no hint of a regional dialect that I could distinguish. Not New England, New York, the South, nor the Midwest. It was like she had sprung from the den of a steel magnate of unknown origin.

It was too flawless. People from Boston dropped their *r*'s. New Yorkers had nasal vowels. Even my own speech had the hint of Yiddish dialect patterns combined with the slightest Southern slurring of *you all* into *y'all*.

My spine tingled. She was from nowhere. Carmen was telling the truth. This was her.

"I'll have to try the Willard's sometime," I said as the bartender set our drinks in front of me.

She gave no indication that she had heard me. I placed two dollars on the bar, wishing they were less crumpled and desperately hoping that was enough money. The bartender swept it up, and I exhaled, taking the two drinks back to the table.

"That was stupid," Fields said immediately. "What did you say to her?"

"I just asked how her drink was," I said quietly. "But Carmen was right. That's her."

"How do you know?"

I explained the utter lack of an accent. Fields leaned back in his seat, studying me. "That's a good observation."

"Why do you sound so surprised? I'm a fantastic journalist—when I have the chance to show it."

"I—" He shook his head, then stopped talking as he watched something in the center of the room. I followed his gaze to see a man in a suit approach a table of young women. We weren't close enough to hear what he said, but he indicated two of them, both bottle blondes. They reached into their purses and pulled out IDs, which they handed over. He studied them, pocketed the cards, and indicated for both women to go with him. They did so, arm in arm, practically squealing with excitement, while the other three girls at their table looked on dejectedly.

"What was that?" I whispered.

"That," he said, "was the president's secretary."

My eyes widened. "You mean—?"

He nodded. "They won a trip to the Lincoln Bedroom. Or whatever room he uses for trysts."

"Two of them? Together? Or . . . ?"

"I don't know for sure. Sometimes yes. Sometimes he'll choose one. Sometimes they'll both come back, and one of the other girls could have a chance."

I studied the three women who remained. None of them had left. "And they . . . want that?"

Fields looked at me, amused. "There are girls here every night hoping for the chance."

I thought about Patricia and her congressman. She wouldn't turn down a private tour of the White House. Even if it meant . . . I shuddered slightly.

A jacketless man with a loosened tie who looked vaguely familiar pulled out a seat at the table with the remaining three girls, and they perked up slightly. I couldn't place him, and Fields leaned close. "Secretary of the Interior," he whispered, his breath tickling my ear. "A few Cabinet members will walk over from the White House and pick off the leftovers."

"And the girls just make it so easy for them," I murmured back. "Whatever happened to playing hard to get?"

"That's what the good girls do."

I felt like there was an implication there. I wasn't *playing* anything. I *was* hard to get because I didn't want to be gotten. Even if I was starting to enjoy Fields's company.

A hotel porter crossed the room to the bar, handing an envelope to the bartender. I could feel Fields tense beside me. "Here we go," he whispered. "Pretend you're looking at me."

I turned my head. In my peripheral vision, I saw the bartender open the envelope and pass something with a closed hand to the blonde at the bar.

"What is it?" I asked, trying to hide my alarm as Fields moved his head lower, his lips just grazing my neck below my earlobe.

"A note or a key probably," he said. "When she gets up, we go. If you still want to do this."

"What are you doing?" I whispered to him as his lips touched my ear. My whole body was tingling. I wanted him to stop. I wanted him to never stop.

"Playing the part."

Right. We had to be going to a room together. I put my hands on either side of Fields's face, pulling him up so we were eye to eye as the blonde stood from her seat at the bar. I nodded, nervous, but trying not to let him see it. "Let's go upstairs."

He swallowed. "You're sure?" I didn't know if he was saying it for show or if he was really asking.

"I'm sure." We were in this too far to quit now. She walked out of the bar, and we followed close behind, Fields's arm around my waist.

The blonde was at the elevator, the button already pushed. Fields tickled my side, and I giggled reflexively. I started to object to the tickle, but he turned me so our foreheads were almost touching, and I understood he had elicited the laugh to make me sound giddy. I needed to play the part too, I realized, and I wrapped my arms around his neck.

"Jack," I said quietly.

He stiffened slightly at the use of his first name. He leaned closer, and I found myself looking at his mouth when the doors to the elevator opened.

Alejandra stalked in, pretending we didn't exist, and we tumbled in after her, laughing softly as I fell against the wall. "Too much champagne," I giggled.

She didn't acknowledge us, just reached for the buttons of the automated elevator. "Two," Fields said, not even looking at her. She glanced over, offended that he thought she would push a button for him. But it was the floor she was going to as well, of course.

"Jack," I whispered again, pulling him closer. The elevator lurched upward, stopping suddenly as the doors opened and the blonde walked out and turned right. We followed her, Fields's arm around my waist again.

Two large men in dark suits stood outside a door at the end of the hall. *Secret Service,* I thought. It didn't mean anything for sure yet though. We had to know. I kept walking, and Fields pulled me back at a doorway about twenty-five feet from the men as the blonde walked directly toward them.

"This is us," he said, louder, then began patting his pockets. "Where is that key?"

One of the men turned his head toward us, and I acted quickly, pulling Fields in by the tie. For a split second, he hesitated, almost asking the question, and when I nodded infinitesimally, he pressed his lips to mine.

I had been kissed before. But not well. A couple boys in high school. Another few in college. Those had felt sloppy, invasive, and more annoying than desirable.

This was nothing like those.

I pulled him closer as his lips explored mine, forgetting—

No, I thought suddenly, opening my right eye just enough to see down the hall. The blonde was gone, but a man was leaning out of the doorway, talking to the Secret Service agents. He laughed, then turned to shut the door, and I caught a glimpse of a face that I had seen on my living room television screen and in newspapers and magazines. Then the door shut, and the two suited men moved their bodies in front of it.

Fields twisted the knob behind us, having found the key at some point, and the two of us fell inside, Fields catching me before I could tumble down, then shutting the door firmly behind us.

We were both out of breath. "Jack—that was him," I panted.

"I know. I saw him too."

For a few seconds neither of us did anything.

And then—

I didn't know how it happened. All I knew was we had come together again, his mouth on mine, my arms around his neck, his hands in my hair. I felt something behind my knees and barely even registered that we had made it to the bed. One of his hands was at my back, and I felt the zipper of my dress move down a fraction of an inch when I came to my senses.

"We can't," I said, pulling away. We were both out of breath again.

He swore. "I'm so sorry. I didn't—I—"

"It's okay." I didn't know if it was or wasn't. And a part of me, seeing how quickly he had jumped away from me and apologized, wanted to pull him back. I didn't know what to do with that feeling though. We had a job to do. Letting anything else get in the way of that would cloud our judgment. "We just—got a little too into the roles we were playing. That's all."

For a second, he looked like he was going to argue. But whatever crossed his face left swiftly, and he nodded. Then he sat on the chair, away from the bed, heavily. "I have a confession," he said, and my body tensed. If this was going to be some declaration of love, the story wasn't happening. "I didn't think you were right."

"What?"

"About a Cuban woman and the vice president. It felt like a reach. I—I agreed the message meant *something*, but I didn't think we'd actually *find* anything."

Then why are you here? I wanted to ask. But I didn't. And he kept talking anyway. I sat on the bed as he did.

"If it was someone like Maricela—someone who had clearly escaped Castro, even with a fake name—I wouldn't give it a second thought. But that's *her* in the room with him. The woman from the picture. And no accent . . ." He looked back at me in wonder.

"We still don't know what she wants or what the 'mass goal' is though."

"No."

I looked out the window; the White House was visible across Lafayette Square, lit from outside.

"Jack," I said, an idea forming, "does the vice president send someone down to find girls too? Not like tonight to someone he knows—like the president does." He nodded. "Then I need to be one of the girls he picks."

"No." Jack stood up and started pacing in front of the window. "What would that even accomplish?"

I looked at the White House behind him again. "I don't know exactly. But we need a feel for what happens in that room."

He stopped pacing, shaking his head violently. "I know what happens in that room. I'm not letting you do that."

I studied him for a few seconds and then laughed. "Jack Fields—are you jealous?"

"Jealous?"

"Well I assumed of him, but maybe you're the one who wants to go into that room?"

"You're not serious."

"I am, actually." He opened his mouth to argue, but I cut him off. "I won't *do* anything. I'll 'get cold feet' and leave. But it's the only way to get any kind of information."

"He's the vice president. What kind of information do you think he's going to give you?"

"I don't know. But that's why I *have* to get into the room with him. Don't you see? We don't have anything if we don't figure out what she wants. And maybe we don't get anything out of this, but what are our options?"

He shook his head. "I say we corner the blonde and talk to her."

"She won't give anything up. She barely gave me the time of day."

"Then *I* try with her."

I suppressed a smile.

"What? I can be charming."

"You can," I reassured him. "But she's a professional who is involved with the vice president. As charming as you are, she's not going to jeopardize whatever she's planning just because you flirted with her. We have to try my way first."

"No."

"Then I'll do it without you."

"Dammit, Judy, you don't understand what these men are like—"

"I can take care of myself."

We stared at each other, neither speaking. Then he gave an almost imperceptible nod. "I don't like it. But I'd like it less if I wasn't involved."

Another silence. "I guess I should be getting home."

Jack looked at his watch. "Not yet. Secret Service needs to see we're in here longer than this. Or it'll look suspicious."

"Oh," I said, color flooding my cheeks. I hadn't considered . . . that.

"I—uh—came prepared," he said, reaching into his pocket. My eyes widened, worried he was about to pull out a prophylactic, when he offered me a worn deck of playing cards, held together by a rubber band.

I started to laugh. He looked at me quizzically, but I shook my head. There were a lot of things I could say about him, but he wasn't a cad.

Even if he did prove to be no match for me in gin rummy.

36

Wednesday was the Fourth of July, but the news cycle didn't seem to care about barbecues or lying by the local pool, so we weren't allowed those luxuries either. Which was just as well—we had a story to break. Jack brought me a story on the vice president on that afternoon. I read the lead, then looked back up at him, questioningly.

He shrugged with a smile. "I may have requested to follow him this week."

But I didn't smile back. "Doesn't that make it harder for me to get in with him? His Secret Service agents saw us together last night." I pushed the context they had seen us in out of my head. All I needed was red cheeks while talking to Jack. It wasn't lost on me that half of the typing pool was pretending not to watch us and that we would be the subject of plenty of postwork gossip later on.

"I'm already a known entity at both the hotel and the White House," he said. "For all they know, you're a barfly."

"A what?"

"A—uh—girl who spends a lot of time at Off the Record."

I got the distinct impression that he didn't mean *spent time there to drink*. "I'll have you know—"

"I know," he said, cutting me off. "You're a respectable girl. And last night was just—"

"A mistake," I finished at the same time as he said, "adrenaline."

For a few seconds neither of us said anything.

Then we both realized the typing pool was awfully quiet. We looked around at the sea of eyes that all looked away at the same time. I cringed. Carol sat closest to me and had likely heard that. They were all going to think that we had done a lot more than play gin rummy on a stakeout.

"Anyway, the president is in Philadelphia for the Fourth of July, so . . . the junior White House correspondent got stuck covering the vice president," he said loudly. Then quieter: "Why don't I drive you home today? We can talk in the car."

I nodded and he left.

But as I typed the article he had brought me, I began to see the value in covering the vice president. We now knew that he would be flying to Atlanta on Friday to try to smooth over an airline strike that the president hadn't been able to fix. Access to his schedule *was* helpful.

I walked the article to the finished bins, picking up another from the board, when I saw Carol and Gladys at Patricia's desk. All three of them were looking at me, then they glanced away in unison as soon as I looked at them.

Great.

Patricia waited until Miss Kelly was in the elevator before she approached me. She put a piece of paper on my desk with a phone number but didn't say anything. "What's that?" I asked.

"That doctor I told you about," she said. "I'm not saying don't have your fun—if that's what Fields is—but I wouldn't expect him to marry you if . . . if you get in trouble." She shook her head. "I've seen too many girls go that way."

"I appreciate the concern," I said. "But nothing ha—" I looked at her more carefully. "Say. What's going on with your congressman anyway?"

She grinned. "Don't tell anyone—but he's taking me to Nassau this weekend!"

"As in New York?"

"No! The Bahamas! You're going to be so jealous of my tan on Monday."

I tended to burn. But—

"Are you sure that's smart?" I asked. Her expression darkened. "I just—that other girl . . ."

"He had nothing to do with that," she said confidently. "Be happy for me. I'm excited."

I put a hand on hers. "Okay. I can do that." She smiled again. "Can I take you to lunch tomorrow? I need some advice."

"About Fields?" she asked.

If anyone knew about being a girl who picked men up at bars, it was her. And I was woefully lacking experience in that area. "Um . . . I might . . . have a bigger fish in mind."

Patricia shook her head, then wrapped me in a hug. "My baby is growing up," she said proudly. I struggled indignantly to get out of her grip, but I was laughing. "Call the doctor," she said, tapping a polished nail on the paper on my desk as she released me. "He may be able to get you in this week. He was willing to prescribe the pill, but no pharmacy will fill it if you're not married, so he'll do diaphragms."

I had heard about the birth control pill, of course—Betty was unequivocal that she wanted a prescription after this baby was born. But it was surprising that Patricia's doctor was willing to prescribe it to an unmarried woman. My mind traveled back to the night before, the feel of Jack's lips, his hand at my zipper.

Absolutely not. If I called that doctor, it was a recipe for disaster.

But I told Patricia I would, then resumed typing, all while waiting for the day to end so Jack and I could figure out our plan.

~

"It's his secretary usually," Jack said, eyes on the road. I was glad he couldn't look at me for this conversation, truth be told. It was the first time I was grateful for the insanity of DC traffic—and with tourists in town to watch the fireworks on the National Mall, it was worse than a normal rush hour.

"And he just . . . asks a pretty girl if she wants to meet the vice president?"

"Not in those words. But he'll ask if she wants to go to a private party. Upstairs."

"And they just . . . know what that means?"

"Sometimes. Sometimes they find out upstairs."

He glanced at me, and I looked out the window. "And what happens if they don't want to be there?"

A sigh. "That's why I don't like this plan."

I looked back at him. "You're telling me the vice president—"

"I don't know. I don't know if anyone has refused him. I don't know if they've just been allowed to leave. I don't know what happens when the door to that room closes."

Neither of us spoke as the light changed, and the old Plymouth lurched forward. "So maybe I tell him I work for *The Digest* if he . . . if saying no doesn't work."

Jack looked over at me, narrowly missing hitting the car that stopped short in front of us to make a left turn. "I'll create some kind of an emergency if you're in there too long."

"Like what?"

"I don't know," he said angrily. "I'll light the damn hotel on fire." He wrenched the wheel suddenly, pulling the car onto a side street and putting it in park, then turning toward me. "I don't want you doing this." His chest rose and fell rapidly as he tried to steady his breathing. "There has to be another way."

"There isn't. We need to get in that room. We don't have enough to write if we don't. And *I* need this if I'm ever going to get out of the typing pool. The fact that he's seeing a Cuban isn't enough." He didn't reply immediately. "You know I'm right."

"Then I'll be the one to do it. I'll say I need to interview him about the airline strike. You can come with me to take notes."

I shook my head. "We need an idea of what kind of information the blonde could be getting from him. You can't get that from a reporter interview. I need to flirt and flatter him and see what I can get him to share."

"Judy, this is crazy. I agree there's *something* going on, but we don't have any idea *what*. And I'm not letting you put yourself in a dangerous situation."

"I'll bring a hatpin."

"And what? Assault the vice president?"

He had a point. "Horizontal stripes *would* make me look even shorter."

"This isn't a joke."

I wondered if the fervor in his expression right now was because he cared about me or if he was worried about his job.

"I'll scream *fire*," I said. "Loud enough for Secret Service to come in. And run out in the commotion."

He didn't respond for a few seconds. "You are the most aggravating and headstrong—"

"Charming woman you've ever met?" I finished.

"You're something all right," he grumbled, but he put the car back into gear.

"You agree that'll work, then?"

"Yes," he said. "I still don't like it. But I'm not going to change your mind, am I?"

"No. So tomorrow night?"

He agreed tersely. "What are you going to ask him?"

I hesitated. "Well, I think I have to mention Cuba and gauge his reaction."

Jack shook his head. "Oh, hi, Mr. Vice President," he said in a falsetto. "How's your Cuban revolutionary mistress?"

I smacked his arm lightly. "Give me a *little* credit here. I'm going to work it into the conversation and see if he flinches at all."

"And when he doesn't?"

"Then he's either a good actor or he doesn't know who his mistress actually is."

"And then what? Say he flinches. What did we learn?"

"I don't know exactly. I get a feel for whether he's willing to talk about Cuba at all. If he's not, maybe it's because he knows something. Maybe he tells me not to worry because they have a plan in place and that's what she's here to stop. But whatever happens, it'll still be more than we know now. Would you be telling Nellie Bly not to go into that asylum because it was too dangerous?"

He swerved around a jaywalking pedestrian. "If I cared about her, yes," he said through gritted teeth.

Something felt warm and bubbly in my chest. "So you're saying you care about me?"

"I—what I meant—I thought I wasn't allowed to use Nellie Bly as an example?" His eyes were straight ahead on the road, and I couldn't keep myself from grinning.

"I'm a big girl, Jack. I mean, not in height, but I can do this." Did I actually know I could do it? No. But I was willing to risk more than he was because I had more to gain if we succeeded. And more to lose if we didn't. So I *had* to find out enough to break this story. "I promise." When he didn't reply, I flipped the radio on, eventually landing on the Isley Brothers singing "Twist & Shout." I sang along, badly, until I got a smile back on Jack's face.

He pulled into my driveway and cut the engine. "I'll pick you up tomorrow night, then?"

"Bring the black dress," I said. "The one with the low back."

"The one you wore the first night at Off the Record?"

He remembered. "That one."

"Okay," he said, still clearly not happy about it.

"Look at you two lovebirds," my mother's voice said suddenly at Jack's open window. We both jumped. Where had she come from? "How sweet of you to drive Judy home. That must be so far out of your way."

"Uh, no—I was going to go see my mother," Jack stammered.

"Such a good boy," she said. "Listen, you should come Friday night for Shabbat dinner."

"Mom, I'm sure Jack—"

"I would love to," he said.

"No, you really don't have—"

"Judith!" my mother said. "Don't be rude."

I glared at her, and Jack laughed. "Unless you don't want me to."

"Of course she wants you to come! Don't be ridiculous. Now come on. Your father is grilling, and we don't want to keep Jack from his mother, do we?"

I sighed, defeated. "I'll see you tomorrow," I said as I opened my door and climbed out of the car. My mother, satisfied, was already halfway up the front steps. I leaned back in the open window. "I'd say I'll get you back for this, but that dinner is going to be punishment enough."

"I can't wait," he said with a devilish grin.

37

Over lunch, Patricia showed me how to perfect a "come-hither look." She had me practice it on a young man at a neighboring table, and I felt utterly foolish, like a child playing dress-up. But sure enough, he excused himself from the group he was with and came over to introduce himself.

Then I turned as red as a tomato, and Patricia had to get rid of him for me.

"It gets easier," she chuckled.

"If you say so." I looked at her, so at ease using her looks to get what she wanted. "Say—how did you ask Clement about that girl?"

"I told you—"

"No." I put my hand on hers. "I know. I mean, how did you bring up such a sensitive subject?"

"Oh, that's easy. Men love to feel big and strong and like they're protecting you." She batted her eyelashes. "I've heard some stories around town about you," she said, her voice much higher than usual. "You wouldn't *ever* let anything like that happen to *me*, would you?"

I could do that. But could I with the second-most powerful man in the country? *You shouldn't be doing this,* Jack's voice whispered in my mind. I shook my head to get him out of there. Yes, this was terrifying. But if I thought about it too much, I would chicken out, and then where would we be? Without a story, that's where. I took a deep breath.

It *did* help that my voice naturally sounded like Patricia's when she was coaxing information out of a politician.

I still didn't know exactly what I was going to say once I got into that room. But my journalistic instincts had gotten us this far. And those same instincts told me I had to be in that room to see what our next steps would be.

Write questions ahead of time, my favorite journalism professor had said. *But always be prepared to come up with more on the fly. You have to think on your feet, or you'll miss the most important details.*

The flirting part was new, but I had spent years preparing for this. I would simply have to follow the vice president's lead and keep my eyes open.

Provided Jack could get me into the room. I threw a sidelong glance at the man Patricia had rejected for me. And if Jack couldn't, I would just have to try to do it myself.

"Who's this big fish, anyway?" she asked.

I wished I could tell her. But I couldn't risk it. So I faked a smile and held a finger to my lips. "I'll tell you later," I said, giving a promise I hoped I'd be able to keep.

~

"What do we do if Havana is there?" I asked as I changed into the black dress.

Jack glanced in the rearview mirror, and I made a face at him. He immediately lowered his eyes. "I—I asked Collins—that's the vice president's secretary—to come tonight. I said I had someone his boss would like to meet."

"Me?" I saw him nod. "And then what?"

"I let you two talk. And if Havana is there, I guess I try to distract her so she doesn't notice Collins taking you upstairs."

"Won't she be suspicious when she sees me with the secretary? I talked to her the other night, and she definitely saw us in the elevator."

He glanced to the mirror again, then looked away quickly. "She'll think you're a . . . working girl."

"I mean, I am."

Jack ducked his head. "Not that kind of work."

Oh, I thought, horrified. Was that what I looked like? I felt dirty suddenly. "And if she tries to stop me from going upstairs with Collins?"

"I think if she gets upset, we're chasing the wrong lead."

I finished getting into the dress and leaned over the front seat. "How do you figure?"

"If she goes up there and gets mad, she actually has feelings for him. If she doesn't care . . ."

"It's all for show to get whatever she's after." He nodded again. I climbed back into the front seat.

"You know, you could just open the door and get in the front."

"And risk being seen by someone who knows my mother while I'm wearing this dress? No thank you."

Jack shook his head with a slight chuckle. "The fact that you're more afraid of your mother than the vice president and a Cuban spy . . ."

I pulled my lipstick from my bag and began applying it. "I'd take Castro himself over an angry Jewish mother."

"You may have a point there." Once my makeup was on, Jack put the car into drive. "You're sure you're up for this?"

I said I was. "So we have photographic evidence that Alejandra was a soldier in Cuba—is Carmen's word enough to establish exactly who she is and publish her name?"

"Now that we verified enough of what she said, yes. We can use Carmen as an anonymous source." We never technically asked if we could quote her. But she hadn't told us we couldn't, and we were open about our jobs. Providing we didn't use her name, she should be protected. As long as we managed to actually stop whatever our woman from Havana was planning, that is. If not, I didn't know that there was anywhere Carmen could run that would be safe. All the more reason to find something that we could use tonight. I just had to keep my eyes and ears open and figure out what that was.

Jack parked across from the Hay-Adams. "You don't have to do this," he said, putting a hand on mine. "We have enough evidence that a foreign national is having an affair with the vice president."

I shook my head. "It's a bigger story than that. I know it. I can feel it. If we don't get anything tonight, then maybe, but I have to try."

"How loud can you scream?"

I smiled. "I may be small, but I've got a mighty roar."

He didn't smile back. "Okay. But remember I tried to talk you out of it."

We looked at each other in the summer twilight of the nation's capital. "I can do this."

He nodded. "I know you can. But promise me you'll be careful?"

"I promise."

He picked my hand up and raised it to his lips, surprising me. But the gesture buoyed me as well. I wasn't going to let either of us down. I got out of the car and squared my shoulders as we crossed the street. The vice president wasn't going to know what hit him.

38

The hotel's desk clerk looked at Jack questioningly as we walked in, and I tried hard not to flinch. I was very definitely seen as a woman of the night at this particular establishment now.

I wondered if, once the story was out, I could come back and explain that I was a nice girl on an assignment.

Then again, the desk clerk had likely heard much crazier stories than that and believed none of them. Besides, I was sure Nellie Bly had certainly gotten worse looks in her day.

Jack shook his head subtly at the desk clerk, and we walked down to the bar. Alejandra de Bernal was nowhere to be seen.

"What if your guy doesn't show?" I asked, nervous.

"Then we try again," Jack said. He led me to a table before excusing himself to get us drinks. I hesitated when he passed me a champagne cocktail, torn between needing the liquid courage and wanting to maintain a clear head for what I needed to do. I settled on a small sip. Finishing my drink last time had only led to trouble, and I was about to try to outsmart one of the most powerful men in the world. "So," Jack said, "Shabbat dinner tomorrow night?"

"Don't you start with that."

He grinned at me. I wondered if he would still be smiling when my mother was interrogating him about his career prospects and how many children he wanted. He probably would. He had no idea how hard it was going to be for me when I had to tell my mother we "broke up" after the story came out. Even with a joint byline, I would never be able to come clean to her that none of this had been real. She would never forgive me. But would he play along with being the one to break my heart? Our mothers being friends complicated it all.

As did Jack admitting he cared about me. I didn't want to consider what that warm feeling in my chest every time I thought about that meant. Because feelings or no feelings, I was *not* ready to get married, give up my dreams, and become my sister, no matter who the guy was.

"Where's your head?" he asked. "Nervous?"

"I'm fine with tonight." I took another small sip of my drink. "It's what happens after the story is done that worries me."

"What happens after?"

"I have to tell my mother we're not together."

Something unidentifiable crossed his face, and he opened his mouth to speak, then he shook his head. "That's him." He gestured toward a man in a suit who had just come down the stairs. "Collins," he called, waving him over.

The man startled, but came to our table. "Nix the name here," he said quietly.

Jack shrugged. It was an open secret anyway, both whom he worked for and what he was doing in the bar. But several women at tables were now looking in our direction and fluffing their hair.

I frankly wondered at the appeal. The vice president had a nice-enough smile, but he wasn't what I would call handsome by any stretch. The president, well, I could see it. But the idea of just wanting to be adjacent to power was foreign to me.

"This is the girl I was telling you about," Jack said. "Meet Judy Greenberg."

"Greenberg, huh?" Collins sat heavily at our table, and the bartender showed up almost immediately with a glass of liquor. No ordering—or bill apparently—necessary here.

I looked him right in the eye. "Yes, sir."

"Well, our man won't have a problem with that, though his predecessor would have." That was another open secret. "Tell me, young lady, why do you want to go upstairs so badly?" He drank half of his glass in one go while he waited for my response.

Jack reached under the table and took my hand, squeezing it.

"Well"—I batted my eyes at him the way Patricia had shown me—"I always thought he looked awfully dashing at the president's side."

"You don't prefer the president?"

I laughed. "Who can compete with the first lady? I know I'm not exactly Marilyn Monroe. No, I like a man who appreciates what he's getting with me." It was a definite dig at the vice president's wife, who was decidedly less glamorous than the first lady, but, well, it did the trick.

"You were right, Fields. This one is a firecracker." He checked his watch. "Well, come on, then. The quicker I take care of him, the quicker I can get home." He looked back at Jack. "Atlanta was a mess yesterday, and his wife wants the whole family in Texas for the weekend. I'd like to at least *see* my family before that."

Jack pressed my hand again, and I squeezed his before releasing it.

"Does he not have a steady girl anymore?"

"Between you and me," Collins said, "he's got three of them. But I told him about this one." He gestured to me. I wanted to punch this man in his smug face for treating me like a piece of meat. But I had to play my part. "And he liked the description you gave me, so he canceled his plans for tonight."

I felt a little queasy at the thought of the vice president canceling a tryst to have one with . . . me. He was in for a disappointment when we got upstairs. I wondered if Collins would get in trouble or if he would be called back from home to fetch Alejandra when I left. I also wondered what "description" Jack had given of me, but that was a question for later.

Collins swigged the rest of his drink. "You coming?" he asked. "I'm sure one of them"—he nodded over his shoulder toward a table where three women sat—"would be happy to if not."

I stood up. "I'm coming."

Jack looked like he wanted to object, and Collins laughed, then patted him on the shoulder. "You'll get used to it," he said. "They always want the man at the top, not us."

I could feel Jack's eyes on me as we walked out of the bar, and a part of me wanted to run back to the safety of his side, his hand in mine. But I had always wanted to write the stories that mattered. And that meant investigating, even if it put me in danger. *I can do this,* I told myself for about the millionth time.

I hardly heard the ding of the elevator arriving over the blood rushing in my ears, and I shook my head to clear it. Jack's warnings had gotten to me, that was all. The vice president was obviously a civilized man. I remembered my grandmother saying she liked him because he had voted to naturalize Jews into America when things got hairy in Europe. There were even rumors that he helped bring some to Texas to save them. This was someone I could have a conversation with. That's all this was. A conversation between politician and constituent. Even if I wasn't old enough to have voted for him.

Before I knew it, we were at the door, two suited men in front of it. I straightened my shoulders, taking care not to touch my dress or hair nervously. Confidence was the name of the game here, and while I wasn't feeling that much of it, I knew my future as a journalist depended on my ability to pretend I was there because I *wanted* to be.

"Special delivery," Collins joked to the men at the door. Neither cracked a smile. "He's expecting this package."

If I ever got a *real* audience with the vice president after this was all over, I was telling him what a louse his secretary was. Granted, with three mistresses, that was probably why he hired him.

One of the Secret Service agents rapped twice at the door, and a few seconds later, a voice I recognized from the radio called to come in.

I swallowed, my mouth suddenly dry, and the agent turned the knob.

The room itself was exquisite. I wondered if the vice president paid for it himself, or if this was taxpayer funded. *The rooms*, I should say, because I walked into a sitting room, with two sofas, a coffee table, and an armchair. An open door led to another room, the foot of a bed just visible, and the curtains were open at the far end of the room we were in, showcasing an even better view of the White House than I'd had two nights earlier.

The door closed behind me, and I jumped slightly, turning around to see the second-most familiar face in the country. He had no tie on, his shirt unbuttoned at the top, showing just a glimpse of an undershirt, and he was in socks. It was jarring to see him so undone.

"Well, hello there," he drawled, his Texas origin evident immediately. "And who might you be?"

"Judy Greenberg," I said. Then, the unbuttoned shirt unnerving me, I added nervously, "I work for *The Washington Digest*." I could have kicked myself for giving that detail away so soon.

"Oh good." I was confused. He was happy I was a reporter? He chuckled at the bewilderment on my face, and I hated that he had read me so easily. "If it was *The Post*, I'd worry. *The Digest* won't run a story against me." He likely wasn't wrong, but this wasn't about *him*; it was about an espionage plot. "Let me guess," he continued, "a typing pool girl, new to the big city, excited to rub . . . elbows . . . with a powerful man."

I swallowed, refusing to cringe at the way he had said *elbows*. But he was describing Patricia to a T. I wondered if she would have been a better choice for this. No. This was *my* story. "Something like that. Mr. Vice President, I wanted to ask you—"

"Drink?" he asked, crossing to a bar cart in the room.

"No, thank you. I—"

"Want to get right down to it, huh? I like a girl who knows what she wants."

I looked around, desperately. "Can—can we talk a little . . . first?" If I just ran out of there with no information, I wouldn't get a second chance at this.

He smiled, amused. "Sure," he said, sitting on one of the sofas. "Why don't you come on over here and sit with me, and we can . . . talk."

I sat at the other end of the sofa from him, but he moved over until our legs were touching, and he put an arm behind me. It wasn't around my shoulders, but was far too close for comfort.

"What did you want to talk about?" he asked.

"Cuba." This was not going how I had planned at all. I hadn't accounted for his leg against mine, the feeling of being pinned between him and the edge of the sofa. And I was clearly running out of time.

His expression didn't change. "What about Cuba? It was a lovely place to visit before the revolution. I assume you're too young to have been."

"I am. Mr. Vice President"—I turned to face him, inching my leg away from his—"are you at all worried that they'll try to retaliate after the Bay of Pigs disaster?"

His face darkened. "No. I'm not."

I was letting my nerves get the better of me. *What would Patricia do here?* "It's just—" I batted my eyelashes. "The whole idea of that sounds so frightening. They wouldn't come after *you*, would they?"

"You have nothing to worry about on that front, little lady." His expression softened. "We've got plenty of plans in motion to make sure Castro and his army are nothing to worry about."

If he was willing to tell me that much . . . "Like what?"

He laughed, moving the hand behind me to play with the ends of my hair. "Now you know I can't tell you anything like that. Why don't we talk about you and that pretty little face of yours?" He put his other hand on my knee, and I jumped up, casting around for some kind of distraction.

"That's quite a view," I said, gesturing toward the window.

"Isn't it?" He had stood up behind me and put an arm around my waist, guiding me toward the window. I realized I was trapped between the glass and him. He trailed a finger up the bare skin of my back, revealed by the dress's low cut. Goose bumps arose where he touched me, and I struggled to control my breathing. I could duck under his arm. It wasn't time to scream. But I could feel it rising up in my throat all the same. I needed to leave. "Play your cards right, and I can bring you there one night for a private tour," he said softly, his breath tickling my ear. "No prying eyes. Just you and me."

A private tour. The girls at the bar had shown their IDs to the president's secretary. Someone arriving with the vice president through a special entrance likely wouldn't have to do that.

I turned around to face him, an idea forming. "Would I get to meet the president?"

He shrugged. "Of course. Assuming he wasn't busy entertaining someone of his own." He mimicked the president's accent, quoting a famous line from his inaugural address.

The president's Massachusetts accent.

Mass goal in sight.

My eyes widened at the realization. He leaned in, his gaze fixed on my mouth, and I ducked under his arm, dashing toward the door, as he, surprised, landed face-first on the window. "I have to—"

A commotion of shouting outside the hotel suite door cut me off.

"—my baby sister in there, and I swear on all that's holy that this will wind up on the front page of every paper in town if you don't—"

The voice turned muffled, and there was a knock at the door. I tried to open it, but it was locked, and suddenly the vice president was beside me. He looked down, amused. "How old are you anyway?"

I thought quickly. "Sixteen," I said, letting my voice go even higher than usual.

He blanched, then opened the door. One of the Secret Service men had one hand pinning Jack's arms behind him, the other clapped over his mouth while he struggled. "Let him go," the vice president said.

Then he shoved me out of the room. "She's too young. Get them out of here. And get Collins on the phone. He's fired."

The Secret Service agent released Jack, and he crashed into the wall. I ran to his side. "What are you doing?" I asked.

He looked up at me. "I couldn't let you do it. I'm sorry. I'm so sorry. But I couldn't—"

The door shut behind us. One of the Secret Service agents had gone inside with the vice president, and the other was still outside the door, glaring at the two of us. "If I hear one word about any of this—anywhere—you'll be seeing me again," he said menacingly. "Now get out of here."

"We're going," I said, giving Jack a hand. He stood up, and the two of us took off down the hall, choosing the stairs over the elevator. Hand in hand, we flew down them, bypassing the lobby and leaving through the emergency exit onto the street.

"Are you okay?" Jack asked, his eyes wild. "Did he—?"

I shook my head. "I'm fine. But Jack—"

"I should have never let you go up there. I've heard enough stories. I should never—"

I grabbed his face with both hands. "Jack! It's not a *mass* goal. It's a *Massachusetts* goal!" He stared at me, not connecting the dots. I moved to the side, my hands still holding his face so that the White House came into his line of sight.

"Massachusetts goal," he said quietly. "The president."

"She's trying to get to the president."

He looked back at me. "You did it. You figured it out. Oh my God—is she—"

But I cut him off, kissing him. For a second, his lips kept moving with what he had been trying to say. Then his arms went around my waist, pulling me in close until the world spun and nothing else mattered except us.

39

Jack kept his hand in mine as we drove north through the city. I couldn't have driven right then. My whole body was vibrating both with the implications of what we had learned and the energy between us from that kiss that I had somehow initiated. Me! What had I done?

"We have to figure out if she just wants information or if there's something more sinister afoot," Jack said, pulling me from my thoughts. Of course that was what mattered. Not the way I wanted to slide next to him on the bench seat and wrap his arm around me. I shivered, and he noticed. "You're sure you're okay?"

I nodded, not quite trusting myself to speak yet.

"I meant what I said up there. I will absolutely dig up dirt on him if he—"

"Nothing happened. Your timing was perfect." He glanced over at me and seemed reassured by whatever he saw. I thought I must look wild, but maybe that was all on the inside. "Information can be plenty sinister though—especially if Cuba *is* working with Russia." I thought of huddling under a school desk because of the threat of nuclear war. If Cuba gave Russia a close foothold, and the president himself told them what he knew . . .

"It's bad either way. But that's a very different story from her being here to try to kill him."

I turned to look at him. It hadn't actually occurred to me that he thought *that*. "You don't think she'd—"

"I've heard rumors. The Bay of Pigs wasn't the only attempt we've made to get rid of Castro. It was just the only public one. If we're trying, it stands to reason he could be doing the same."

He swerved suddenly to avoid a collision, pulling his hand from mine to hold his arm out in front of me, protecting me as he hit the brakes. When the car had steadied, he wrapped that arm around my shoulder, pulling me to his side, precisely where I wanted to be, enjoying the feel of his leg against mine. Amazing how it was the exact same body parts, but when the vice president did it . . . I held in a shudder so Jack wouldn't think it was about him. No. I never wanted to be in *that* position again.

Jack swore softly. "We're going to have to try to get something out of Alejandra."

I looked up at him. "How?"

"I could pretend to be CIA," he said.

"Wouldn't she run?"

"Probably."

We were silent for three blocks, trying to work this out.

"I pretend to be another Cuban agent," I said, an idea forming.

"You what?"

"We'd need help—I'd need a little Spanish. Not much. Just enough to say something to spook her. But what if I tell her the Russian sent me to make sure she's actually going to finish the job? Make her reveal a timeline."

"I should do it."

"They sent a woman to cozy up to the vice president and the president for a reason—I'll tell her the Russian wants me to take over if she fails. She's not going to like that, so she'll make it clear she's not going to fail."

He shook his head. "It's too risky. If she *is* an assassin, what stops her from killing you?"

"The fact that the Russian sent me. With what Carmen told us, we know just enough to make it believable."

"Maybe. But who do you know who speaks Spanish? Carmen left town."

My shoulders slumped. I knew no one except Carmen. We had hit a dead end. And then, as Jack navigated the car around the traffic circle, I saw the sign for Colesville Road—the way we would take if we were stopping to pick up a box of Montgomery Donuts . . . "Frank," I said suddenly.

"Who?"

"You know, Frank. The security guard at *The Digest*."

"Frank speaks Spanish? I thought he was Italian."

"He grew up in Puerto Rico."

"How do you know that?"

I grinned up at Jack. "I take the time to talk to people—all reporters should. You never know what you're going to learn."

Jack rolled his eyes at the dig. "Won't he be suspicious that you want to learn how to threaten a spy in Spanish?"

He had a point. Anything that would get Alejandra de Bernal to think I was her compatriot was going to raise a red flag. I watched as a raindrop hit the windshield, tracing a crooked path toward the bottom of the glass, another soon joining it, then more until Jack switched on the windshield wipers.

Jack shook his head. "No one comes to DC for the weather," he muttered.

The weather. What had Carmen said about the weather? *Whoever she is, she's not here for the weather. Trust me. That's better in Cuba.*

"You're a genius."

He looked down at me in surprise. "I am?"

"The weather. That's one of the first things you learn in another language. I'll get Frank to tell me how to say 'Our friend wants to know how the weather is in Havana' and 'It's awfully cold in Russia.'"

He bit his bottom lip, pondering this, then shook his head. "Greenberg, that just might be crazy enough to work." I grinned at the use of my last name. I was Judy Greenberg, ace reporter in his head right then, not Judy Greenberg, girl he sometimes kissed at the Hay-Adams Hotel. "Change the locations though. Havana and Russia are too specifically hostile."

"San Juan, then?" Jack nodded. "And . . . ?"

"Chicago. Although when we talk to Alejandra, let's change it to Siberia." I looked up at him, questioningly. "More threatening than just Russia."

He pulled into my driveway, but I didn't make a move to get out of the car, not quite ready to leave him. Jack whispered my name, and I turned my head, not even caring if my mother or grandmother—or even my father for that matter—saw us kissing in the car.

I leaned forward, my head tilted up as his came closer to mine and then—

A rap at the window made us jump apart.

My grandmother stood under a giant umbrella, her hair covered in a plastic rain bonnet, indicating that Jack should roll down his window. He complied, and she pointed at my dress. "Best change back into what you left in," she warned, pointing toward the living room window, where a light shone behind the curtains. "Your mother's still awake."

"What are you doing outside in the middle of the night in the rain?"

"Canasta ran late," she said. "My friend Hannah Kellerman just dropped me off. Terrible driver, that one. But don't you worry, young man. I'll make sure Edna knows it was Hannah who ran over her daylilies, not you. Now go let her get changed and then you can kiss her good night properly." Which likely meant it had been my grandmother who ran over the daylilies earlier in the day. I doubted there was a worse driver than her roaming the streets.

I shook my head. "You are the worst."

"If I were, I'd be telling your mother the state I just caught you in instead of saving your *tuchus*."

She had a point there.

Jack stammered out a thank you and put the car in reverse as she shooed him away, then took us to the side street where I typically disrobed.

"I think I like her," he said as I slipped out of the black dress.

"She's something all right."

"I see where you get it from."

"You should be seeing a lot less," I said, meeting his eyes in the mirror. He looked away. "But yeah. She always understood me better than my mother and my sister."

"What about your father?"

That was an interesting question, actually. He seemed proud I was working at *The Digest* after all. "I think he ignores what he doesn't want to see." I turned around. "Zip me up?"

He complied, and I climbed over the seat. "You really should just use the doors."

"And deny you that quick look at my legs? What kind of fun would that be?"

He started to laugh. "I'll tell you this: I'm never bored with you around."

I leaned into him, and he wrapped his arm around my shoulder to drive the three blocks back to my house.

40

"Don't tell the other typing pool girls," Frank said, accepting the box of doughnuts I had brought him as a bribe. "But you're my favorite."

I smiled at him. "You said your—who was it again who made something like these?"

"My *abuela*," he said around a mouthful of doughnut. "My grandmother."

"Spanish is such a lyrical language. I wish I could learn it." I batted my eyelashes like Patricia had taught me.

He wiped at his mouth with the back of his hand. "What do you want to learn? I can teach you."

"Oh, I don't know," I said, waving a hand in the air like I was trying to think of something. "One of those silly phrases like they used when they taught me French in high school. Something like . . . 'Our friend wants to know how the weather is in San Juan.'"

He looked at me askance, and I wondered if I had pressed too hard. "That's the kind of sentence they use?"

"Things like that. And 'Where is the library?'"

Frank shrugged. *"Nuestro amigo quiere saber como esta el clima en San Juan."*

"A little slower?" He obliged, and I repeated it until he was satisfied.

"You're a quick learner," Frank said fondly. Then he nodded toward someone behind me. "Think your fella is waiting for you though."

I turned around to see Jack watching us. "He's not—"

"I see a lot of things," Frank said with a wink. "But don't you worry. I don't tell Miss Kelly what I know."

I was going to have to ask about the cold part on Monday. But that was well worth the price of another box of doughnuts.

~

"Are we going to be able to pull this off?" I asked Jack as he drove us to my parents' house after work on Friday for Shabbat dinner. We hadn't talked about what those kisses meant. Had they been the heat of the moment in that hotel room and nothing more? Pure adrenaline after I left the vice president's suite? I desperately wanted to know, and yet I was terrified to have that conversation. What if he thought it was nothing? But what if he thought it was *something*? We would have to sort this mess out once the article was over, but for now, it was easier to keep living in the excitement of what we were working toward. The fact that I liked the feel of his arm around me was a strange bonus, but not one that had to mean anything.

Okay, even I knew that was a lie. But it was a lie I could keep telling myself a little longer, until we were forced to acknowledge that our situation was more or less than I thought it was.

But would we be pretending for my parents' sake tonight? Or was I the only one pretending? And why did that distinction make me so nervous?

He glanced over at me. "It's a lot stronger if we can figure out what Cuba wants with the president. But we could run what we have. We don't *have* to talk to Alejandra if it's too dangerous."

I exhaled forcefully at his cluelessness. "I meant dinner tonight."

"Oh," he said with a laugh. "Why not? Your mother loves me."

"My grandmother is a wild card, however. And she knows too much."

"Maybe we should send Alejandra de Bernal after her next."

"Not funny. Just be prepared. She likes to push buttons."

He grinned. "Which is going to be harder? Getting a spy to confess or surviving Shabbat dinner with your family?"

"It's truly a toss-up," I said, remembering the cantor. "But make sure you wait until after we say the motzi to eat."

"You forget, Jacob Feldstein knows all the rules. Besides, what kind of cretin eats before the motzi at Shabbat?"

The kind my mother thought I should marry before I met you, I thought.

We arrived at the house, and a flutter at the window told me my mother was watching for us and was now inside yelling, "Leonard! They're here!"

I straightened Jack's tie, realizing as I did it what an intimate gesture that was for two people who were pretending to date. Or a perfectly normal gesture for two people who *were* dating. *Get yourself together, Judy.*

"Ready?" I asked, not quite meeting his eye.

"Absolutely. I need to see if this brisket is as good as you say."

The little boy next door was playing catch with his cousin on the front lawn, and I narrowly dodged a ball as I stepped out of the car. "Jordan!" his mother called from the front porch of their house. He grinned sheepishly at us through a mouthful of braces as Jack tossed his ball back, and we climbed the steps to my house.

My mother flung the door open before we even reached the top. "Jack," she said warmly, ignoring me entirely. "We're so happy to have you here tonight. Come in, come in. What can I get you to drink?" She took his arm, leaving me on the front porch and practically shutting the door in my face. Jack looked back at me helplessly.

"Hi, Mom," I said pointedly.

"Go change your dress. I laid one out for you."

My hackles rose. I had specifically worn a nicer dress so I wouldn't *have* to change. And I wasn't six years old. But I could oblige her to make this go smoother.

She led Jack to the white sofa that she had meticulously scrubbed the chocolate stain out of with a toothbrush. I wondered if I would be allowed to sit there with him. She could go either way, honestly.

I changed into the dress—which was technically Betty's—that she had selected, though it wasn't my favorite. Then I scrubbed the ink from my fingers, freshened up my makeup, and went down to rescue Jack—

Who was sitting on the white sofa, flanked by my mother and grandmother, a glass of liquor untouched in his hand, and my baby album across his lap.

"Mom!"

"What?" she asked. "He should know what your children will look like."

I blinked heavily as Jack tried not to laugh. This was going to be a long evening.

My father arrived home with Uncle Gil, followed shortly by the chaos of Betty and her family, which provided a welcome reprieve. Betty stopped short when she saw Jack sitting beside me.

"Oh," she said, putting a hand on her stomach self-consciously. "I forgot you were bringing someone tonight." That wasn't even a little bit true because my mother talked to her on the phone at least six times a day. But she probably assumed he would be more on par with the cantor. She crossed to us and held out her hand. "Betty—Judy's sister."

Jack stood up to shake it and offered her his seat. She said no, if she sat on anything that low, she would never be able to get up again, but she raised her eyebrows at me and mouthed, *Keep this one.*

Granted, she mouthed it in full view of Jack, who, if he was smart, was going to run for the hills any second now.

My mother announced dinner was ready, and we all filed into the dining room, which was set with the fancy Shabbat candlesticks, not the ones we used regularly, as well as the Rosh Hashanah china. I looked at my mother and—yes, she had gotten her hair done earlier in the day. She was going all out. She had seated us together, Jack next to my father and across from her. My grandmother was on my other side, Betty and her husband across from us, and Uncle Gil opposite my father at the end of the table.

Jack looked at home at our table, and for a few minutes, I let myself imagine that this was real. That the electricity between us wasn't just adrenaline from chasing a crazy lead. That this could be my life. Working at a newspaper and coming home to someone who supported and believed in that.

My mother brought out the brisket, and Jack took my hand under the table. I looked at him, and he smiled at me as my mother lit the candles, covered her eyes, and said the traditional Shabbat prayers. When she finished, my father led us in the motzi, and then everyone started to reach for food. I realized I should have warned Jack that we were absolute heathens once the blessings were said, but he simply followed suit, as if everyone's family was this uncivilized.

"Judy was right about your brisket, Mrs. Greenberg," Jack said. "This is the best I've had. Just don't tell *my* mother I said that, please."

My mother positively giggled like a schoolgirl. Betty caught my eye—the corners of her mouth had turned down in a way that I recognized meant trouble.

"So, Jack," she said, "do you make enough at the newspaper to support a family?"

"Betty!" my mother said, horrified, as Jack choked slightly on a bite of food and reached for his water glass.

"What? Unless you expect them to live here, it's a valid question."

"If he doesn't, he'll go work for your uncle Gil."

"He'll do what now?" Uncle Gil said around a bite of brisket. "I'm not your family labor union, Edna."

"Leonard?" she asked helplessly.

My father glanced from his brother to his wife, unsure what he was supposed to do here.

"Maybe I'll die before they get married and leave them an inheritance," my grandmother offered helpfully.

I blinked at all of them. "No one is getting married—or dying—anytime soon," I said. "Unless you all keep it up and Jack chokes to death to get away from us."

He had fully recovered, and I could tell he was trying not to laugh. "I've been pretty frugal," he said. "By the time we would be ready to discuss that, I think we'd be okay."

"Of course he's been frugal," my mother said. "Didn't you see the car out front?"

"Mother!"

She turned to look at me, completely mystified by my tone. "What?"

"Doesn't *anyone* here care what I want?"

"I do," Jack said quietly. No one else responded.

"I want a career. I don't want to be . . ." I trailed off, realizing if I said more, I was in trouble. But my hand had gestured in a direction that spoke volumes.

"Me, she means," Betty said, standing up and tossing her napkin on the table. "Come on, Reuben. I've had enough."

"Betty," my mother said imploringly. "Judy didn't mean that. Tell her you didn't mean that."

"I didn't mean that," I said quietly. I *had* meant that—not as an insult, but as an example of what *everyone* else seemed to want. No one seemed to be able to understand that my end goal wasn't to get married, have kids, and be content as a housewife. This was a disaster.

"Yes, you did," Betty said. "And you've got a lot of nerve to say that while wearing my dress!" My mother turned pale but didn't say anything. Betty turned to Jack. "Get out while you can. She lies, she steals, and she'll do worse to get her way." She picked up her youngest and headed for the door. But she stopped at the living room, doubling over and dropping Gary onto my mother's white sofa, where he spit out a mouthful of half-chewed brisket.

"Betty!" my mother cried, rushing to her side, with only one glance at the mess on her sofa.

We all left the table to see her holding a hand to her stomach, a red stain spreading across her dress. "Hospital," she gasped toward her husband. "Something's wrong."

I ran to the kitchen and called the fire department. Within minutes, we heard an approaching siren signaling their arrival. We all watched helplessly as they put her onto a gurney, and they whisked her and Reuben off to the hospital, my parents following behind in their car. Which left me, my grandmother, and Jack to deal with two very scared and forgotten children.

I was about to tell Jack he didn't have to stay; my grandmother and I could handle getting them to bed. But he picked Gary up. "Hey, champ," he said softly. "Your mama's going to be just fine."

He couldn't have known that. I didn't know that. The look on Betty's face combined with all that blood had me beyond frightened. If she died—I shook my head. I wasn't going to think about that. Especially because she had been right. I *was* thinking I didn't want to be like her. Was that going to be the last thing we said to each other?

Instead, I followed Jack's lead, picking Sandy up. "Sounds like *you* get a sleepover here tonight. *And* Grandma isn't here, which means no rules." Her thumb was in her mouth, something she had stopped the previous year, and Gary was studying Jack with great curiosity. "Who wants ice cream?"

"We didn't finish dinner," Sandy said around her thumb. At least I think that's what she said.

"Just don't tell Grandma that. Deal?" She nodded, and I handed her off to my grandmother, who was watching me and Jack with a twinkle in her eye. "I'll go get ice cream. Jack, do you want any?" He said no. "Okay, two bowls of ice cream, coming right up."

"Make it three," my grandmother said. I looked at her. "What? I'm taking advantage of your mother not being here too."

I shook my head. She was too much.

41

With Jack's help distracting them, I got both kids bathed and into the spare pajamas Betty had brought over for when she went into labor, while my grandmother cleaned up the kitchen. Then the kids insisted that Jack read them a bedtime story, not me. My mother had converted Betty's old room into a bedroom for grandchildren, hinting without subtlety that my room would become her long-desired sewing room if I *ever* got married. I tucked them into the two twin beds, glancing at the crib in the corner that Gary had recently graduated from. I did hope it wouldn't remain empty. I didn't know much about childbirth, but I did know that blood, a month before the baby was due, couldn't be a good sign.

Sandy asked me to stay with them until she fell asleep, so I sat in the rocking chair, while Jack left the room, leaving the door cracked to allow me to make a quiet escape. It was impossible not to worry in the dark room, but eventually their breath slowed enough that I could creep out.

I came down the stairs stiffly, the stress of the evening leaving me with tense muscles. A bath would be lovely, but I was waiting for news of how Betty was and didn't want to be away from the phone. There was a light on in the den, and I opened my mouth to ask my grandmother if I could make her a cup of tea, when I saw her sitting in her chair, a cup of tea already in her hands. Jack was on the sofa near her.

"I thought you'd have left."

He offered me a half smile. "Figured you—and Mrs. Greenberg here—could use the company. Unless you want me to go."

I found myself shaking my head. The TV was on, tuned to a rerun of *The Detectives* on NBC. My grandmother was in her chair, eyes glued to the screen, and I sat on the sofa next to Jack. I nodded toward my grandmother. "She's got a crush on Robert Taylor."

"Who doesn't?" she asked.

Jack ducked his head to avoid her seeing his smile. Not that it mattered. Her eyes never left the screen while Taylor was on it.

"Thank you," I said quietly. "It's not always this . . . chaotic . . . here."

He looked over at me. "Somehow I doubt that's true."

Okay, he wasn't *wrong*. But the fire department didn't usually have to transport someone to the hospital.

"The Star-Spangled Banner" was playing from the TV when the sound of the front door woke us. I had dozed off sometime during *Here and Now*, as had Jack. My grandmother had apparently gone off to bed after draping a crocheted afghan over us. I moved away from Jack quickly to avoid awkward questions from my parents.

My father came in, bleary eyed, and snapped off the television, startling when he saw us on the sofa. "How's Betty?" I asked.

"Not good," he said, clearly exhausted. There were no footsteps behind him, and I realized my mother wasn't home. "They had to deliver the baby early. She had something called a placental abruption. They finally got the bleeding to stop, but she lost an awful lot of blood first."

The room started to spin slightly, steadying only when I felt pressure on my hand. I looked down to see Jack holding it. "Is she going to be okay?"

My father sank into the armchair, absolutely crumpling. "I don't know," he said, his face in his hands. "The doctors said as long as she didn't start bleeding again, she should be, but she's not out of the woods yet. Your mother told me to come home, that she'd call if—" He couldn't finish the sentence.

I thought back to Betty complaining that this pregnancy was harder, but her doctor had dismissed her concerns. I swallowed. If she didn't make it, what became of the kids upstairs?

"The baby?" I asked thickly.

"Healthy," he said, his voice shaking. "A little girl. She didn't even get to name her yet." He raised his head, and there were tears on his cheeks, jarring me to my core. I had never seen a man cry, let alone my father. And suddenly I couldn't breathe. That sight told me what he couldn't: Betty really might not survive tonight.

I thought of the nights I had spent in her bed as a child, curled up against the warmth of her body, terrified because it was thundering outside. Yes, we had grown apart in recent years, but the idea of losing her . . .

A voice startled me out of my reverie. "Aunt Judy? I scared."

I jumped up, racing past my father and Jack to the stairs, where Sandy stood at the top, thumb in her mouth. I went to her and crouched down to hug her. "There's nothing to be scared of," I said, knowing that was a lie. There was a lot to be scared of right now. For her especially. "Let's get you back to bed, okay?"

She nodded against my shoulder. "Will you sleep with me? Mama does that."

It felt like I was drowning. I couldn't get enough air into my lungs. But I managed to agree, and carried her, as quietly as I could, back into the room that I used to sneak into when it thundered, putting her into bed and climbing in next to her. She nestled in against me as I lay there, waiting for her breathing to slow.

My eyes were open in the darkness, no chance of falling asleep myself, as I thought about Betty. If she died, Reuben couldn't do this on his own. He had to work to support them. My mother would help, but I would need to also.

I closed my eyes, and in the darkness, Sandy was me, afraid of the thunder, looking to her big sister for comfort.

I knew I hadn't done this. I didn't believe in jinxes or hexes or even the evil eye, despite the older women in my life always saying *kinehora* and sometimes spitting. But how I wished I could rewind a few hours and not say that I didn't want to be Betty. Because if Betty didn't come back to us, I was going to have to step up and be as much of her as I could.

~

By the time I crept out of the room again, I felt like Rip Van Winkle—it had clearly been a hundred years since dinner that evening. I held the railing as I went downstairs and was surprised to see Jack still sitting with my father.

"Come on, Daddy," I said to my father, who suddenly looked like he had aged as much as I felt like I had in the last couple of hours. "You should get to bed."

"What if your mother calls?"

The phone was in the kitchen. "I'll sleep on the sofa down here tonight," I said. "And I'll wake you if there's any news."

"Why don't I stay down here?" Jack asked.

I shook my head. "It's okay. You should go home."

"I can stay if you want me to."

I did. Desperately. I wanted to curl back up with him on the sofa and let him comfort me. But the reality was if he stayed, I had to go upstairs—imagine if my mother came home and found us asleep together? And more importantly, Betty's life hung in the balance. She was what mattered most right now. Not what I wanted.

"I'll be okay," I said. "Let me just get my father upstairs."

"I'm fine," my father said, looking anything but. "But promise you'll wake me if she calls."

I said I would, and he left, lumbering up the stairs.

"You're sure you don't want me to stay?"

I nodded, hating that I was lying to Jack but too emotionally battered to analyze why that was.

"Okay," he said and kissed my forehead. "I'll check in on you tomorrow."

Tomorrow. My shoulders slumped in defeat. "We have to run the story with what we have. I won't be able to—"

"Shh," Jack said, pulling me in close. "One step at a time. A lot can happen in a few hours."

I nodded, terrified at the thought that we might be planning a funeral by then, but held myself together until the door was closed behind him. Then I sank to the floor against it and let myself cry, sobbing for all that we would lose if Betty didn't pull through. *Be okay,* I thought desperately. *You have to be okay.*

42

I eventually pulled myself off the floor and fell asleep on the sofa. For a blissful second, I didn't remember why I was on the sofa, and then I heard the front door shut. Its opening must have woken me. *Betty,* I thought, sitting bolt upright. I threw off my grandmother's afghan and dashed toward the door, colliding headfirst with my mother.

"Betty?" I asked desperately. "Is she—?" I couldn't finish the sentence.

"She's okay," my mother said. She looked so diminished in the faint morning light. So much older than the night before, with her makeup washed away by tears. "She's going to be okay."

We collapsed against each other. I couldn't remember the last time I had felt comfort from my mother. In recent years, everything had been about finding me a husband. But we held each other up in our shared relief, letting the fear of almost losing Betty evaporate off us together.

"Edna?" My father asked from the top of the stairs. We both turned to see him in his robe, unshaven, looking haggard.

"She's stable," my mother said. "She needed transfusions—a few of them—but she finally leveled off. She even got to hold the baby." My mother released me, smiling ruefully. "Then she told me to go home. Said I was fraying her nerves too much."

I let out an involuntary bark of a laugh. Betty *was* okay if she had said that. They both turned to look at me. "Did she name the baby?" I asked, trying to compose myself.

My mother nodded. "Brenda Jeanine. For my mother and Reuben's grandmother." That had been neither of their names, but I was sure the Hebrew would line up.

I glanced at my watch. It was early, but the kids would be up soon. I patted my mother's shoulder. "You go get some rest. I'll start breakfast."

She shook her head. "Who could sleep? But I'll freshen up." She went upstairs, where she and my father embraced, while I went to the kitchen and started on a batch of pancakes.

My mother provided a *lot* more detail than I wanted about Betty's condition over breakfast, describing the birth and blood loss to my grandmother in full gory detail before the kids joined us. I pushed my own food to the side, horrified. Having children sounded awful, even with modern medicine. And she wanted that for *me*?

Now that the danger had passed, however, both my mother and grandmother were thrilled that not only did they have a new baby to dote on, but this wasn't anything to prevent Betty from having more babies. I didn't know how many more they expected my sister to produce—especially after this ordeal that could have killed her.

The phone rang, and I took that as an opportunity to exit the conversation. "Hello?" I asked.

"How's your sister?"

I held the receiver away slightly, looking at it with surprise. It was Jack. I had forgotten I gave him my number for emergencies. "She's okay," I said. "She's going to be okay."

I heard him exhale in relief through the phone. "Are you okay?" I nodded, then realized he couldn't see me and said I was. "Thank you. For last night."

"Listen," he said. "I think you were right. We should draft something based on what we have. You have too much going on and—"

"Like hell," I said. Silverware clattered to the table as my mother and grandmother turned to stare at me.

"Aunt Judy said a bad word," Sandy said, eyes wide.

"Sorry," I said through gritted teeth. Then I took the receiver as far as the cord would stretch into the dining room. It was futile though. My mother and grandmother would be straining to hear every word. And while my grandmother pretended her hearing wasn't as sharp as it used to be, when she wanted to hear something, that woman didn't miss a word. "That was when I thought Betty—" I couldn't quite say out loud that I had thought she was going to die. "We're too close to give up now," I whispered.

"Judy—"

"Please," I said quietly. "We have to see this through. It's the only way I have any hope of getting out of the typing pool."

There was a long pause during which I could practically hear him shaking his head. "I'll see you Monday, then." There was a click, and the line went dead. I knew I shouldn't care that he hadn't said goodbye. But I did.

Neither my mother nor grandmother had resumed eating and were both watching me as I replaced the receiver.

"So," my grandmother said. "What exactly was 'like hell'?"

"Bubbe said a bad word now," Sandy said.

"Bubbe is old and can say whatever she likes," she said to the little girl. "Your aunt Judy on the other hand . . ."

I rolled my eyes. "Jack thought maybe I had too much going on to make time for him right now. Is that what either of *you* wants?"

"No," my mother said immediately. "Oh no, absolutely not. But don't use that kind of language. Men don't like that."

She had clearly never set foot in a newsroom before. My grandmother, however, was eyeing me shrewdly, believing none of it. But I cleaned up the breakfast dishes, my back to them, giving nothing away.

Shortly after breakfast, the two of them left me with Sandy and Gary to go to the hospital. I took the kids to the playground down the street and fixed them sandwiches for lunch. My mother and grandmother returned mid-afternoon, promising my niece and nephew that they would be allowed to go meet their little sister soon.

And I found myself with an afternoon to stew. All I wanted was to call Jack, even if it did mean walking down to the pay phone at the gas station for some privacy. I wanted to make sure he wasn't mad at me. To thank him again for the night before. To ask why he had stayed. What it meant.

But I was also scared of the answers. If I put becoming a journalist over him, would I lose him? If I put him over what I had wanted for so long, would I lose *me*? I had never been one to lament the accident of being born a woman—heaven knew I liked dressing up and looking pretty, even if the clothes were typically stolen from my sister. But it wasn't fair that he would get to live out his dreams *and* have a family, and I had to choose one or the other.

If I ever actually made it to being a reporter, that was.

I called up to my mother that I was going for a walk, wandering the neighborhood aimlessly in the oppressive heat of summer in the DC area, not realizing where I was going until I found myself standing outside the gas station, location of the nearest pay phone. I hadn't brought a purse. This was foolish. It wasn't like I could call him anyway.

The merciless sun glinted off something in the small patch of grass between the station and the road, and I bent down to see a lone dime. I didn't particularly believe in signs from above, but—

I plucked the dime from the ground and gripped it tightly in my palm, then walked over to the pay phone, inserted it, and dialed the number I had committed to memory in case I needed it.

It rang three times, and I was about to hang up, when Jack's voice answered. "Hello?" There was a clacking sound in the background that I immediately recognized as typewriter keys.

I swallowed. "It's me. Judy."

"What happened?" he asked, instantly, the typing stopping.

I shouldn't have called him. "Nothing," I said quickly. "I just—I didn't like how we ended things when you called this morning."

He let out a heavy sigh. "I'm sorry. I just—this is all new to me."

"What is?"

"All of it. I cover politics mostly. Not—whatever this is. If I cowrite with someone, it's someone with more experience. I'm the junior White House correspondent after all. I've never covered a dangerous story before. Especially not with . . ." He trailed off, and I held my breath. Not with someone with no experience? Not with someone he cared about?

"Not with . . . ?"

"You," he said after a long pause. "From a journalism standpoint, I know you're right. We're onto *something*. And pushing Alejandra a bit is the next logical step. But I still feel responsible because I got you into that room the other night. And if anything happens to you . . ." He stopped himself again.

"It'll be my own stupid fault," I said firmly. Did I hope he had been planning to finish that statement by saying how devastated he would be? Yes. But the implications brought me back to my earlier pondering about what my life would look like if I chose him over a career. And the reality was—"I told you to get me into that room. You tried to stop me."

"I have the feeling not many people have been able to stop you when you decide you're going to do something."

I finally smiled. "Now whatever gave you that idea?"

"Lady, you going to be long?" a man asked from behind me, causing me to jump.

I scowled at him. "I should go," I told Jack. "But this plan is going to work."

"How can you possibly know that?"

"Because if I'm not letting *you* stop me, I'm certainly not letting—" I glanced over my shoulder to see if the man who wanted the phone was listening. He was. "*Her* stop me."

There was a long pause. "Okay," Jack said. "I still don't like it. But . . . if you can't beat 'em, join 'em."

I grinned. "I'll see you Monday."

"Monday it is."

43

But even with things less up in the air with Jack, I couldn't sit still on Sunday. Between knowing I was going to confront a spy with only what Spanish I had learned from Frank, the fight I had with Betty right before she went to the hospital, and the noise from Betty's kids, my nerves were shot. Betty had almost died thinking that I was insulting her life and choices. And if things went south with Alejandra, bravado to Jack aside, I didn't want that to be our last conversation. My mother said Betty was doing well enough for visitors, so I decided to go see her. I took the bus down to Hofberg's, got two sandwiches, and then took the bus back across town to Suburban Hospital in Bethesda, where Betty was recovering.

I was directed to the maternity ward. I knocked before entering, though I didn't wait for her to respond because her door was open.

"Hungry?" I asked, holding up the Hofberg's bag. Betty was in the bed, the baby in her arms as she fed her a bottle. She was incredibly pale, with dark, haunted circles under her eyes, but she was sitting up and alert.

"Pastrami?"

"On rye with sauerkraut and spicy mustard dressing." I did know her favorite.

"Are you just trying to keep me too fat to take my clothes back?"

I sat on the end of her bed and passed a sandwich to her. "Am I that transparent?"

But instead of biting my head off, Betty chuckled. "Do you mind holding her while I eat?" I nodded, and she handed me the baby. "Support her head now. And angle the bottle so she doesn't get too much gas."

I looked down at her scrunched little face. My only experience with newborns was with Betty's first two, and they all kind of looked like little old men until they were a month or so old.

"Meet your aunt Judy," Betty said as she unwrapped her sandwich. "Judy, meet Brenda."

"She's beautiful," I said as she curled her little fingers around my pinkie.

"Mom says she looks like you did."

"Then she's *definitely* going to be a looker." Betty laughed. "Let's hope she's taller than me though."

"You've done all right for a half-pint," Betty said around a mouthful of sandwich. "God this is good. Hospital food is miserable."

I smiled at her. "There are chocolate top cookies in there too."

"You really *do* want to keep my clothes, don't you?" She shook her head. "Did you know those are only in Maryland and DC? Reuben had never had them when he moved down here."

I didn't know that. She finished her sandwich while I admired my new niece, wondering what it would be like to someday hold a baby of my own in my arms. I didn't want to forgo all of this, I realized.

"I can take her if you want to eat."

I shook my head. "I'm okay. Have a cookie."

She took one from the bag, closing her eyes as she bit into it. She swallowed, then looked at me. "So what did you steal my green cocktail dress for?"

I kept my face neutral. "I don't know what you mean."

"A thief *and* a liar, huh? Do you really think I didn't go through my closet after you came over that day?"

Betty *had* known me my whole life.

I opened my mouth to speak, but she stopped me. "The truth, please. Or I tell Mom."

I decided not to lie for once. If things went badly the next night . . . No. I didn't want to think about that.

"I'm working on a story."

"I thought you were in the typing pool?"

"I am. Jack and I found a lead, and we're following it."

She looked me over appraisingly. "So dinner the other night was for show?"

My shoulders dropped. "No—maybe—I don't know."

For a minute, neither of us said anything, and I was grateful she didn't press me.

"What's the story?"

I shook my head. "I can't tell you that yet." She took another bite of cookie. "I was really scared the other night."

She looked at me sympathetically. "I was too, to be honest. I'd been having a lot of back pain—I probably owe you an apology. I think that's why I've been so cranky lately—but the doctor said it was all in my head. I *knew* something wasn't right. But no one listened. And it almost killed me."

I looked down at the baby in my arms, her eyes closed as she drank the last of the bottle and continued sucking. "Her head isn't even that big. Grandma was wrong too."

Betty let out a hearty laugh. "No, thankfully this one *does* take after our side." Then she sobered and shook her own head. "I *knew* something was wrong though." She looked back at the baby, then set the rest of her cookie on the bag. "Give her here. She needs to be burped." I passed Brenda to her, and she held her expertly to her shoulder and patted the baby gently on the back. "It's funny. You think you know what you're doing and then, BAM! Life throws a curveball at you."

I watched her cuddling the tiny little thing that had almost killed her. Then she looked up at me. "You like this Jack, don't you?" I nodded, suddenly afraid. Kissing him had been one thing. Even falling asleep on the sofa like an old married couple. But admitting that I felt something somehow made it real. "He likes you too. I could tell. But you want this career too, right?" I nodded again, surprised by how easily Betty could read me. We had always been polar opposites. "Maybe he's okay with that. For now at least."

My voice came out as almost a whisper. "What if I'm never ready for—" I gestured to her and the baby.

She shrugged. "Then you die an old, lonely aunt."

I barked out a small laugh. "How comforting."

"Listen, you've always done everything your own way. Which has been frustrating for me, as someone who had to follow the rules. But why would this be any different?"

She had a point there.

"Truth be told," she continued. "I've always been a little jealous of you."

"Of me?"

Betty nodded. "You've known what you wanted and didn't let anything get in your way since you were what? Five?"

But Betty had wanted what she had since then too. Hadn't she?

"Six," I said, and she laughed.

"I met Reuben freshman year of college," she reminded me. "I didn't get a chance to figure out if I wanted something else."

I disagreed. She didn't *have* to marry a ridiculously boring man. I had met my share of boring men at school and didn't give up. But saying that wouldn't help anything. Three kids in, the deed was definitely done by now.

"There's still time," I said. "When the kids go off to school, you could do some part-time work."

She shrugged. "Maybe. I need to convince Reuben to agree to the pill first. I need a break. And honestly—after all this—I don't think I want to risk it again." Her face had a vulnerability to it that I hadn't seen since we were kids.

But that was an area I could help with. Or Patricia could at least. "If he won't, I may know someone who can get you a prescription even if Reuben doesn't go with you. Or at least a diaphragm."

"I don't want to know how you know that."

I laughed. I couldn't remember the last time Betty made really me laugh. It was definitely before she had kids.

"Keep the green dress," she said, reaching for her half-eaten cookie. I slid the bag closer to her so she didn't have to disturb the baby, who was now asleep on her shoulder. "It suits your complexion better anyway."

I looked at her, still so pale from all the blood loss, in the hospital bed, and it hit me again that we really almost lost her the other night. "Thank you. And Betty?" My voice was thick as I held back tears. "I'm awfully glad you're okay. I do love you. You know that, right?"

"And here I was thinking you were rooting for me to go so you could have my whole wardrobe." She set the cookie down and put the hand that wasn't holding the baby on mine. "I love you too. Promise you'll tell me about the story when you can?"

I nodded and quite honestly would have started telling her about it, except Reuben walked in with Sandy and Gary, who immediately scrambled up onto the bed and woke the baby, who began to cry.

"She does have a set of lungs on her," I said.

"Tiny but mighty, like her aunt," Betty said as she tried to hold all three kids.

"I should be going," I said, moving out of their way. The room was too small for so much chaos, and I knew firsthand how much the older two missed their mother these last couple of days.

"Don't you want your sandwich?" Betty called, pointing toward the bag.

I shook my head. "It's another pastrami for you. You know I like their corned beef better."

"Cookie!" Sandy shrieked as she lunged for it, making the baby cry harder as I left the room, feeling lighter.

44

Monday morning, I greeted Frank with another box of doughnuts and told him our friend wanted to know how the weather was in San Juan.

"Perfecto," he said with a wink.

"How would I say—oh, I don't know—'It's awfully cold in Chicago'?"

He had already taken a bite of a doughnut and had to finish chewing. "Chicago *esta frío terrible*." That wasn't so hard.

"Chicago *esta frío terrible*," I repeated. Then I realized I needed to ask something else to cover my tracks a little. "What about, 'Where is the library?'"

"Donde esta la biblioteca?"

I repeated the phrase and smiled at Frank. "Thank you."

"Anything for my favorite typing pool girl." I hoped he would be calling me his favorite reporter if all went well tonight.

There was a copy of *The Digest* on my desk, an article that I hadn't typed by Jack on the cover. A note paper clipped to the page behind it just said "Lunch today. Duke's."

It wasn't a question. But it also didn't need to be.

I started working, but doubt began to creep in about my ability to do this. I had put on my bravest face for Jack, but if Alejandra responded in Spanish, I was in trouble. There was no way she would risk that in a public place with high-ranking government officials surrounding us. But it was an awfully big gamble.

Patricia stopped by my desk, and I looked up, distracted. "Nassau was lovely, by the way."

I stared at her for a few seconds, trying to figure out what she meant. *Clement,* I remembered. *She went to Nassau this weekend with Clement.*

"Oh! I—" I shook my head. "Sorry. It was good?"

"Dreamy," she said, sitting on the edge of my desk. "I know better than to believe promises married men make, but Judy, I think he might just mean it."

"Mean what?"

She laughed. "I thought you were far enough from the farm by now. He said he's leaving his wife. Of course I told him I'll believe it when I see it, but that man sure knows how to show a girl a good time."

"That's great," I said weakly.

"What's wrong with you today?"

"Just tired," I lied. "My sister had her baby early so her older kids are at my house while she's in the hospital for the week. Not enough sleep."

"Sounds like a nightmare," Patricia said. "Say, Roberta gave her notice if you're looking for a room. Though if Phillip *is* telling the truth, I could be moving out too. But that'll take a while. It'd be fun to have you as a neighbor."

"When is she moving out?"

"In another month."

I might just have enough saved by then. I told her I would try to swing it. "Better tell them you're interested soon—I don't want to wind up with some square next to me."

~

Jack was at the back corner table again at Duke's, tucked away from prying eyes. I crossed the room to join him. "He got back to town yesterday," he said, by way of greeting. "Which means we try tonight. If you still want to."

"Well hello to you too."

"Hi," he said tersely. "Now listen—you're not going to get anything out of her in public. It's too risky."

He wasn't wrong. But it was me on the line here and I didn't exactly want to go someplace private with the woman Carmen had called *la diabla*. "Then what do you suggest?"

He reached across the table and put a hand on mine. "I'm not sending you anywhere alone."

"Meaning what? You pretend to speak Russian? Do you know any?"

"No. I would hide."

"Where?"

"I'm thinking a bathroom stall."

I shook my head. "She'll check the stalls if we go talk in the bathroom. Even Carmen did that."

"Right. We put up an Out of Order sign and lock the door. And I hide in there with a dictation machine."

I looked at him. "And if she catches you, you bludgeon her with an IBM Executary? This is insane." I took my hand back, frustrated.

"Less insane than you going in there alone. If you still want to do this, you need to agree to having me there as backup."

We stared at each other for a few tense seconds until a waiter came to take our order. Neither of us had so much as glanced at a menu, but we ordered from memory. Fields took a long sip of water when the waiter left. "I can get ahold of something."

"Something? Like what?"

He lowered his voice. "A gun. I know a guy who has one."

"Jack, no."

"I'm not willing to risk your life over this."

"And I'm not willing to risk yours."

There was a long pause. "Maybe we walk away. Hell, maybe we run away. If you hadn't taken that message, we wouldn't have known about any of this. It doesn't have to be our problem." His eyes were unfocused, looking at something I couldn't see.

"Did you just ask me to run away with you?"

He flushed slightly. "Maybe."

I reached across the table and took his hand. "But I did take the call. And we're the only ones who *can* do something about this."

He chuckled mirthlessly. "So this is when you give me the *Casablanca* talk? About how I'll regret it for the rest of my life if we don't go through with it?"

I smiled. "Won't you?"

He took a deep breath, then exhaled it forcefully. "As much as you will."

"What's the range on the dictation machine? I only used one briefly when I was in Pullman's office."

"It's not perfect, but we should get something. And it's portable."

"Okay, but how do we get you into the bathroom? Roberta's dresses won't fit you."

Fields finally laughed. "No. You make sure there's no one in there first, then I go in when no one is looking."

"And just sit in a bathroom stall until I can get one of Che Guevara's guerrillas to follow me in there?"

"I'll bring a book."

"Okay, Atticus Finch." He looked confused. "*To Kill a Mockingbird.* Atticus sits outside the jail with a book."

"I haven't read that one."

I shook my head. "I'll bring you my copy for tonight."

"Okay," he said. "But even if the dictation machine doesn't capture it, we'll both be witnesses, and that puts the story on much firmer ground than if there were just one person."

It was a solid plan. "Don't bring a"—I lowered my voice to a whisper—"gun."

"I think I should."

"Do you even know how to use one?"

"I haven't done it before. But how hard can it be? Criminals use them."

I blinked heavily. "You're not exactly Al Capone, *Jacob Feldstein.*"

"Fine. Arnold Rothstein, then. He was Jewish."

I shook my head and made a *hah* sound. "How did we get here?"

"You were nosy and took a phone call."

I squeezed his hand. "And aren't you glad I did?"

Our food arrived, saving him from an answer. But the look in his eyes told me what I needed to know.

45

There were no guarantees that either the vice president or Alejandra de Bernal would be at the Hay-Adams that night. But we were ready if they were.

I fixed my hair and put on a respectable dress but rolled the green one up under my skirt. Maybe Betty's blessing to keep the dress would bring me luck.

When Jack arrived, I kissed my parents and grandmother each on the cheek as I left.

"What's that for?" my mother asked, surprised by the gesture.

I shrugged, taking a good look at them. "Don't wait up."

"She's acting suspicious," my mother said as the door closed behind me. "You don't think she would elope, do you? I'm definitely waiting up."

I smiled a little. She would be asleep by nine based on how ragged Betty's kids were running her. My grandmother, on the other hand, would probably be awake until I got home. Which meant I had better make it home. No, I *would* make it home. This Alejandra de Bernal may have fought alongside Cuban revolutionaries, but she hadn't yet met Judy Greenberg.

Okay, she had, briefly. But still.

"You sure you want to do this?" Jack said, holding the passenger door open for me. "We could go out for a nice dinner and see a show instead."

I sat and looked up at him. "When this is over, I'm going to take you up on that offer."

He shut the door and went to the driver's side. "You've got the Spanish down?"

I repeated the phrases Frank had taught me, substituting Havana and Siberia for San Juan and Chicago.

"I hate this," he said. "It should be me."

"Always trying to take my credit."

"And only you would make a joke right now." He turned onto the side street, and I climbed into the back seat. "How do you want to do this?"

"Well, it helps if you don't look in the rearview mirror, for starters. But first I take off the old dress and then put on the new one."

"You are the most irritatingly—"

"Delightful woman ever? Aww, thank you. Eyes up front, please." He obliged. "I sit next to her at the bar and ask about the weather in Havana in Spanish. Then tell her we need to talk in private."

"What if she pretends she doesn't know Spanish?"

"I use her name." He met my eyes in the mirror, but I turned around and asked him to zip me.

"Okay," he said as I climbed into the front seat. But I sat close to him, our legs touching, and changed the subject, telling him about Patricia and her congressman.

"I don't believe a word he says."

"Me neither," I agreed. "But she mentioned the room next to hers is going to be available soon. I was thinking I might try to rent it."

"Your parents would hate that."

"They would. But I wouldn't. And hey, if I start making reporter money, it'll be a little easier to afford."

"We're not there yet. We still need a plan for how to go over Pullman's head with the story—if he alerts the Russian, we're in big trouble."

I hadn't actually thought about that. "What if he just wasn't in the office when we turn the story in?"

"Pullman is always there."

I thought of Florence, warning me not to go into Pullman's office with the door shut. Something about the way she had said it told me she had spoken from experience. "I think I could slip something into his coffee—if you could get something that would do the job without killing him, that is."

Jack laughed tightly. "You're too much. But yes, that would work." As he parked, he said, "Last chance to change your mind."

I shook my head. "No," I said. Then I remembered what else I had brought, and I handed him my copy of *To Kill a Mockingbird.*

He flipped it over. "I thought you were a library girl."

"This one was worth buying."

"I'll take good care of it," he promised.

We crossed the lobby, and I went into the bathroom, Jack waiting outside, the book held in front of the extremely noticeable bulge of the portable dictation device under his jacket. The coast was clear. I poked my head out and gave him a thumbs-up. He looked around, but there was no one in sight, and we hid him in the first stall. He handed me an Out of Order sign and a roll of tape. "Where did you get this?" I asked.

"Swiped it from the bathroom on the newsroom floor."

"What happens when someone tries to use the stall you stole it from?"

He shrugged. "They get an unpleasant surprise."

I shook my head and pointed to the dictation machine. "You know how to work that?" He nodded. I didn't ask if he had brought a gun. I didn't want to know.

"You're okay?"

"I am."

He pulled me in quickly and kissed me. "For luck," he said sheepishly.

I kissed him again, then shut the stall door, told him to lock it and keep his feet up if he heard anyone come in, and then fixed my lipstick at the sink.

It was time.

My palms were clammy as I crossed the lobby and went down the stairs toward Off the Record, my first time entering a bar alone. I had to hope none of the girls from the typing pool were there. But no one had mentioned plans to go out for the evening.

I ordered a champagne cocktail at the bar, then went to the table where Jack and I typically sat—it was secluded but also had the best view of the whole bar. And I thought about the first time I was here—I had still been mad at Jack for taking credit for my work. It felt like a lifetime ago.

Patrons came in, one woman nodding at me—I was a regular now. I sipped my drink, practicing my Spanish in my head, and waited, wondering how Jack was faring with Scout and Jem and Atticus. I wished I had something to read as well—it was awkward sitting alone. But then again, I needed to be on the lookout. So I sat there, shredding a cocktail napkin into tiny pieces until Alejandra de Bernal walked into the room and took a seat at the bar, looking bored.

The bartender poured her a martini as I watched from the corner of my eye, trying not to stare.

I waited until she had taken a sip, then I discreetly spilled what was left of my drink under the table and stood up, tossed my hair, squared my shoulders, and went to the bar, where I climbed onto the stool next to our target.

She didn't turn to look at me. I ordered another champagne cocktail, stayed quiet while the bartender made it, and then waited until he was as far from us as possible. I swallowed, my mouth suddenly dry, took a deep breath, and leaned closer to Alejandra.

I didn't look at her. *"Nuestro amigo quiere saber como esta el clima en Havana,"* I said. *"Siberia esta frío terrible."*

She didn't turn her head. "I'm afraid I don't understand," she said slowly.

"I think you do. Extremely well, in fact."

"Sorry," she said, sounding anything but.

"Hmm." I shifted to look at her. "Our—friend—will be quite interested to hear that, *Alejandra*."

Her head swiveled toward mine. "What do you want?" she whispered, her eyes steely, dangerous.

"Just to talk. A little more privately, I think."

She looked me up and down, clearly assessing the threat. What I wouldn't have given for another six inches in that moment.

"I'm not going anywhere with you."

"That's fine," I said. "I'll let our friend know that you aren't cooperating, and he'll talk to you himself. He can be very . . . persuasive. Even if his methods are a bit . . . more severe than mine."

Something indecipherable crossed her eyes. It wasn't quite fear, but yes, she knew it was a threat.

"The lobby bathrooms can be locked from the inside," I said. "Public enough for safety. Private enough to talk."

"Fine. But they'll be looking for me here soon. And if anything happens—"

I smiled at her, feeling powerful. This woman, who had fought alongside men in a war, perceived me as a threat. "We're on the same side, *amor*. Just a friendly chat between . . . compatriots."

The use of Carmen's endearment seemed to convince her, and she stood from her seat, signaling to the bartender. "If my . . . friend . . . comes looking for me, tell him I'll be back soon," she said quietly to him.

"And put my drink on her tab," I added boldly.

She stalked up the stairs ahead of me, looking around the lobby. But there was nothing out of the ordinary. We entered the bathroom, and I locked the door behind us. I held my breath when she tried to turn the knob to the stall Jack was in. If she pulled out a hairpin and picked it . . . but she didn't. I exhaled as she peeked under the small crack, and seeing no feet, seemed satisfied.

Then suddenly, she was on me, throwing me against the door. She towered over me, holding me pinned there.

"Who sent you?" she demanded, her face contorted into a snarl.

"I told you," I said, adrenaline coursing through my veins, as I worked desperately to maintain a tone of calm, all while mentally begging Jack not to come out, gun blazing to defend me—he was just as likely to shoot me as her. My life very likely depended on my ability to intimidate her—and on Jack's ability to keep his cool. "Our Russian friend. He wants to make sure you're going to get to the 'Mass goal.' If not, then I'm to take over."

She looked at me for a long moment. "It was you last week, wasn't it? When he canceled on me?" I nodded once, honest this time, and she released me. "Tell *our friend*," she hissed, "that it'll be Thursday. The first lady is up north this week, and that's the night he's free."

"And you haven't made it to the White House yet?"

She glared at me. "If I had, I would have finished the job and been back home or dead by now."

Finished the job. *Finished* the job. She wasn't getting information or starting an affair with the president.

Everything inside me was screaming, but I managed to keep my face neutral and nodded. "I will relay the message."

"Relay that I don't appreciate"—she waved a hand in my direction—"this as well."

I shrugged. "I'm not sure our friend cares about what you appreciate. *Dosvedanya*, comrade," I said with a smirk. The Russian sounded more threatening than "goodbye." She blinked at the term, stared at me for a few seconds, then turned the lock and strode out of the room. I counted to twenty before peeking out of the bathroom to see her going back down the stairs toward Off the Record.

"She's gone," I said, and there was a click as Jack unlocked the stall door. "Did you get it?"

He nodded, eyes wide. "I think so." He reached shakily for the play button, but I stopped him.

"We'll listen in the car."

"Judy, she—"

"We have to get out of here," I said. "Now."

I opened the door again, waited until the few people in the lobby had cleared, and then gestured for him to come out, both of us watching to make sure no one followed us.

The July air was oppressive in the District, even at night, as we burst out into it, the White House illuminated to our right. For a second, we both stared at the building.

"She's—"

"An assassin," I finished.

He took my hand, and we ran across the street to his car.

46

Safely in the car, with the adrenaline of the moment fading, I started shaking. Jack put his arm around me but pulled over onto a side street as I inexplicably began to cry.

To his credit, Jack held me, stroking my hair, soothing me wordlessly until I quieted.

"You were incredible," he said softly. "Where did you get *dosvedanya*?"

I hiccuped. "*From Russia with Love*."

"The James Bond book?" I nodded. Jack laughed. "Where on earth did I find you?"

"In the typing pool."

He kissed my forehead. "You never belonged there. But you know that."

"We have to write the article. Now. Tonight. Before the president comes back to town."

"We have a few days."

I shook my head. "We don't. She said Thursday. It's Monday."

He swallowed, looking past me at the dark city street. "We can't turn it in until we can take out Pullman," he said slowly. "Even if we write it tonight."

"Ipecac," I said suddenly.

"Gesundheit?"

"No, we put ipecac in his coffee. Well—I ask someone else to do it. Or I sneak up there and get someone else to serve it to him. It won't *hurt* him. He'll just throw up a lot and have to leave."

Jack looked unconvinced. "How do you know it won't hurt him?"

"Didn't your mother ever make you take it when you swallowed something you shouldn't have?"

"No?"

I smiled. "I guess I never liked following rules. There would be too many questions if we tried to write it at my house. We wouldn't get anything done. Can we go to your place?" As soon as the words were out of my mouth, my mind flashed back to the hotel room. I shook my head to clear the image. This was too important to get distracted.

Jack's face was mildly horrified.

"Or we grab a typewriter from your apartment and go sit at the Tastee Diner?" I asked, naming a Silver Spring staple that was known for being open all night.

"Is that okay?"

"Sure." I was never one to turn down a Belgian waffle.

But I watched him as he put the car back into drive. Something was off. Had I done something wrong?

I turned my face toward the window, watching the city pass by. Soon the city was behind us, and I realized we hadn't reached an apartment.

"I—uh—you should probably know," Jack started. "I don't have an *apartment,* per se. It has its own entrance and all, but . . ." I looked at him, confused. He was still staring straight ahead. "I rent the basement from my mother."

I tilted my head. "Okay."

"I just—she was going to take in boarders, when my father died, and I didn't want strangers in her house so this . . . worked."

"That's sweet of you."

"You don't think it's weird?"

"Of all the things that make you weird, that's the least of them."

He finally smiled. "I just didn't want—there would be just as many questions if we worked at my place, that's all. And it's really only a bedroom, a desk, and a bathroom."

"I understand. Can you still go grab your typewriter and some paper?"

"Of course."

"Then let's get this thing written already."

He looked over at me. "Yes, ma'am."

~

Twenty minutes later, we slid into a secluded booth at the Tastee Diner, Jack placing the dictation device and the zippered case of his typewriter on the table. We both reached for the typewriter at the same time.

"I'm typing," I said. "Ninety words a minute, and I always have to rewrite your leads."

He shook his head but let me take it. I unzipped the cover, revealing a mid-fifties light-gray Royal Quiet Deluxe. It wasn't my Underwood, but it would do the job. "College?"

Jack shrugged and smiled ruefully. "Still works. And honestly, I like it better than the newsroom ones."

I knew what he meant. Typewriters had their own personalities. I positioned my fingers over the keys and typed three words. Yes. This machine and I would get on just fine. I rolled a sheet of paper into it.

The waitress came with menus, and Jack ordered two cups of coffee with extra cream and sugar. I ordered a Belgian waffle, and Jack said he'd have the same. She left, and we looked at each other, suddenly shy. Writing was a deeply personal experience, and cowriting articles in high school and college had always led either to fights or to me just taking over. I couldn't see me and Jack actually fighting, but, despite my critiques, he had more real-world experience in this area than I did.

Our coffees appeared in front of us, and Jack reached for his and took a sip. He set the cup down, then looked at me. "After the

US-backed Bay of Pigs invasion failed to depose Cuban revolutionary Fidel Castro—"

I held up a hand. "Absolutely not."

"What?"

"You can't start with the background. This is the problem with all your leads. Start with *who* or *what*."

"I did start with *what*."

"You started with a presumed reason *why*. Not *what*. The *what* of this story is the planned assassination."

He leaned back, his face a mix of mild amusement and annoyance. "So how would you start it?"

I thought briefly. "A Cuban spy on a mission to assassinate the president of the United States—"

"We don't know she's a *spy* even if that's what you and I have been calling her. I'd say she's a national. Or a revolutionary—we have evidence of both."

"Fine. A Cuban revolutionary on a mission to assassinate the president of the United States began an affair with the vice president in the wake of the failed US-led attempt to depose Cuban leader Fidel Castro."

He looked at me, going over it in his head. "Try not to say *Cuban* twice."

"Okay." I began to type, removing the first use of *Cuban*. Then I counted the words.

"What are you doing?"

"That's your other problem. Your leads are too long. Keep them shorter. Under thirty-five words is the sweet spot." Then I continued counting. "Okay, we've hit *who*, *what*, *how*, and *why*. Do you think we need to include DC, or is it implied with the president and vice president in *The* Washington *Digest*?"

"Implied," Jack said. "Do you always do everything by the book?"

My fingers itched to start the next sentence, but I waited. "I think that's why I like journalism so much. It's like a puzzle. You have to fit all the pieces into the right places or it doesn't work."

"That explains why you liked *this* story so much, then. We had to crack it first."

I smiled. He wasn't wrong. "It was a lot more exciting than finding a way to get stains out of a mattress, which is what I'd be investigating in the women's section."

Jack grabbed a sheet of paper and pulled a pen from his pocket as the waitress brought our waffles. I watched as he began scrawling notes. "What are you doing now?"

"My leads may not be the strongest, but I've got a few tricks up my sleeve yet. I like to make a list of everything I know about a story and then put it in order to—"

"Follow the inverted pyramid," I said. He nodded. "I like that." I reached for the syrup at the end of the table and covered my waffle with it. "What do you have so far?"

Jack went through his list, then we traded off adding elements. "What do we want to do about Carmen?"

I bit the inside of my lip. I knew why he was asking. Now that it was an assassination plot, not just an affair, we were absolutely going to be questioned by multiple agencies.

"Using her name lends credence," Jack said. "A lot of it."

"And then whoever Alejandra is working with goes after her next."

"She's not exactly an innocent."

I leaned forward. "She helped us. Whatever she did . . . then . . . is in the past. And certainly isn't tied to *this*."

He took a bite of his waffle, chewing slowly. "If we don't use her name, they're going to suspect that the unnamed source who identified Alejandra was her regardless."

"Let them suspect. We don't have to tell them."

"Okay."

I had expected more of a fight. "Do you agree or are you just giving in because it's what I want?"

"Both. But giving her name up to the FBI if we get questioned *might* not be the worst thing we could do."

I looked at him askance. “How do you figure?”

“If she’s willing to provide our government with information, they’ll protect her—we can’t offer that ourselves.”

I nodded. Under normal circumstances, no, I would never give up a source. But Jack was right—this could keep her safe. And it wasn’t like she was going back to Cuba anytime soon.

“Pullman is the more interesting question though,” Jack mused. “It’s always possible he’s not actually involved in this and just got a tip.”

“From a Russian? No way. He’s either working with Russia, with Cuba, or with both. Otherwise why would he demote me for taking the call?”

“Maybe he’s got someone else following this one on the sly and had you pegged all along as someone who wasn’t going to follow rules and would go rogue to try to write the story?”

I ignored the second part of that. “Did you see anyone else going after Alejandra? Did we see anyone else we knew at Off the Record or the Hay-Adams or anywhere important?”

“There’s always a chance it wasn’t *newspaper* related.”

“I don’t understand.”

Jack shrugged. “It’s Washington. You never know who’s got FBI ties. Or CIA. Or any other government agency for that matter. Maybe he’s on the right side of this.”

Another valid point. Half of my childhood friends had parents whose jobs were shrouded in mystery. And one of Betty’s friends’ fathers retired, only to reveal he had never been an accountant, but was a CIA analyst instead. “So if he’s working at the newspaper as cover but is actually working for *our* government to stop this, he won’t want it getting published either.”

“Exactly. If we out him and we’re wrong . . .”

He didn’t have to finish the sentence. Not only would we be interfering with a government agency, we’d both be out of jobs. And likely blacklisted at every newspaper in town. Even in the typing pool.

Especially in the typing pool. If we didn't get this perfect, I was done. Jack would land on his feet at some small-town newspaper with his anglicized name and by virtue of his sex. Me? There would be no second chances.

I took a deep breath. "If we worry about potentially sabotaging intelligence agencies while working in DC, there's nothing we *can* cover. They haven't stopped her yet. We can."

Jack nodded slowly and then reached his hand across the table. I took it.

For a few seconds, we just looked at each other, saying nothing. Then I gulped down the rest of my coffee and signaled to the waitress that I could use a refill. It was going to be a long night, and I needed to be my sharpest. Everything depended on that.

47

It was nearly three in the morning by the time Jack brought me home. "My grandmother is going to kill me if she's still awake."

"I have a feeling she'll be singing a different tune when she sees your name in print this week."

I hoped he was right. The article was strong. Jack was going to mark up our copy in the morning with fresh eyes, and then I would retype it and return it to him—we could get away with a few rounds of that at work—with plans to meet at lunch for a final revision before we turned it in. I was confident my mother had a bottle of ipecac because of Betty's kids, but if not, we could grab one on the way back to the office after lunch.

And then . . . glory or ruin. There was no in-between.

Exhausted as I was, I doubted I would be able to sleep, and it had nothing to do with all the coffee I had drunk. My future rested in the lines on the papers Jack had tucked in his coat pocket.

"Listen, Judy," he said, cutting the engine. "About what I said earlier—running away—"

I shook my head. "It's late. We don't need to do this."

He looked away, down the street. "What if I want to?"

I swallowed, my mouth suddenly dry. "What if you want to . . . what? Run away together?"

He turned back to me. "Not run away, but—I know we were . . . pretending . . . for your family. But after the story is done, what if"—he gestured to the space between us—"this . . . wasn't done?"

I could feel my chest rising and falling rapidly, but it felt like there wasn't enough air in the car. In the neighborhood. In the world. *Yes,* I thought. But also no. That future led to marriage and babies and me tending house while Jack went off to break stories and do all the things that I wanted to be doing while my typewriter gathered dust in a closet.

I had never met someone who understood me. Who *saw* me. But I knew how this ended. It wasn't fair. He would give up nothing by being with me. I would have to give up everything. Except him. And I didn't know if that was enough.

But it was late. And I was tired. Hell, a Cuban assassin had me pinned against a hotel bathroom door just a few hours earlier. I shook my head and covered his hand with mine. "Let's talk about . . . that . . . later. After the article is done and in. Okay?"

His eyes held mine, searching for something that I couldn't yet give. "Okay," he agreed.

He didn't try to kiss me as I got out of the car. And once I was inside, I sank down against the softly shut front door, wrapped my arms around my knees, and wondered why I couldn't be like every other girl, who could just say yes, and be happy as a wife and mother.

~

Morning came all too soon, and I studied myself in the mirror after I washed my face. I didn't understand how the changes that had occurred this past month weren't visible from the outside. Though that was a good thing—I had a bottle of ipecac to steal after all. I poked my head into my parents' room to make sure it was empty, then crossed quickly to their bathroom, found the brown bottle, and sloshed it to make sure there was enough. I was in luck—it was full. I had no idea how much a grown man would need to ingest without knowing he had drunk it, but

I had to hope this worked. If it didn't, we had one more day before we were out of time to get this printed and stop the plan from happening.

And if they refused to run it even without Pullman because it made the vice president look bad, well . . . we would have to try our luck walking into *The Washington Post*. Either way, I would type a second copy of the final draft just in case.

"You'd better work," I whispered to the bottle as I returned to my bedroom, slipping it into my purse.

I was too anxious for breakfast, grabbing only a piece of toast, most of which I hid in a napkin when my father stood from the table saying it was time to go to work.

"You're awfully quiet," he said as we headed down Sixteenth Street. "Everything okay with that fella of yours?"

"Yes. Just tired."

He patted my arm. "Things will calm down once Betty is back from the hospital, and the kids go home."

For us, I thought. Betty was going to have her hands full with three little ones.

We eventually pulled up in front of *The Digest* building. "Thank you for the ride," I said. I hoped it wasn't the last one.

He grinned and patted me on the shoulder. "Knock 'em dead. You'll be writing stories before you know it."

I tried to imagine him reading the story on the front page the next morning, his mouth slowly dropping open as he realized the implications. Then his eyes drifting up to the byline and seeing Jack's name and . . . mine. He would look across the table, holding the paper up for me to see. If they got permission to use Burt Glinn's photograph, Alejandra's face would be staring back at me. And my father's mouth would stretch into a proud smile.

Or I would be unemployed and potentially facing charges for poisoning a federal agent. That was always a possibility too, and one I shouldn't discount.

But there was no turning back now. And I needed to get up to the seventh floor before Mr. Pullman arrived.

"Thanks, Dad," I said, hurrying out of the car.

Jack was waiting in the lobby, and Frank inclined his head toward him, then winked at me. Jack raised his eyebrows in an unspoken question, and I nodded. We were doing this. He took a deep breath and nodded back, then pushed the up button for the elevator. Once inside, he pushed five and seven, and the two of us rode up to the newsroom where he got out. "Good luck," he whispered.

I was going to need it. The door opened on seven, and I stepped out, glancing around nervously. The women at desks looked up, then back down, disinterested, except for Florence, whose eyes widened. "I thought you'd been fired," she said quietly as I approached her desk.

I shook my head. "Can we talk—privately?" Florence looked wary, but she followed me to the kitchenette where the coffeemaker was. "I need your help."

"With what?"

"I just need to—" Another secretary walked in, crossed to the coffeemaker, which had already brewed a pot, poured a cup, and left. Florence looked at me, expectantly. "Do you remember when you told me not to go into a room with Mr. Pullman with the door shut?" She nodded. "Were you speaking from experience?"

For a long time, she didn't react. Then she slowly nodded.

Good, I thought. He deserved what we were about to do to him. "I need to slip something into his coffee."

Florence shook her head. "I can't help you."

She turned to leave, but I put a hand on her arm, stopping her. "Look, I can't tell you why. You don't even have to do it. I'll do it. But it has to be today."

When she looked back at me, something was different in her face. It had hardened. "Is that why you aren't up here anymore?"

It wasn't. But I wasn't above telling a white lie if it got us what we needed. Lives were at stake here. "Yes," I said.

She finally nodded. "I can't do it. But I won't stop you." The elevator dinged, and men's voices drifted into the kitchenette. "Hurry," she said, grabbing a mug. I pulled the bottle from my purse and uncapped it, dumping some in. High heels clacked down the hall, and there was no time to measure. Florence grabbed the coffeepot and filled the mug, leaving just enough room for cream and sugar. "He'll taste that," she said, noting the bottle I had used.

"An extra sugar?"

She nodded, adding three and the cream, then stirring it as a leggy blonde walked into the room.

"Here," Florence said, holding it out to her. "I got you started."

"Well aren't you just the sweetest?" the woman said, taking the cup, her voice a nasal Southern twang. She turned and left the kitchenette.

"Get out of here before he drinks that," Florence said, giving me a small shove. "Take the stairs. Fewer witnesses." She was right. Peeking out into the hall, she gestured to me. "Coast is clear. Go now."

"Thank you," I said quietly.

She shook her head. "If anyone asks, I haven't seen you since you worked up here."

"I'll say the same."

"See that you do."

She gave me a half smile, then shoved me toward the stairs. I went down two flights, then checked my watch. Miss Kelly was going to be mad. But I had always been early before. I would just have to hope that bought me enough good grace for one day of showing up three minutes late.

48

Jack laid the article wordlessly on my desk at ten. It was heavily marked up, his cramped handwriting in pencil all over the margins. "High priority," he said, bouncing slightly on his toes.

I glanced left to see Miss Kelly watching us. "Yes, Mr. Fields."

"I'll be back for it myself," he said, louder than he needed to. Miss Kelly's left eye twitched in annoyance.

"Twenty minutes," I said.

"You're usually faster than that."

"You usually don't have this many changes." She was still watching us. "Better lead though."

He turned and walked away, and I could tell, even from behind, that he was trying not to laugh. Miss Kelly stopped him at the elevators, his posture straightening as he sobered. I could only catch a few words, but "follow proper protocol" was definitely part of what she was saying. He gestured around the typing pool, then made a point of looking at his watch.

I realized I had better get to work. The majority of his edits were improvements, tightening for conciseness and clarity, though I did stet a couple of changes.

Twenty minutes later, he returned as I was pulling the last sheet from the roller. I handed the pages directly to him. He nodded briskly, then left. I watched him go, my heart beating faster than I wanted to admit. The story was good. That was all. And we might just change the course of history with it.

The elevator opened, and Miss Kelly nearly bowled Jack over, knocking the papers out of his hand in the process. He bent to retrieve them, and Miss Kelly glared. "I don't have time for your nonsense today, Fields."

"Sorry, Miss Kelly. Is everything all right?"

"No," she said brusquely. "We're down a managing editor, and the newspaper needs to run. So whatever that story is, get it done and turned in and stop wasting time bothering Miss Greenberg."

"Might need one more round of edits," he said.

She threw her hands up and stormed back to her office.

Down a managing editor. Jack and I made eye contact across the room, and I could have sworn he was just barely restraining himself from kicking up his heels. *Duke's*, he mouthed. I nodded.

~

We sat on the same side of the table this time, poring over the article together, settling on three more tweaks.

"Don't we look cozy," Duke said, bringing over an order of knishes. "I heard there's a congratulations in order too."

I looked at Jack, horrified. What had our mothers done? He shrugged at me.

"Your sister," Duke said, and my shoulders dropped in relief.

"Oh. Betty. Yes. She gave us quite the scare."

Duke chuckled. "I'll cater it when there's something for you two to celebrate." He walked away, greeting Anna Wainwright, who was at a table with—I squinted—Mildred Gelman, the wife of the former Speaker of the House, whose daughter, Beverly, was making waves as a campaign manager for a Senate candidate. I would love to interview her when this was all over.

My eyes drifted to the next table, and my breath caught as I recognized the man sitting there, watching me and Jack.

I elbowed Jack sharply, and he looked up from the pages he was studying. "What—?" He followed my gaze, and I felt him stiffen next to me.

Then a waiter brought his order, and J. Edgar Hoover directed his attention to the sandwich set down in front of him.

"You don't think he knows, do you?" I whispered.

"There's not much he *doesn't* know."

"But they'd have stopped it, right?"

"I *think* so. They took oaths."

I shook my head. "This feels like a bad omen."

Jack looked over, amused. "Do you go in for all that? He eats here all the time. It's a coincidence."

Coincidence or not, we were going to be on Mr. Hoover's radar when this story ran. I wondered if he would remember us from the restaurant. Then again, there was no way he would be interrogating us himself.

I took a deep breath and blew it out forcefully. "Okay. I'll type these changes. And then . . . I think it's ready."

Jack agreed, though neither of us had an appetite for the food that was then placed in front of us. Mr. Hoover didn't look back as we watched him tear into his food, completely unaware that we were about to make his men extraordinarily busy very soon.

49

"—some kind of stomach bug or something," a reporter was telling Frank as we reentered *The Digest* building after lunch. I glanced at Jack, and he gave me a half smile. The ipecac had worked its magic. If Florence told anyone, I would still be in trouble for poisoning a managing editor, but I had used ipecac to get out of school before. He would be miserable for a day and then fine.

"How long do you need?" Jack asked me quietly by the elevators.

"Not long. Twenty minutes at most with a second copy as security." We got into the elevator, and a few people stepped in after us. Jack slipped his hand into mine, squeezing it. I hadn't realized quite how nervous I was until that gesture. The doors opened on three, and I slipped past the reporters going up to the newsroom, feeling Jack's eyes on me as I walked toward my desk, papers in hand.

I typed slowly, carefully, going over every word to make sure it was right. And by the time I typed the final *-30-* to signify the end of the article, I knew it was as good as it was going to get.

Jack appeared at my desk. "Ready?" he asked. I nodded, handing him the pages, our names together as a joint byline on the top of the first. The slug was "assassination plot." For date of publication, we had put "immediate."

I wished I could go with Jack to turn it in and watch his editor's face change as he read. I also wished I could hide under my desk like a school-style bomb drill. My stomach rumbled angrily, and there was a distinct chance I'd go the way of Mr. Pullman . . . While it would lend credence to the stomach flu story going around, I would rather not join him.

"When will we hear anything?"

"I'll come down and tell you as soon as I know," he promised.

I reached out and touched his arm as he turned to go. "Whatever happens, thank you."

He nodded, then shook my hand off, and I turned to see Miss Kelly watching us. *They had better hire me to write,* I thought. Because I was definitely getting fired for fraternizing otherwise.

But Jack headed to the elevator, Miss Kelly said nothing, and I went to the board for an article that I needed to retype four times because I couldn't focus.

The minutes ticked by interminably. Then the hours. Miss Kelly went marching through the typing pool at three, jabbing impatiently at the elevator button until it arrived.

Beads of perspiration began to creep down my back, having nothing to do with the oppressive heat of DC in July. Where was Jack? Something was wrong. Had we misjudged Pullman? Was he a line of defense against someone higher up? What could possibly be taking this long?

I couldn't hear the clock across the room ticking. I rationally knew that. But each move of the second hand thudded in my chest like something from an Edgar Allan Poe story. Tick. Tick. Tick. Each time the elevator doors opened, I jumped, thinking it was Jack.

But he never came.

Instead, just after four, Frank walked out of the elevators. Everyone stopped typing and stared. I had never seen him away from his post.

And then he slowed to a stop at my desk.

"Miss Greenberg," he said crisply. Gone was the friendly tone of the man who had told me about his grandparents and taught me Spanish. No winks of approval or telling me I was his favorite typing pool girl today. "Come with me."

"Frank," I said. It came out too squeaky. I tried again. "What's this about?"

His face didn't soften. "Bring your things."

That was it, then. I was out. Whether it was because I knew too much, because I had poisoned Pullman, or because I had been "fraternizing" with Jack, I didn't know. And from the hard set of Frank's face, I wasn't finding out from him. I closed my eyes and took a deep breath, my dreams evaporating right in front of me.

My stomach churning, I pulled my purse from my desk drawer and walked, Frank holding my arm like I was some kind of criminal, with my head held high through the typing pool as everyone stared.

Patricia threw herself in front of the elevator door as we reached it. I shook my head to ward her off. She shouldn't get fired too over me. That congressman was never going to leave his wife and support her. She needed this to avoid going back to her parents' farm in disgrace. "What's this about, Frank?"

He shook his head stonily. "Mind your business, Patricia."

"Judy is my friend and therefore it IS my business."

I reached out to her with the arm Frank didn't have a vise grip on. "It's okay. I—I knew what I was getting into." We held each other's eyes for a long moment. "Don't lose your job over me," I whispered.

She opened her mouth to say something, then closed it and nodded, pulling me in for a quick, tight hug. "You have my number," she said.

I did. I also didn't trust myself to speak right then. So I offered her a half smile, the most I could muster, and she stepped aside, letting Frank push the button for the elevator.

He didn't let go of me, even once we were inside. But we didn't go down to the lobby, where he would eject me. Instead he pushed the button for the top floor. I looked to him in surprise. I didn't even know what was up there. But he stared straight ahead.

"Frank," I said pleadingly. He still didn't look at me. And suddenly, I was afraid. This wasn't right. Something was very, very wrong. Beyond me being fired for whatever infraction they had decided on based on my sex. Something else was happening here.

The elevator opened into a waiting room of sorts, with two sofas, potted plants, and breathtaking views of the White House and beyond it the Washington Monument. A woman sat at a reception desk, but she didn't look up as Frank frog-marched me past her, knocking on a closed door down a hallway.

"Yes?" a male voice asked, and Frank opened the door.

John Worthington, the newspaper's publisher, sat at a polished mahogany desk in front of a gigantic picture window. Photographs of him with celebrities and politicians lined the shelf behind him. The president and vice president, Cary Grant, Marilyn Monroe, Audrey Hepburn, Martin Luther King Jr., and more. The man sitting opposite his desk turned. It was Jack.

I had no idea what was going on.

Frank released my arm, and Worthington indicated I should sit in the seat next to Jack. I did, crossing my legs demurely at the ankle.

"You two," he said, pulling a cigar from a box on his desk and cutting the end off with great care before continuing. "Are in a lot of trouble." He removed the band from his cigar and left it on the desk, facing me. The writing was Spanish, and the word *Havana* was clearly visible on it.

I looked at Jack, inclining my head slightly toward the band. A Cuban cigar. He was part of this. We had to do something. But Jack didn't look at it. His shoulders were down, and he wore a hangdog look of defeat. Worthington said we were in a lot of trouble. Whatever this was, it wasn't good.

I looked at the cigar band again. We had to get out. To run. We may have failed, but if we could make it out of the building, we could go to Duke's. He would know how to find J. Edgar Hoover himself. I might not get a writing career, but we could still stop this from happening unless—

"Enough with the dramatics," a woman's voice said from the corner behind us.

I turned, fully expecting to see Alejandra de Bernal pointing a tommy gun, like something out of an old gangster movie.

But it was Miss Kelly.

50

"Leave us," she said, and I started to stand. Jack and I would have to make a break for it. That was all there was to it. I didn't know why Miss Kelly was here, but she was providing the distraction we needed.

But Mr. Worthington stood up, cigar in hand. He lit it at the door, its woody aroma lingering as he shut the door behind him.

Miss Kelly came around the desk and sat in Mr. Worthington's chair, fanning the air in front of her face. "I'll never understand why he smokes those. They smell awful."

"They're Cuban," I said.

"They are," she agreed. "When you have the kind of money he has, you tend to want the best. And we're willing to look the other way in exchange for certain favors."

Jack and I exchanged a look. It was clear neither of us knew what was happening. The phone on Mr. Worthington's desk rang suddenly, and I jumped at the disturbance. Miss Kelly picked up the receiver. "Yes?" she said, as if she answered the publisher's phone all the time and had no need to identify herself.

She listened for a few seconds before saying, "No. She doesn't need to come in. Not yet anyway." She hung up without saying goodbye.

Then she looked at the two of us, pulling a pack of cigarettes from the top right drawer of the desk and offering us each one. We both shook our heads. She removed one for herself, lit it, and took a long drag before setting it down on an ashtray. "We will not be running your story," she said coolly.

My blood turned hot in my veins, and I could feel my chest rising and falling rapidly. "You're working with them," I said, jumping to my feet.

"Them," she mused. "Yes. But likely not the 'them' you're referring to. Have a seat, Miss Greenberg. You're in no danger today. At least not from me."

"Then who—?"

"In due time," Miss Kelly said. I looked to Jack uncertainly, but he was as bewildered as I was. Who was she working with if not the Russians and Cubans? How had she dismissed Mr. Worthington like he worked for her? None of this made sense. Miss Kelly gestured with her cigarette, and I sat at the edge of my seat. Ready to spring up at a moment's notice. And do what, I didn't know. But I wasn't going to take whatever it was lying down, that was for sure. I had worked too hard to let everything end like this.

"Little spitfire, aren't you?" She was almost smiling as she turned to Jack. "I do see why you like this one."

"So what, then? You're firing me because I fraternized?"

She leveled her head at me. "I think we took it a bit past fraternization with a room at the Hay-Adams, don't you?"

"We didn't—" Jack started as I said, "That's none of your—"

We both stopped. "We played gin rummy for an hour and then left," I said.

"And you expect me to believe that?"

"I don't care if you do or not, it's the truth."

She knocked ash off of her cigarette into the tray on the desk. "That's irrelevant anyway. We aren't running the story because it will make the country look weak. Not to mention likely start a war with Cuba, who is currently in bed with the Soviets. Do either of you want that?"

The implications of what she was saying sank in, and we both shook our heads.

"Good. The FBI will handle it from here." She studied us for a few seconds. "Mr. Fields, you're free to go. Miss Greenberg, I believe there's more we need to discuss before you leave today."

"No," Jack said.

She looked at him in surprise. "What do you mean, no?"

"I'm not letting you fire her. Judy found this story. She's the one who convinced me we needed to follow the lead. She made the connection between Alejandra de Bernal and the vice president, and she's the one who got her to confess the plot *on tape*. She should be working in the newsroom, not the typing pool."

I reached over and put a hand on his arm. I appreciated the show of support. But he didn't realize he was doing more harm than good. The more evidence he gave that I went outside of what I was supposed to be doing in the typing pool, the less likely I was to keep working here in any capacity. I may have saved the president, but my job was beyond salvation, and I knew it. The most I could hope for was a referral to another newspaper, and I doubted she was giving me that.

But a flicker of expression—was that a smile?—crossed Miss Kelly's face. Yes, she looked almost amused.

"I suppose you can stay, then," she said, her head tilted as she considered this. "You do know too much anyway. Though I need to warn you, Mr. Fields, that your career as a reporter is likely finished if you choose to stay."

He looked at me and I shook my head. "Don't give this up for me."

His eyes met mine. "Don't you get it? I don't *want* this if you can't have it too." My breath caught. Betty had said maybe he wouldn't mind me working, but never in my wildest dreams had anyone *felt* something like that for me, let alone said it.

"Both staying, then?" Miss Kelly asked.

I reached across the chairs, and Jack took my hand. We nodded. Whatever came next, we would figure it out together.

"Well, then," she said briskly, stubbing out her cigarette. She picked up the phone and dialed a number. "Permission to extend to both?" she asked. No greeting. "Yes," she said after a pause. "I think that will work if not." Then she hung up the phone.

"Mr. Hoover and I would like to offer you a new job," she said.

"Mr. Hoover?" I asked, the face of the man at Duke Zeibert's flashing before me. She couldn't mean—

But she nodded, pulling a badge from her pocket and holding it up for us to see. "Agent Ann Kelly, FBI."

51

Jack and I looked from the badge to each other to Miss Kelly. "But—Mr. Pullman—the message I took—"

"We arrested him at his home this afternoon on the evidence of your story," she said.

"But we didn't name him."

"You didn't have to," she said. "That's why I sent you up there to work for him."

I shook my head. "I don't understand."

"You think any of the girls in the typing pool would have the wherewithal to follow a lead like that? You think anyone in the newsroom would have either?" Jack flinched.

I didn't. But then again, I hadn't seen this coming at all. "And Mr. Worthington? With his Cuban cigars?"

"John's on the Bureau's payroll. He doesn't know why, exactly, but he knows to stay out of our way, and in exchange he gets all the illegal cigars and rum he wants. Those old money types just like to feel important, and this lets him have his fun while still feeling like a patriot."

"But Pullman—"

"Has been on our radar for a while. We just couldn't prove it with a solid-enough case to arrest him until today. We believe he has a Cuban handler and was passing information to the Soviets."

"No," I said. "The man who left the message definitely had a Russian accent. I think it's the other way around."

Miss Kelly shrugged. "No matter. We'll get him to talk regardless. A treason charge still carries the death penalty."

Treason. I had worked for a man being charged with treason. And the death penalty.

My stomach felt queasy again.

"I gave him ipecac today," I blurted out.

Miss Kelly smiled. "I assumed as much. Easy and it worked. I knew I picked the right girl for the job."

"And Alejandra de Bernal?"

"In custody as of an hour ago. Took down two of our men in the process."

"Are they—?"

Miss Kelly shook her head. "You were lucky the other night. We'll make sure you have actual training with weapons before you go into the field again."

Into the field again. Weapons. What?

"I—I'm sorry, you want *me* to work for the FBI?"

"Was that unclear?"

I looked at Jack, who was absolutely stunned, then back at Miss Kelly. "I—but I want to write."

She steepled her fingers, considering this. "You'd be doing a great service to your country as an agent."

I sat back in my chair. I *had* enjoyed the thrill of finding Alejandra. Of pretending to know enough in that bathroom to get her to talk. Being alone with the vice president had actually been far more frightening than that. But the stolen moments in the Library of Congress, the excitement of finding her picture in the annals there. And the feeling of my fingers flying across the keys at the diner as Jack and I found the words to save a world leader's life. The rest was a means to an end. I had dreamed of this for so long and now . . . now I had done it too well, and it was being taken away.

"I want to write," I repeated more firmly.

"I do too," Jack said, squeezing my hand.

Miss Kelly stood up and turned to study the landscape of the city behind her. She didn't respond for a full minute. "That *is* an idea," she said finally, still facing away from us. "It's more work, of course, but it provides a layer of cover for you both."

"What does?"

She turned back around. "I suppose the time *has* come for a woman in the newsroom here. Though you may have to start on some women's issues—at first, at least."

I heard Betty's voice in my mind. *The doctor said it was all in my head. I* knew *something wasn't right. But no one listened. And it almost killed me.* And an idea began to form.

"Real women's issues," I said. "Not stains and child-rearing tips. I want to write about injustices and the bigger problems that women face."

She shrugged. "You won't hear me objecting to that. Though you would also be investigating for us. If you accept, I'll tell Worthington he's starting a women's section as soon as your training is complete."

I looked at Jack. "I accept," a voice said. It was too high to be his, and his mouth hadn't moved. *I* had said it.

"Then congratulations, Miss Greenberg. Welcome to both the FBI and the newsroom."

I had done it. I was a reporter. And somehow an FBI agent. It was all rather dizzying. "Don't you need to run a background check or . . . something?"

"Miss Greenberg, we did that a month ago."

"You did?"

"Did you think it was a coincidence that the director of the FBI was at the same restaurant as you today? While he *is* a fan of the roast beef there, no. He wanted to see you with his own eyes." Then she turned to Jack. "Mr. Feldstein?"

He startled, his eyes wide, at the use of his real name. "I—I don't know. I need some . . . time . . . to think about all this."

The corners of Miss Kelly's mouth turned down. "I see. Yes. I did feel you were more of a risk. You had less to lose than Miss Greenberg." She sat back down and drummed her fingernails on the desk for a few seconds. "As I see it, you have two options at this point in time. You can accept, and work under the same conditions as Miss Greenberg if you still want to write news stories, or you can marry Miss Greenberg and remain a reporter."

"He can what now?" I asked, jumping up.

"Sit," she said, pointing at the chair and turning her attention back to Jack once I had. "We can't have you knowing a field agent's identity if you aren't either working for the Bureau or married to her."

"What does getting married have to do with anything?" I asked.

Jack looked over at me. "Spouses don't have to testify against each other."

Miss Kelly nodded. "And they're granted certain information privileges in the intelligence communities. So if you wanted to share anything for a story that you learned in the course of your duties with the Bureau . . ."

She didn't finish the sentence, but the implications were clear. If I shared any information with him and he published it, if we weren't both employed by the FBI and we weren't married, there would be dire consequences.

"Listen," I said, standing again and beginning to pace the room. "Do I have feelings for Jack? Yes. But I know how this one ends. We get married, and then I wind up sidelined while he does all the work." I turned to Jack, pointing a finger. "You'd better take this job, you hear me?"

He studied me for a moment, then turned to Miss Kelly. "Are there any restrictions if I take the job and *then* we get married?"

"No. I think we can work with that."

"Excuse me. I'm in the room. And this is *my* life we're talking about here. I'm not taking this just to wind up sitting at home popping out babies while you go off and—"

"Come to think of it," Miss Kelly said, pulling another cigarette from her pack. "If you're working at *The Digest and* the Bureau, you'll each have to collect two separate paychecks." I stopped and looked at her. Was that supposed to convince me? She lit her cigarette. "At that point, a nanny would be well within reach, if unconventional. Mr. Fields, I believe you have a wealthy great-uncle."

"No, I don't."

She took a deep inhale of her cigarette and blew out a tremendous amount of smoke. "Yes, I believe you do. A childless one at that. On your dear departed father's side. And I believe he just passed. Leaving you as his sole male heir . . ."

Jack and I looked at each other. "With enough money to pay for a nanny so you can still work as a reporter," he said softly.

I turned back to Miss Kelly. "Do we have to decide that part today?"

She smiled, fully this time. "No. Though if your mother ever finds out about that hotel room, you probably want to decide quickly." She leaned in confidingly. "Edna would have an absolute fit."

"She would," I agreed. Then I realized she had used my mother's first name. "Wait. How do you know my mother?"

"I don't." She shook her head. "But your grandmother has some strong opinions."

I blinked at her. "You know my grandmother?"

"Sylvia and I go all the way back to our grade school days in New York." My mouth dropped open. "Close your mouth, dear, you'll catch flies," she said, using an expression my grandmother used as well. "She was the one who told me to take a chance on you in the typing pool without secretarial training."

No. There was absolutely no way that was true. "My grandmother doesn't have any friends who aren't Jewish," I said slowly.

"No," Miss Kelly agreed. "But she is dear friends with Hannah Kellerman."

Hannah Kellerman. Ann Kelly. I blinked several times, connecting the dots. Was I the only one who hadn't changed my name to get ahead?

"Mr. Fields? You're officially accepting, then?" He nodded. "I need you to say the words, please."

"I accept," he said quietly.

"Excellent." She stood up and reached across the desk, handing us each a card with the address for the Department of Justice printed on it. "You'll report here tomorrow to begin training. Now if you'll excuse me, I have work to finish before your grandmother and I play canasta tonight. You can have the room for the afternoon as you discuss your future options."

She started to leave, but I called her name before she reached the door. "Miss Kelly?" She turned around. "Can—can you look into Congressman Clement from South Carolina?"

Her brow furrowed. "Why?"

"I—don't get her in trouble, but—Patricia—from the typing pool—she's been seeing him, and I have a bad feeling. That other girl who went missing and all, and he took Patricia to Nassau last weekend and I just . . ."

Miss Kelly was shaking her head, irritated. "I told him to back off," she said to herself, then looked back at us. "He's CIA. Been trying to poach one of our people for months to have someone on the inside here too."

"CIA? Then the girl who went missing . . . ?"

"Foreign agent. But he's why I had to fire Louise and Myrtle. They were feeding him information from our articles before they ran."

"Then Louise isn't pregnant?" Fields asked.

"Not that I'm aware of." She glanced at her watch. "I do need to be going. Ask for Agent Lewis tomorrow." And with that, she was gone, closing the door behind her.

I sank back into my chair. "What just happened?"

Fields looked at me, equally wide eyed. "That was not how I saw today going."

I was a reporter. And an FBI agent. Me. Little Judy Greenberg. And I found myself grinning. No one would ever see me coming, that was for sure. Then I looked back at Fields. "And you want to *marry* me?"

"I—I mean, not *today* but"—he looked down at his hands, then back up at me—"eventually. Yeah. I do."

I started to laugh, and his expression turned to hurt, until I got up and went to sit on his lap, wrapping my arms around his neck. "*Eventually* sounds perfect," I whispered before kissing him.

Epilogue

Washington, DC, August 1963

"This is ridiculous," I murmured to Jack.

"I agree," he said back, his mouth hidden behind his glass, before taking a sip of his old-fashioned.

"So why are we doing it?"

"The Big Man wants to be sure." The Big Man was our nickname for J. Edgar Hoover. It was a bit of a joke, as he stood a whopping five foot seven. Which, granted, meant he towered over me, but still.

"*I'm* sure. When have I been wrong?"

Jack grinned at me. "He's going to want more evidence than that."

"The leader of the civil rights movement isn't going to suddenly tell us he's a Communist in an interview about the march he's planning later this month."

"That's where we use our secret weapon," Jack said.

"No."

"It's too late," he said, nodding across the room of the Round Robin Bar at the Willard Intercontinental Hotel, where our target was staying. And I saw an older woman, dressed in her finest, order a cocktail at the bar.

"Why she thinks she's better at this than us, I will *never* understand," I muttered, irritated. It was just like her to completely steal my thunder. Though she stayed out of the newspaper at least.

Jack was amused. "What can I say? She's good."

I rolled my eyes at him as the woman took a sip of her drink, looked over, and winked at me. "Oh no. She's coming over. She can't just—she's going to blow our cover."

"How *is* my favorite granddaughter doing today?" My grandmother asked, leaning down to plant a kiss on the top of my head.

"I'm telling Betty you said that."

"Psh." She waved a gloved hand in the air. "I tell her the same thing." She patted Jack's shoulder. "And my favorite soon-to-be grandson-in-law?"

He chuckled, and I looked down at my left hand. I still wasn't used to seeing a diamond there. Not that we had set a wedding date yet, to my mother's eternal chagrin. "Did you get in?"

She nodded, turning her chin up proudly. "Here on behalf of the United Jewish Appeal looking for ways to unite our two groups in a quest for equality." She leaned in close. "Much better cover than yours. A profile? He's not going to tell you anything at all. Unity and equality? That's practically a description of a commune. Though I do think our boss is barking up the wrong tree here."

"You can tell him that, then," I said darkly. Better her than me.

"I intend to," she said. "Once I can confirm it. I'll wait for you after your interview though."

"You don't need to do that."

"Sure I do," she said. "I had them bump you until after my meeting anyway."

I was ready to kill her. "You can't just interfere—"

"Hannah said to do what I needed to," she reminded me. "But no matter. I'll drive you home."

I was shocked that my grandmother was still alive with the way she drove, weaving in and out of DC traffic like she hadn't a care in the world, barely looking at the road. She had definitely graduated from the F. Scott Fitzgerald's Jordan Baker school of driving, believing it was everyone else's job to stay out of her way.

"Jack drove," I said. "We're fine."

"No, no, no," she said, pinching my cheek. "Have you *seen* his car?"

Author's Note

As I was casting around desperately for book ideas one day, I hopped on the Peloton. I don't remember the ride I did, but the instructor mentioned Marilyn Monroe. And because I've been writing books set in the early 1960s, my brain traveled to John F. Kennedy and his affairs—largely to avoid focusing on how hard the climb section of my ride was.

And then I remembered something a random guy had told me at Kelly's Irish Times in DC back in my twenties, when I was fun and still left my house for non–kid-related things. This long-forgotten guy told me that Kennedy used to send men out to Irish Times to pick up girls from Catholic University for him.

And as I pedaled, I thought, *Huh. That would make a hell of a story.*

A quick Google search proved that couldn't be the case, as the bar opened in 1978. And I found no evidence anywhere of girls being picked up at a bar for the White House. But I texted my best friend, Jen, and her husband, Will (he was the only reason we University of Maryland grads found ourselves in a bar by Capitol Hill), and asked if they remembered hearing that. They didn't, but Will said Off the Record, in the basement of the Hay-Adams hotel, would make more sense as it's directly across from the White House.

I looked up Off the Record, and as a journalism major in college and a (now former) journalism teacher, I suddenly had a book idea. I wouldn't name the president and vice president, because the bar pickups would be pure fiction, but we've got some little wink-wink nod-nods about their identity anyway.

I had used *The Washington Post* in *Behind Every Good Man* (under fictional leadership out of respect to the absolute icon that was Kay Graham), but I wanted to create a different newspaper so that the workings of it could be all my invention, from the typing pool to the selection of secretaries for the editors. Plus *The Post* had a women's section. I wanted a newspaper that was less progressive so that Judy would really have to work for what she got. And I had Ann Kelly in mind from the very beginning—including her real job.

Early on, I looked for a restaurant to send the characters to and found Duke Zeibert's. All of the real-life people who are mentioned as being there were known to frequent the restaurant. Hilariously, I wrote the scene where Judy explains that the community isn't *that* small, and Jewish people don't all know each other—then I called my dad to ask if he had ever eaten there so I could snag details, and he said, "No, but I did go to junior high with his daughter." Jewish geography will get you every time!

In college I took a class on America in the 1960s. When I signed up, I expected hippies and Woodstock. What I got was mostly about the Kennedy administration and assassination. And while my professor was eccentric, he was a firm believer in multiple shooters and Cuba's involvement. So I had some background knowledge, but I had trusted the shirts at Urban Outfitters and thought Che Guevara was a hero. Let's just say what I found on him was *not* what I expected. However, when I read that women fought alongside him, the story got a lot more interesting. Alejandra de Bernal is entirely fictional, but I did go through Burt Glinn's photographs from the day Havana fell to inform both her description and the scene where Jack and Judy go looking for evidence of her at the Library of Congress.

Maricela is a complete work of fiction as well, and there's no evidence that Desi Arnaz ever played the Bohemian Caverns (which by all accounts was a VERY cool spot in what is still the music corridor of DC).

Off the Record and the Hay-Adams are both real places that I took liberties with to make certain plot points work. The bar was and still is, however, a hangout for people needing a drink after leaving the White House (apparently that's universal no matter the administration). And President Lyndon B. Johnson did frequent Off the Record and allegedly kept a room at the hotel for various purposes.

Ann Kelly's and Sylvia's FBI involvement was largely influenced by a friend of the family, who revealed, when she retired, that she had been a CIA analyst all along. This was literally the least likely person I would expect to be working for the CIA. Like . . . ever. And I thought, wouldn't that make more sense than the people you *would* expect? (I think everyone from the DC area has a story of discovering someone's REAL job much later.)

Then I realized I might have a problem: Were there Jewish FBI agents back then? Thankfully, there were! J. Edgar Hoover may have been somewhat suspicious of us, but I found Morris Childs. He was born in Russia/Ukraine (those border towns were always changing hands) and was a huge asset to the Bureau. Were there Jewish *women* agents? Not that I could find. But anglicizing names was a very real thing to become more desirable hires, both in Hollywood and elsewhere.

And finally, a journalism note: I went several rounds on "lead" versus "lede." My high school journalism teacher, Kevin Keegan (to whom this book is dedicated), taught it as "lead," so I did as well. The textbook I used said the same. But I've seen it both ways and have been told "lede" is the "professional way" to introduce an article. So I felt vindicated by this article by Roy Peter Clark, which justified spelling the word the way I was taught: https://www.poynter.org/reporting-editing/2019/lead-vs-lede-roy-peter-clark-has-the-definitive-answer-at-last/. I'd argue both are correct, but going with Keegan's usage felt right in this case.

I hope you enjoyed coming along on Judy and Jack's adventures as much as I enjoyed researching and writing them. This was definitely the most fun I've had while writing a book, and I really think that comes through on the page.

Thank you always for reading!

—*SGC*

Acknowledgments

This absolute labor of love owes thanks to so many people in my life. (So buckle up—it's a long drive!)

First, foremost, always, my rock star of an agent, Rachel Beck. I love that I can text you a scrap of an idea at any hour of the day or night and that you will support me from faint concept to publication. You are incredible and I sing your praises constantly to anyone who will listen. Best. Partnership. Ever.

Thank you beyond words to my editor, Nancy Taylor Holmes. I don't do well with new people. You have to basically approach me with an open palm and a treat like I'm a skittish dog. But we clicked instantly, and what somehow started as me describing the general idea for this book to you at my cousin's wedding blossomed into me writing my favorite book so far. I adore you, your vision, your team, your vibes . . . Wait, I'm starting to sound like Taylor Swift. Thank you, thank you, thank you.

Thank you to my developmental editor, Christina Henry de Tessan, for taking my vision of Judy and making her come through even better than I imagined on the page. I never took a creative writing course in school, but I feel like I'm in one (in a good way!) with you. Thank you for your wisdom and insight.

Thank you to Carissa Bluestone, for filling in so seamlessly with Nancy on leave and for letting me be insanely picky on the cover. I appreciate you!

Thank you to the entire teams at both Lake Union and Liza Dawson Associates. I hear so many publishing horror stories and I'm sitting here like, "Can't relate *insert hair-flip emoji*." From selling the book, to copyediting, production, and marketing, I truly have the most incredible team in the business.

Thank you to my publicist, Ann-Marie Nieves, for reading my insane, rambling emails and for taking me to places beyond where I could have dreamed. You are the very best!

Thank you to my husband, Nick, for being my partner in this crazy life. I love you, and I definitely thought back to some of our newspaper-sponsoring bickering during Jack and Judy's writing adventures! Thank you for supporting me through it all.

Thank you to Jacob and Max for being my biggest fans—even if you haven't read anything I've written yet. Seeing how excited you get when I succeed is the second-best feeling in the world. (The first-best is when you hug me without farting on me.) I love you more than anything in the universe.

Thank you to Gracie and Sandy for cuddle breaks and making me stroke you like a Bond villain whenever I do virtual events. I'm sorry there are no schnauzers in this one, but I'll get you next time!

Thank you to my mother, Carole Goodman, for picking up every bit of slack when I can't do it all. From reading my work the day I write it, to going on quests for whatever clothes I need, to Costco runs and school pickups and drop-offs and everything in between. Thank you, Mama.

Thank you to my father, Jordan Goodman, for always having the answers. And if you don't know them, you either know who to ask or where to find them. Mom may joke that I'm Google, but when it comes to insider knowledge when I'm writing, you are the master. (And thank you for letting me use your Amazon account!!!)

Thank you to my brother Adam, sister-in-law Nicole, and nephews Cam and Luke. It's hilarious how many people still come up to me at book events and say they know you. It doesn't matter how famous I get; I'll always be Adam's sister. Love you.

Thank you to my grandmother, Charlotte Chansky. In so many ways, my storytelling voice is yours. And you would have absolutely pulled the chocolate trick on my mother's white sofa if she had tried to fix me up with that cantor!

Thank you to my aunt and uncle Dolly and Marvin Band for always telling me how proud you are of me and for having all the answers when I need details. I love being able to share these stories with you.

Thank you to my aunt and uncle Mike Chansky and Stephanie Abbuhl for always being proud of me—even if Dani spilled the beans that Mike sends my accomplishments to the Chansky family group chat while not replying to my texts. Thank you for sharing your homes and lives with me.

Thank you to my cousins, Allison Band and Andy Levine, Ian and Kim Band, Mindy and Alan Nagler, Andrew and Dani Chansky, Peter Chansky, Ben Chansky, and Shira Pomeroy, for being excited about every step of this journey with me.

Thank you to Mark Kamins for letting me vent, for commiserating, for loving me exactly how I am, and for understanding money so I don't have to. Hope you caught your cameo in this one!

Thank you to my lifelong best friend, Jennifer Lucina. I could write a whole other book listing all the reasons why I am thankful that I have you, but you already know them all. Pink really IS good with green. Love you forever.

Thank you to Sarah Luczak McKinley for being one of the most dependable people in my life. It doesn't matter what it is, I know you're there, and that lets me feel strong in my weakest moments. I love you, my dear friend.

Thank you to Jeremy Horton for being the person I can send the most unhinged memes to without judgment and for knowing to check in when I go dark.

Thank you to Haben Asghedom for being my partner in motherhood, crime, and online overspending. I count my blessings every single day that you bought the house next to ours. Thank you for absolutely everything. And thank you to Mike and my favorite girls, Aurora, Elena, and Zara, for the best built-in playdates ever. We all love you!

Thank you to Jessica Markham for keeping me on track by yelling at me whenever I don't have pages for you. For dressing me. For selling my books. For encouraging me to actually spend money on myself. For motivating me. And for being one of the most important people in my life.

Thank you to Aimie Runyan-Vetter for *always* getting it, whether we're talking about books, about publishing, or about life. I don't know how I could do any of this without you.

Thank you to Elyse Brum for picking up right where we left off like not a day has passed. It's amazing how much can change, and yet our friendship hasn't. I love you.

Thank you to Kim Thibault for being one of the best things to come out of this journey. Thank you for (secretly) beta-reading and for being my friend. Put your oxygen mask on!

Thank you to my friends: Fabiola Perez, Sarah Elbeshbishi, Sonya Shpilyuk, Joye Saxon, Christen Dimmick, Jamaly Allen, Caroline Dulaney, Katie Stutzman, Jennifer Kramer, Mary Dempsey, Michael Gizzi, Kerrin Torres, Jan Guttman, Reka Montfort, Max and Angie Giammetta, Spirit Cottrell, Jenna Levine Liu, Brittany Rassoolkhani, Heather Bergman, Alex Tsironis, Beth Davis, Sandy Young, Nicole Lau, Rob and Diana Pajewski, and Steve and Carolyn Korman, and Aaron McKinley.

Thank you to my author friends, who have made this journey so much sweeter: Lindsay Hameroff, Jenni Walsh, Jaime Lynn Hendricks, Samantha Greene Woodruff, Jean Meltzer, Annie Cathryn, Heidi Shertok, Meredith Schorr, Felicia Grossman, Stacey Agdern, Alison Hammer, Lisa Barr, Rochelle Weinstein, Helen Laser, Jane Rosen, Zibby Owens, Pam Jenoff, Ellen Won Steil, Rea Frey, Georgina Cross,

Dara Levan, Ali Rosen, Harper Kincaid, Jacqueline Friedland, Jenn Bouchard, and Jessica Guerrieri.

Thank you to my literary "big sis," Andrea Peskind Katz, for being the best sounding board for books and life.

Thank you to the Confino family.

Thank you to Renee Weiss Weingarten for being the best book cheerleader and for creating one of my favorite places on the internet—and thank you to all of Renee's Reading Club for feeling like family!

Thank you to my beloved Peloton Moms Book Club. I'll see you on the leaderboard!

Thank you to Melody Wukitch and the whole team at Park Books. It's amazing how your store can feel instantly like home, and I love that it gets to be home for my books. Love you!

Thank you to Sue Perez and Luisa Ramos for keeping me looking fabulous.

Thank you to Kelly Kervin, Stacy Smith, Jamie Rosenblit, Susan Zabolotzky, Susan Peterson, Moran Vidaletz, Kelly Mikolich, Chase Waskey, Jodi Cutler, Leslie Zemeckis, Christine Adams, Danielle Medina, Dara Granoff, Leighellen Landskov, Leslie Shogren, Michelle Jocsun, Sophia Becker, Susan Ballard, Kate Vocke, Cheryl Koch, Alexis Campbell, Jennifer Hecht, Fay Silverman, Aimee Fogel, Ticey Geyer, Katie Polito, Larry Hoffer, Lauren Margolin, Emily Halperin, Ginny Velazquez, Jessica Roy, Ivy Kaprow, Tiffany Van Tine, and Blythe Colyer.

Thank you to all my readers, for letting me live my dreams every single day.

And finally, thank you to Kevin Keegan, to whom this book is dedicated. My life changed forever when you walked into Doc Goodwin's freshman English class and said a future editor in chief of *The Rampage* could be sitting in that room right then. Judy exists because you told me I could do better. She exists because you taught me. She exists because you pushed me. She exists because you encouraged me on my teaching journey. She exists because you read those early books in binders (complete with necessitating your own epilogue to *Beyond the Palace* so you could sleep at night). And she exists because of the pride I see in your eyes when we meet each summer and I give you the latest book. Thank you for being my teacher, my mentor, my friend, and my biggest fan. I am certainly yours.

Book Club Questions

1. Judy has no problem stealing her sister's clothes and lying to her family to interview at *The Digest*—is this Machiavellian streak part of her character or a response to how her family treats her?
2. Why does Judy trust Jack to help her after he took credit for her work?
3. Why would Miss Kelly be okay with Judy fixing Jack's articles?
4. Judy's grandmother is her ally against her mother when it comes to the cantor, yet still nearly outs her to her parents when she slips on Patricia's name. Does she just like stirring up trouble or is she actually helping her granddaughter?
5. Why do you think Maricela agrees to help Jack and Judy?
6. Did Miss Kelly leave the newspaper photo from Maricela's show on Judy's desk to let her know she knew what Judy was up to? Or was it a coincidence?
7. What was your reaction to the reveal that Jack Fields is Jacob Feldstein? Did you suspect it?
8. Betty's placental abruption presents with classic symptoms of this pregnancy complication—why did her doctors dismiss her complaints? How common is this still today in healthcare?
9. When does Judy actually start to have feelings for Jack?

10. Was Judy right or wrong that she needed to get into the vice president's room? Would Alejandra and her handlers have stopped if they published just the story about the affair?
11. Did Jack bring a gun when Judy confronted Alejandra? Or did he listen to her?
12. Is it selfish of Judy and Jack to write the story instead of going straight to the FBI or Secret Service? Or is this something the public deserves to know?
13. Did J. Edgar Hoover eat lunch at Duke's that day on purpose to spook Jack and Judy?
14. Did Miss Kelly mean that Judy's grandmother told her to take a chance on her in the typing pool or with FBI work?
15. Did you expect their story to get published? Did you have any inkling of who Miss Kelly was before she reveals her real name and position?
16. Judy and Jack are able to work out a solution where she still gets to be in the field—what choice do you think she would have made if that wasn't an option? And would she regret it?
17. How does Judy's family experience shape her desire to write about more important women's issues? How is that coverage of women's health still evolving today?
18. *The Digest* is an extremely misogynistic place to work, despite Miss Kelly calling many of the shots. Why do you think she allows it to operate in that way?
19. Was Sylvia working for the FBI all along? Or did she join when Judy did?
20. How did your background knowledge of 1960s events shape your views of the novel? Did you make any real-world connections in it?

About the Author

Photo © 2025 Kate Samsock

Sara Goodman Confino is the bestselling author of six novels: *Don't Forget to Write*, *Good Grief*, *Behind Every Good Man*, *She's Up to No Good*, *For the Love of Friends*, and *Off the Record*. After spending more years than she's willing to publicly admit teaching high school English and journalism, she is currently writing full-time and trying to make a living off the crazy stories in her head. She lives in Montgomery County, Maryland, with her husband, two sons, and two miniature schnauzers. When she's not writing or frantically parenting, she can be found on the Peloton, at the beach, or at a Bruce Springsteen concert, sometimes even dancing onstage.